WILLOW

THE METCALFES || BOOK 2

RONIE KENDIG

TASK FORCE
press

For more information about Ronie Kendig, please visit: www.roniekendig.com

Cover design: Jennifer Zemanek/Seedlings LLC

Author is represented by Steve Laube of the Steve Laube Agency, Phoenix, AZ

PRAISE FOR WILLOW

I loved this book! It kept me flipping pages and reluctant to let go! Ronie Kendig's heart and desire to be a voice for these people shone! It is a reality that attention needs to be drawn to, and for that I say, thank you! Chiji fit the bill so perfectly! Book boyfriend loading! Honestly, from the first moment I met him on the pages of this book, he screamed protector and proved his mettle!

~OCHEGBA ADEJO, BETA READER & REVIEWER

Willow is an emotionally charged, down-to-the-marrow compelling, well-executed story. Kendig kept me turning pages and wondering what was going to happen next. The burgeoning romantic relationship is complex and riveting. The Metcalfes are an incredible fictional family. The subject matter of this unique romantic suspense novel will be a clarion call that'll long ring in readers' hearts, inspiring awareness and action (prayer) against human trafficking.

~JULEE SCHWARZBURG OF SCHWARZBURG EDITORIAL

SPECIAL THANKS

Special thanks to dear friend Toni Shiloh for introducing me to the inimitable Ebosereme Aifuobhokhan, who provided invaluable help in keeping Chijioke Okorie authentic and accurate to his Nigerian heritage. Thank you, Ebos, for your many suggestions and ideas on ways to show respect and honor your homeland. I loved how in sync we were as Chiji's story came to life.

Also many thanks to Ochegba Adejo, who joined my influencer team for *Stone*, then got excited about Chiji's story and mentioned she was Nigerian. She so graciously agreed to read *Willow* for authenticity and accuracy of her native country! Absolutely delighted when she said Chiji was perfect then even called him her "Book boyfriend loading!"

I pray, Ladies, that I have done your people and country justice.

Reader, any mistakes are completely mine.

DEAR READER ...

The contents of this book will not be easy to read.
Readily I admit—this story was hard to write, finding that
delicate balance of sharing the brutal truths behind human
trafficking and respecting the survivors. Between helping people
understand the depths of depravity, yet not glorifying the
shadows.

You may find this story *too* hard to read, but I hope you will
brave the journey and allow your heart to be moved by the
plight of so many. If you need a breather in the midst of the
trials happening for Willow and Chiji, take it—and in the pause,
I beg you to remember the people trapped in this nightmare and
PRAY FOR THEM!

Ronie

CHAPTER ONE

MILE SAFEHOUSE, NIGERIA

"THINK HARD because I've seen ops like this destroy the best of men."

"I know, Ndidi." Chijioke Okorie felt the full weight of his friend's warning and appreciated the manner of concern in which it was relayed. This spoke not of doubt in Chiji's ability, but of the darkness that would invade his life should he accept this heavy mantle.

"If this works, you realize what will happen, what you'll be forced to do, right?" Tox Russell knuckled the table as he stared hard at him. "Tell me you understand what the undercover role means—that you *can't* protect the children and women—boys. They'll be beaten and raped right under your own nose and you will not be able to interdict." Ndidi gripped his shoulder. "I know your heart, brother. I know your convictions. The best, the purest. But this—"

"It is what I must do." Chiji steeled his spine and courage. "There is no other road before me. *This* is how I must help my

1

people, and it starts with saving my sister. If I cannot protect her, then how can I do this thing and help the rest?"

Ndidi rolled his shoulders and looked away with an aggrieved sigh. "Just remember—we need the name of their contact. All they have is his codename—Viper. We need his identity. But ..." His gaze darkened as he leaned in. "We can find another way. *Will* find another way, if—"

"I can do this."

"No doubt. But I know *you*, Chiji. This"—he thumbed toward the map around which stood a half dozen special operators and men willing to do violence on behalf of the innocent—"*this* will rip that big, proverb-spouting heart out of your chest and send a herd of elephants over it. That is—if they don't figure out who you are and don't kill you first."

That his American friend's confidence in his ability did not waver bolstered Chiji. "You fear for my safety."

"Yes!" Ndidi's emphasis on that lone word seemed a clap in the heavens.

"I am not afraid of this," Chiji said. "Chineke put me here and gave me friends to help. I have helped you fight your wars for many years. Now, I need you to help me fight this one, to help my people. If Jesus can let them put Him on the cross for the children, I can do this for the children of Nigeria."

"Just one hiccup there, Jiminy. You're not Jesus."

"No," Chiji said with a smile he knew irritated his friend, "but each day, I follow in His footsteps. And if it costs me my life, then I am at peace."

"That's the part I don't like."

"You never did."

"Hey," a voice from behind called. When they both glanced over their shoulders, an operator in tac gear thumbed over his shoulder. "Call came." He nodded to Chiji. "Everything's set, *Colonel Adebayo*. Readying the bird now."

Resolve firmed in his gut. Adigwe Adebayo was the name of

the notorious colonel said to be the mirror image of Chiji. The notorious colonel heavily involved in the corruption among the Nigerian government, including a brother in the Housing and Urban Development office. The notorious colonel who answered to only one person: General Kalu Agu, the very serpent in charge of the Nigerian mafia who had developed one of the largest, most profitable trafficking businesses that spanned several countries.

Ndidi lifted an eyebrow at Chiji. "Say it—that you understand—*fully* understand—what this means."

Chiji gave his friend a sad smile. "It was my plan."

"That's not what I asked." Ndidi narrowed an eye and leaned in, quieting his voice. "When—not if—*when* they learn who you are, there will be no rescue. It'll become a recovery mission." He scowled. "Of your sorry carcass."

"When a needle falls into a well, many people will look into the well, but only a few will be ready to go down after it." He jutted his jaw. "I am ready to go down after it."

A shadow darkened the gray eyes of the friend closer than a brother. They had worked enough missions together to be able to read each other well, and it was clear he did not like this one. "It's a bad idea." Expression like stone, Ndidi huffed. "Don't expect me to come get you when it goes wrong."

Something warmed in Chiji's chest—he had spoken those very words to Ndidi at the start of a mission that radically altered the man before him. And he knew that nothing would stop Ndidi from rushing to his aid if the situation demanded it. He grinned. "You came out of that mission the same—mostly. Except with a wife—and now a son."

"Don't change the subject."

"Just as you had to take that impossible mission upon your shoulders, so I must do this."

Ndidi rubbed his jaw with another sigh. "Just don't come back with a wife, okay?"

Chiji laughed. "The only bride I want is my people."

"Sir." The barked voice again drew their attention. "Time to roll. Readying the bird and awaiting final clearance from air traffic control, then we're wheels up."

If only it was as easy to ready his soul. The toll of this mission would be enormous on his mind. And on his body when they discovered the spy in their midst. Because in order to save his people, to cut off the head of this serpent poisoning his country and its name, he must become the serpent.

PRESENT DAY

MiLE Humanitarian Camp, Imo State, Nigeria

"You pray for death."

Even the intrusion of haunting words could not pull Willow Metcalfe from staring after the two preteen girls, Ginika and Adesina, now under the care of Dr. Paul Gallagher, medical director for the Obioma compound. "I've seen a lot," she murmured, eyes still stinging after processing the girls, "but this ..." She shook her head.

Nkechi crossed the room to a metal cabinet, from which she retrieved care kits filled with toiletries for the girls. "Here, they have a chance, a start of a new life." Her Owerri-born friend opened a small mesh bag and added a towel and wash cloth. "Do not forget—Nigerians are a strong people with a stronger faith."

Willow heaved a sigh as they prepped the backpacks. "I know, but it still breaks my heart knowing what they went through." She laid the clothes they'd sized for the girls inside. "Every other assignment I've worked with every other organization, I sort of grew numb to the pain—ya know, in order to make it through each day. It mortifies me what people can do to one another."

"But, to the glory of God," Nkechi asserted happily, loudly, "Mr. Cord comes here and starts Obioma. He is helping Imo State do more to stop this evil thing."

After years in the Peace Corps and all that she'd seen, Willow would be lying if she ascribed praise to God in light of all the hurt and suffering plaguing the world. How could one praise Him for a compound when people across the world were brutalizing each other? She had long ago taken a personal vow against violence. She loved her brothers but could not understand what they did, being soldiers, sailors ... operators. And her lack of faith in God over this would shame her Southern, Scripture-quoting mom right into the grave. But that was an argument for another day. Or never.

Especially if that look on Paul's face was any indication. Her stomach churned as he came toward them, head low. "I've done all I can." He ran his hand through his dark, unruly mop. "Just called HQ for a transfer to the Federal Medical Center for a surgical evaluation."

"*Surgery?*" Willow gaped and covered her mouth. "Is it really that bad? They're so young," she whispered.

"Most are," he said gravely and touched her shoulder. "Maybe you and Nkechi can get them a backpack and books to help make their transition more comfortable."

"We are ahead of you, Dr. Paul." Nkechi beamed, hoisting up the ones they'd finished moments ago. "You do your thing, and we do ours. The rest is up to Chineke."

Oh, that she had the enduring strength of this woman. Willow was flagging. Two months in this compound felt like two years, and she found herself ready to go home to Virginia. But going back would only remind her that she wasn't needed. Mom had Stone now, and with four heroic brothers and a high-powered-attorney sister, Willow had always been one Metcalfe trait shy of measuring up or being needed.

"Mama Willow! Mama Willow!"

The sweet, lilting voice yanked her toward the floral fabric curtain door as a blur-of-a-boy burst past it. She crouched just in time to catch up the ball of energy. Straightening, she squeezed the boy into a bear hug. "Ife! How's my favorite student?" She kissed his sweet, sweaty cheek, then tickled him.

Ifechukwu "Ife" Nnadozie laughed and squealed as she dug her fingers into his side. "No, stop!" His infectious laughter trilled in the tropical air as he arched backward and wriggled to free himself.

Laughing, Willow set him down before she dropped the wiry guy and squatted. "Now," she said, peering into his dark eyes, "what has you so excited?"

"Look!" He brandished a piece of paper—but when he saw it was now crumpled, his face fell. He pouted, that lower lip trembling. "It is ruined."

"Not at all." She extended her hand, so he'd give it to her. "I see letters and is that—"

"No, no." He patted her shoulder, his expression so serious and instructive. "I must tell you. Major Matt said."

Hiding her smile at his heart-melting sincerity, she nodded. "Of course. Go ahead."

"I did it! I passed my last test. Now"—his chest puffed—"I will be in class with the big kids."

Willow gasped. "That's amazing! I knew you could do this. It was a lot of hard work, wasn't it?"

He clapped a hand over his forehead. "No, not too hard." That chest puffed again. "I'm smart."

"And so humble, too. But you did it—worked hard and learned and"—she thrust her fists up, careful not to lose her balance—"victory!"

He mimicked her. "Victory!"

Through the V his arms formed, she saw Matt Rubart edge into the doorway, hands in his jean pockets. "Well," Willow said, "not only am I very proud of you, but so is Major Matt. And I know Mama Nkechi is, too. Right?" She eyed the other woman over her shoulder.

Nkechi tapped her temple with a conspiratorial nod. "Soon, you will be smarter than all the other boys, and maybe one day, you will be governor!"

"But I don't want to stay here." Ife edged closer to Willow. "I'm going home with Mama Willow." He hooked his arm over her shoulder and peered deeply, soulfully, into her eyes. "Right?" With a gentleness that had stolen her heart the very first day she'd arrived, he smoothed her long blond hair.

"You know you can't do that, Ife," Nkechi warned softly, likely wanting to keep the boy's expectations where they should be. "Besides, Imo State needs smart boys like you."

"But I don't want to stay in the orphanage. I want a home."

Heart wrenched in two, Willow hugged him. "And what about when you grow up? Nigeria needs strong leaders, and I'm sure you could—"

"I don't want to be a leader." He pouted. "I just want to play soccer."

She laughed and gave him a squeeze, hearing other children playing outside. "Well, it seems you're missing a very good game. Tell you what, I'll protect your paper, and you can go play."

"Okay!" With a sweet-but-noisy kiss on her cheek, he darted past Matt and out into the afternoon sun. He plowed right into the soccer game—a stark contrast to the shy, scared little boy she'd met a few short weeks ago.

Standing to her full five-nine height, Willow crossed her arms and smiled at him. "Come on, admit it."

He gave her a sidelong look even as he turned his head after the boy. "What am I to admit this time?"

She sidled over and jabbed him in the side. "You like it here."

After a short hesitation, he gave a cockeyed nod. "I like helping them, but ..." His blue eyes twinkled in the morning light that hit them, his gaze tracking over the courtyard of the compound. "I can't say I like it. Or what's happening."

Nkechi clicked her tongue. "There are not many who *like* what is happening, but we do our best and pray each day for Chineke to help us." Backpacks zipped, she lifted them and moved through the side door that led to the infirmary.

"She doesn't like me," Matt said conspiratorially.

Willow leaned against the doorjamb, watching the children playing, the older ones sitting on steps. Twenty children in all were resident here, until they could find permanent placement or relocation to an orphanage—one under MiLE's umbrella, not one that was a front for selling children for sexual exploit. She had not personally seen these, but Cord Taggart, the founder of MiLE—Mission: Liberate Everyone—warned it was commonplace. There was too much pain in the world these days. Too much. It wore on her, especially this horrific industry of trafficking.

"Maybe it's an epidemic."

Willow started. "What?" She straightened and looked around. "What epidemic?"

With a sheepish grin, he swiped the bridge of his nose. "Not liking me."

She gave a laugh and went back to monitoring the children. "You know I like you."

"But not enough to—"

"Matt," she sighed. "I told you—"

"I know." He nodded to the yard again. "*This* is what you're married to. Not me."

His words had a strange effect and somehow really, truly hurt. "I am sorry—"

"You're not, actually." He considered her then ran a hand over his stubbled jaw, a tiredness rimming his eyes that she hadn't noticed before. "But I get it."

Something in his words made her pause. "What am I hearing in your tone?"

"I'm going back," he said with a heaving breath, then nodded. "Home." Hands in his pockets again, he shrugged. "You asked me to give it a try, and I did. Though I have no regrets about coming, this isn't where I belong. I like helping people—it's why I went into medicine. But ... I can do that in a clinic in Virginia."

"Virginia." Part of her resented him for being able to go home. She couldn't. Wouldn't. Not yet. She traced the boundary wall of the compound, knowing she had unfinished business here. "That sounds ... planned."

"And that sounds as if you care."

"Of course I care." She'd always thought the world of Matt, even loved him—part of why she'd encouraged him to come out and join MiLE to see if they could make a go of it—but this one side of him always ... stung. "*This* is why, Matt. This is why I can't marry you. All through our relationship, despite saying you understood that I wanted to help people, that understanding never made it to your heart." She hated how this point had driven a wedge into what had been a perfect relationship. "It's *embedded* in mine. I belong here, have a purpose—"

"What is that purpose, Wills?"

"I'm here for the people. Here to help."

"You definitely have a call to help people, but how long is this—here—going to last? You move from place to place, job to job. That restlessness, Wills, is really about you needing to be needed. Feel like you matter, or are useful."

Her heart drummed hard. "What's wrong with wanting to be needed or to feel like I matter?"

"Nothing, in and of its own. But your worth—your intrinsic worth—isn't tied up in *doing*. The doing is born from trying to fill a wound. Your brothers—"

"Are *heroes!*"

"I know." He held up his hands. "Hear me. Please."

"No." She drew in a couple of ragged breaths. "No, I don't think so. I asked you to come out here to see if we could find common ground, make things work." She brushed her hair back. "Clearly, I was wrong."

"Yes," he said calmly, gravely. "You were. I came because I was willing to explore it, but you won't reciprocate. That aside ..." He shoved his hand through his hair, a move that reminded her of something from one of those sappy Christmas movies. "Look, I know you love these kids, but seeing the abuse, the sufferings, year after year, the impact on your tender heart ... I'm worried about you—"

"It doesn't matter what happens to me as long as I can help them."

He paused, considering her, then sighed. "It's *destroying* you, Willow." His worried, caring tone made it all the worse.

She scoffed, hating it when her vision blurred as she looked to the children again. "I'm fine," she bit out. A long line of dust plumed in the distance. "I'm needed here. It's fine—I'm fine."

"Will—"

"If I die here, helping them, I'm fine with that."

Sorrow creased his brow. "Then why are you so angry?"

"What?" She recoiled. "I'm not—"

"Your hands are fisted. You just used four 'fines.'"

She startled, only then realizing it was true. "Because *you*—"

A clanging alarm bell yanked Willow around. She scanned the area, heart in her throat, and saw one of the operators jogging toward them. "What's going on?"

"Got a call," Braden said as he cradled his M4 in his hands.

"Serious trouble headed our way. HQ said to pack up everyone and leave. Unfriendlies inbound."

Her gaze leapt to the ever enlarging plume of dust. "Leave? But there are sick people, children—"

"Then best we start moving now, ma'am, and stop chattering."

Anger shot through her, but she stifled it. "What trouble could be so bad we have to abandon the only home these kids have known?"

"Nigerian mafia."

CHAPTER
TWO

Outside Obioma Compound, Imo State, Nigeria

PANIC POUNDED the drums of war in his heart as the vehicle jounced and pitched them toward the compound. Had his message gone through? Had he sent it soon enough? It was tricky, sending the message while surrounded by mafia. Men who would as soon slit his throat as ask questions.

Please, Chineke, let the compound have had enough warning.

Integrating with the mafia cell had been much easier than Chiji expected. But had it been *too* easy? The mafia lieutenant, Ahmet Omo, was eager to have General Agu's possible attention and endorsement, so he'd readily accepted "Adigwe Adebayo" into the group. The man was very anxious to run their first "recruiting" op and have the general's man witness his cunning and effectiveness.

Ahmet thumped his shoulder and laughed. "You are so serious."

Chiji dragged his gaze back out the window, heart focused on prayers to know how to keep things as civil as he could manage once the attack began without compromising the mission. But his soul writhed, knowing what would come. It

12

would be hard, but he must do this, must find who had taken Chiasoka.

"Soon," Ahmet said as he two-handed the steering wheel to keep it on the dirt road, "I will show you how we do things here. How we can make money and have fun at the same time. Then—then you can tell the general, so he will help us."

"Help you what?" Chiji knew a sneer cut into his words, but it could work for him, for his role as Adigwe, who would be looking down on a lesser.

"Get more money, more weapons!" The lieutenant again thumped Chiji's arm. "Help make certain officials look the other way, eh, brother?"

It took every ounce of willpower not to recoil—or strike out. Chiji had not been among those he considered "brothers" in over two weeks. To be forced to accept "brother" from one responsible for the evil tearing his country apart …

A means to an end. A means to an end. He repeated the phrase over and over as the truck jounced along the rugged, dusty road toward the compound. Behind them, two more trucks, beds filled with mafia and soldiers, barreled toward the unsuspecting. Men wild, eyes fueled by greed and lust, and shooting into the air. All feeding the frenzy of depravity.

MILE COMPOUND – OBIOMA, NIGERIA

"Move it, people! Move it!" Braden barked as he and the other guards funneled everyone into the armored bus.

Ife clung to Willow's leg as she helped Nkechi ensure the children were boarding safely and quickly. It was so surreal, knowing they were about to be attacked. Knowing trouble was actively coming for them.

She shook herself, refocusing on the children. Each one had a pack slung across their backs as they climbed in. Paul and another doctor had boarded and were helping the children into safety positions. Clinging to each other, Ginika and Adesina scrambled inside and all but threw themselves at the back of the bus, then disappeared in one of the seats. Hiding, no doubt, in the hopes of protecting themselves from being taken again. It made Willow's heart ache.

"Mama Willow." Ife's eyes widened. "My picture! I forgot it."

"It's okay, I—"

He shot off.

"Ife, no!" She shouted over the heads of the other children climbing into the small bus, watching him dart around people, his speed and agility impressive and frustrating. "Ife! I have the picture." She started after him.

Braden put up a well-muscled arm that thumped into her midsection. "No, ma'am."

She scowled. "I have to get Ife! He ran back."

"No, ma'am," he repeated, firmer this time. But then … annoyance dug into eyes that had seen much. "I'll get him." He pivoted and jogged in the general direction of the bunkroom.

Should she help?

"Willow, please help!" Nkechi called from inside the bus.

Foot on the first step, Willow saw the problem. The two new girls were weeping puddles, clawing and crying for Nkechi, who was tending a younger child at the back. After another glance to the main building, praying Braden found Ife, Willow climbed up into the bus and hurried to the sobbing girls. Ginika was the first to spot her and threw her arms around Willow, and her sister followed.

Peering out the window, she offered reassurances to the preteens that all would be well while her heart worried over Ife.

"Is it them?" Ginika asked, her whole frame trembling. "Did they come to punish us?"

Easing onto the seat with them, Willow held the girl's head to her shoulder. "No, no. Shh." Saying it was another group of bad men only seemed to reinforce that they were not safe, that trouble was everywhere. "We're on the bus and will leave soon. We'll be fine."

"Please don't let them take us back," Adesina cried.

The creak and thud of the door closing drew her head up as the bus lurched away from the inner courtyard. She drew in a quick breath, searching the front for Ife. She spotted Braden standing in the door well, talking on his comms. She scanned the bus for the wiry little guy, but could not see him. He wasn't here …

No, that couldn't be. Braden wouldn't have gotten back on without him.

Her heart rattled. Surely he was here.

But even as she offered herself the reassurances, Braden's gaze rammed into hers. His lips tightened.

"No." Willow rose from the seat. "Wait here," she muttered, having to literally pry Ginika and Adesina's arms from around her. "Wait. Stop the bus!"

"Willow, what's wrong?" Matt called from the back.

Maybe she was making something out of nothing. But she had to be sure. She hurried, visually tracing every face in the seats as she made her way forward. Each wrong face made her heart thud harder, faster.

The bus jolted to a stop and the doors flung open.

"Oh, thank God!" She waded through the sea of legs to reach the front.

Braden stepped out to help Dr. Paul in. But no Ife. He had to be close. He'd been gone so long. Willow threw herself past Paul, her gaze locked on Braden. "Where is he? Where's Ife?"

He faltered. "I … I couldn't find him."

"*What?*" Willow reeled around, facing the main building.
Crack-boom!

Dust and debris erupted from the main gate just beyond the

main dorms ... where she spotted a round face in the upper window.

"No!" Willow darted forward.

"No way!" Braden shouted, catching her. "You go back and we can't do anything. You'll die."

"I'm not—"

Gunfire and trilling shouts peppered the air, stilling her. Lodging into her mind the futility of this. But how could she not help Ife?

"Go go go! Back on the bus." Braden tucked his M4 into his shoulder and fired back.

Willow turned and palmed the armored side. Heard a scream.

If you leave, he *will die.*

And if you stay, you *could die.*

"You can't do anything." Braden hooked Willow's arm as he protected them.

"Give me two minutes."

"Not happening!"

"We're out of time," the driver shouted.

"Two minutes for two lives. It's worth it."

"Two minutes will cost twenty lives!" Braden countered.

Heart tangled in the impossible situation, Willow looked to the window again, but Ife wasn't there.

"Willow!" Matt's voice somehow spiraled through the chaos engulfing the area. Drew her gaze to his through the bus window. He shook his head, his expression fierce. Scared.

He knew. *Knew* what was she going to do.

And now, so did she.

She wrenched free and bolted back to the main dorm. Plastered against the southernmost wall, she panted hard, sucking in air for courage and her aching lungs. Even as she did—unbelievably—she realized a plume of dust had replaced the bus. She stared at the fading end of the bus and saw Matt's face etched in horror, banging on the window.

The sight tugged at her as dust swarmed the escaping bus.

Terror yanked on her common sense. They'd left without her!! Stunned, stupefied—she hadn't expected them to do that, but ... but she'd known she couldn't leave Ife behind.

Matt must've found a window to open because his shout faded with the dust. At least he'd be safe. Go home—he hadn't wanted to be here anyway. Not really. And now he could go home and start that practice. Guess he didn't need her bad enough.

Willow scurried to the corner of the dorm and crouched. She peered around the plaster. The view opened before her of the courtyard's center. Men flooded out of a half dozen vehicles, running into the buildings.

She yanked back and plastered herself against the sun-warmed building. This had to be her stupidest idea yet. But she was not going to let Ife die at the hands of the Nigerian mafia, or worse—get groomed into becoming one of them.

The groundskeeper, Mr. Abara, was dragged out of his home and into the open by two mafia members. They were so young! Infuriating to see lives ruined at such a young age. The two teens pitched the aged man forward, sending him sprawling in the dirt.

What about Mr. Abara's wife and daughter? They were on the bus. Had to be. Right? *Please, God, let them have been on—*

Screams within the home squashed Willow's hope. Sickened, she could only imagine what was happening in there. Did not want to believe it. Forced herself to not imagine ...

Do something, idiot!

What? What could she do? She'd vowed to never answer violence with violence. And that wouldn't exactly serve the Abaras. Tears pricked as powerlessness clogged her veins.

I have to do something!

Jeers and mocking laughter filtered through the air. Her stomach roiled when she spotted two more men stalking into the small home. Whatever they were doing to the woman, it would only get worse.

Willow pulled back and thumped her head against the wall. Clenched her eyes. *Oh, Father*, please ... *Please help them.*

A hand clamped over her mouth.

She started. Bucked, blind with panic that they'd found her, she fought the man, afraid they'd rape her. Kill her. Then Ife wouldn't have a prayer. *No!* She wiggled. Thrashed.

"Willow, shh! *Shh!*"

The hissed voice wedged past her panic. She looked up into blue eyes and stilled as his hand fell away. "Matt!" Relief warred with her fear—he was here. She wasn't alone. But then again— he was *here*. He could die! Because of her! "What're you doing? Why aren't you on the bus?"

"Couldn't let you get all the glory."

She shoved him back. "You should've left. You were safe!"

"I'm trying to keep you alive!"

"That's not your job," she hissed at him, crouching lower as if that would shield her voice from the mafia. "I don't need your help."

"This isn't about *you*. Well, not completely about you." He nodded to the bunkroom. "Ife wasn't the only one left behind."

Properly chastised, Willow looked where he indicated. Spotted two more faces peering out to watch the chaos below. "Oh no," she whispered.

A frenzy of voices snapped their attention to the courtyard. Another youth aimed a weapon at Mr. Abara, his compatriots cheering him on.

She sucked in a breath.

Matt tapped her shoulder. "C'mon." On his haunches, he pivoted.

"We have to do something."

He looked over his shoulder. "We are. Hurry before—"

"I mean for Mr. Abara."

Matt's eyes told the truth. "We can't help him, but we might be able to get to the boys via a rear stairwell. If we hurry …"

"Then what?" Willow balked. "The bus left!"

"One thing at a time. C'mon."

Glancing back at the courtyard, Willow couldn't move. Couldn't make herself abandon one person to save the other. How on earth did her brothers do it?

Matt tugged her sleeve, pulling her after him. Conflicted, she went with him, each step a torment, anticipating the shot that would end the dear groundskeeper's life. There wasn't much to keep up here on the compound, but MiLE had given Mr. Abara a living, a way to provide for what was left of his family after his home and family were attacked last year by Boko Haram.

Crouch-running, they made their way past the administration building where, inside, they heard things breaking and being destroyed. They wound behind the stockroom, grateful there were no walls or doors on this side. Sounds of looting and men yelling, fighting over Obioma's meager supplies. It broke her heart and she stumbled, her courage giving out as they dropped behind the well for cover. They knelt, and she eyed the yawning gap between this well and the rear stairs to the dorm. Crossing it would put them in clear view of the mafia, who were gathered—

Willow sucked in a breath as the sea of men parted to allow three more. Two were better dressed but not what she'd consider well-dressed. The third was a giant—easily over the six-two height of her eldest brother, Stone—and stood next to a man who held his hand out to the side. At this silent signal, one of the youths passed him a rifle. Was he the leader?

"Where are they, old man?"

Mr. Abara looked at them but only shook his head.

"How did they know we were coming?" the leader asked.

19

Again, the older man shook his head.

"You cannot protect your woman or daughter. And you cannot protect yourself. You are a waste of life." The leader fired a burst at Mr. Abara.

Willow yelped and jerked back, covering her mouth. Tears burning.

Matt wrapped his arms around her.

"Heshothim.Heshothim." Shock spiraled through her. "Just … shot him."

"The boys," Matt urged, pulling her with him toward the open. "Hurry."

Even as they sprinted across the road, Willow found her gaze back on the brutal scene. Saw Mr. Abara laid out on the ground, the crowd of mafia dispersing, and most curiously … the tallest mafia leader moved forward, crouched next to the elderly man, and touched his forehead. His lips moved in some silent prayer or mantra. His gaze rose … and across the humid, hot day, dark, fathomless eyes connected with hers.

With a gasp, Willow ducked back and hurried up the stairs, heart hammering. Praying he had not seen her. That shadows had masked her face. He hadn't really looked into her eyes, right?

"Spread out," came the shout. "Find the rest! There are more here. I hear them!"

CHAPTER
THREE

WHAT WAS *SHE* DOING HERE?

He had seen her. A ray of glorious sunshine in one of the darkest missions of his life. And he knew her. Had prayed since seeing her in that photo for a chance to meet her, get to know her. Convince her that she was meant to marry him. A fool's hope. A fool's fancy. If her brother knew the hope Chiji harbored, he would have killed him rather than train him to run this op.

And now ... now she was here, scurrying around the dark places of this compound like the rats, seeking shadow and safety. From him. From these men he must play brother to.

He prayed she could find it. Because as much as he had prayed to God for the last two years for a chance for their paths to cross, it was not in this way he wanted it to happen. This ... her being here was bad. Ahmet would brutalize her. Share her with his captains.

And then ... then Chiji would have to do violence on her behalf. While he could make peace with that eventually, it would upend everything he had worked to create here. Every pawn put

21

into place. Every nuance enhanced … all to find his sister, Chiasoka, who had been taken from the village near their home compound. After easing the elderly man into God's arms with a whispered prayer, Chiji rose to his full height and towered over Ahmet. Used the psychological impact of that to cast some doubt on the man's confidence. Make him hesitate.

And hesitate Ahmet did. He frowned at Chiji. "You pray for this man?"

"Would you want to meet God knowing you had failed your family so completely?" Chiji hoped the answer was enough. He would never apologize for praying.

"There are over 400 orisha. Which are you praying to, Adigwe?"

The Yoruba worshiped many gods, but Christianity and Islam had deep roots in Nigeria as well. For Chiji, being raised by parents heavily impacted by Christian missionaries from London had lodged faith's thick tendrils around his heart.

But Ahmet … Ahmet was not interested in gods or God. He was interested in conflict and confrontation.

Crack! Boom!

Heart grieved, Chiji watched men toss Molotov cocktails through the window of what looked like a home. The homemade bombs went off, engulfing the structure in flames. A half dozen men emerged from the infirmary with boxes and sheets filled with medical supplies and drugs.

Chiji turned a fierce eye on Ahmet. "I thought you wanted to impress the general. This is not the way to do it." His suggestion that he was less than impressed hung sourly in the air. Knowing this man honored only himself came with a stiff warning that the blood and violence wrought at his hand would be overwhelming.

That realization turned Chiji toward the building where he'd seen the light of the sun grab her hair as she slipped into shadow again. She was not supposed to be here. None of them were. The warning had made it through—that's why the bus had been escaping. He'd been relieved, but then Ahmet sent a truck to intercept. Whatever her purpose for staying here, he prayed she could succeed, escape. Get away. Far away.

Please, God. Protect her. Show me the light.

OBIOMA COMPOUND, IMO STATE, NIGERIA

Unbelievably, the mafia were not yet on the second floor of the bunkhouse. Hand on Matt's back—he'd insisted she follow him down the hall, popping into each room, scanning the six bunks and checking closets—they had cleared all but the last two when thudding echoed in the hall.

"Mafia," she whispered.

Matt reached behind himself, caught her wrist, and brought her around in front of him. "Go." He whirled around and put his spine to her, walking backward. "Check the rooms. I'll cover."

Heart in her throat, Willow ducked into the first one. Gray mattresses gaped at her as she took in the room, the bunks and under, the dresser, then the closet. She rushed back to Matt. "Clear." She moved on to the next room. Saw the same thing, but ... this was it. The last two rooms. "Ife?" she hissed, trying to keep her voice low but loud enough for him to hear. "Ife, where are you?"

"Out of time," Matt warned quietly.

"I haven't found him yet!" The shriek in her voice matched the one in her heart as she sprinted back to the first room. Grabbed the jamb and flung herself back to the second. Then past Matt to—

"No!" he spat.

"I can't find him!" she cried, whirling around the empty room.

"Stop! You there!"

Willow spun and the blur-that-was-Matt materialized in front of her, blocking the hefty man with a machete and a malicious gleam in his eye. As he lifted the blade, she saw movement behind him in the room. The second-to-the-last room she'd checked.

Ife peeked out of a wood chest she'd ignored.

Willow drew in a sharp breath and touched Matt's back. How had she missed him? He gave an almost imperceptible nod even as he spoke to the machete man.

"You have no weapon," the Nigerian taunted as he took a step forward.

"I do not need a weapon to kill you." The warning in Matt's words made the man hesitate.

A slow grin smeared into the man's face. He hefted his machete and drove forward.

Matt surged at the man. Caught his weapon arm. Pinched the soft flesh beneath the arm, which elicited a piercing howl as the man went to his knee though he still tried to chop at them.

Matt ended the melee, forcing the man's weapon around and into his paunch. This time, the man's howl lost its fierceness and life ebbed away. He slumped to the floor even as three more mafiosos swarmed the stairs.

At the sweet, coppery scent of blood, Willow felt sick—but when she saw who trailed the three, she nearly emptied the contents of her breakfast on the floor next to the dead man.

Straightened, Matt backed into her, protecting her, pinning her.

He'll die and it's my fault. God, forgive me.

The tall, praying Nigerian stalked up the steps, his gaze locked on them in a lethal duel. Confidence oozed from his mahogany skin and rich, dark eyes challenged them. Dared them to test him. "You should not be here. Why did you not go on the bus, too?"

He knows about the bus ... Was that a bad thing? Was it a

warning? No ... no, this was taunting. And if he knew about the bus ... she worried about Nkechi and Dr. Paul. Ginika and Adesina. The other children.

"There's no reason to hurt us," Matt asserted. "We're no trouble. Nor do we want any."

The tall man looked from Matt to the dead mafioso on the floor. "I would disagree." His attention slid to Willow, though he spoke to Matt. "You killed one of Ahmet's men."

Matt shifted, trying to block his view of her. "He tried to kill us."

"What are you doing up here, Adigwe?" a voice rammed into the calm but tense confrontation. "What is taking so long?"

"I found two Americans," the taller man said over his shoulder—rich eyes never leaving her—as the boss, the same man who'd shot Mr. Abara, stomped onto the second floor.

The boss leered at them, lingering far too long on Willow as he walked a circle around her. "Kill the man, but this ..." Nodding, he sniggered. "Very nice, Adigwe. Thank you for this sweet—"

Adigwe stepped into the man's path. Touched a hand to his chest. "I found her, Ahmet."

Staring at the back that, compared to the others, was long and lean yet seemed powerfully broad and well-muscled beneath his blue linen shirt, Willow fought the urge to pound his back. Yell that neither of them would touch her. They disgusted her!

Matt's touch against her arm was gentle as he slipped between her and the tall Nigerian. In response, she curled her fingers around Matt's shirt. He lengthened his frame, trying to shield her.

Danger glimmered in the boss's eyes. "You challenge me, Adigwe?"

Adigwe had to angle his neck down to speak to the boss's face. "I would think this woman is enough of a price to buy my good word to the general." He cocked his head and was all ease and confidence, as if he bartered over a pair of shoes, not a woman, a *life*. "Yes?"

"We take turns then, yes?"

"No."

"You ask too much—"

"No." He bared his teeth as he said, "I *ask* nothing. I have said." He winged up his eyebrow. "You prefer then I speak to the general of what your men do here—"

"What do you mean?" the man growled.

"Did you think I missed the inventory you tucked aside on the last raid? Or what they are stealing here? Or the side business your men do with the women before you turn them in to the general?"

Over Matt's shoulder, she saw Ife peek up again. This time, another head was there, too—another boy. How could they both possibly fit in there? Hand low and at her side, Willow flicked her fingers, hoping he could see them, praying he'd get the message to stay put.

Ahmet wasn't yielding. "You wanted nothing of the old man's women, said you would not defile yourself with them," the boss said. "Why this one?"

The tall one caught Willow's hair and knuckled her chin. "Is it not obvious?"

Shocked at his touch, Willow did her best not to shy away, her mind still pinging on Ife. She tried to surreptitiously signal him to stay, not to move or say anything. If he remained there, maybe … maybe he could find his way to another compound or village.

Only then did she notice the hall had fallen quiet. Once more her gaze collided with his.

Oh no. *God, no—please don't—*

He studied her, those dark eyes probing, somehow delving past every protective barrier and practiced technique she'd learned over the years to portray that she was an ally, a friend.

The eyes ... rich, dark, fathomless. Not terrifying or void-like, empty of soul and heart. There was a kindness ...

She scoffed. *Right. He's with the Nigerian mafia, idiot!*

Had he seen her signaling the boys? But maybe he'd just flirt with her. Forget she'd been staring into the room.

Even as that hope bled into her consciousness, he angled his head around to look where she'd been looking.

Impulse almost yelped out an objection, but if he hadn't seen what she had seen, she would give it away.

He shifted around the leader, who asked what he was doing, then stalked into the room.

Heat streaking down her back and stabbing her belly with adrenaline that they'd find and kill Ife, Willow took a step forward.

Three blades sang in the air and came to stop just shy of her throat and side—and Matt's. The men swelled around them as the tall Nigerian stood in the middle and glanced around. Looked to her.

No. No no no no. She begged with all that was in her for God to hide the boys. That these monsters wouldn't find them or convert them.

Her heart rent when he shifted to the chest. Glanced at her.

Willow realized she was leaning forward, body tense. She yanked her gaze down. Refused to allow her body to betray Ife any more than it already had.

But she heard the creak of the lid. Heard Ife cry out.

Willow stifled a sob when the tall man hauled the two boys out into the open. Fury coursed through her—at herself for betraying their hiding place, and at the man who she suddenly found herself praying would meet his end. Soon. Violently. "You beast!"

CHAPTER
FOUR

Obioma Compound, Imo State, Nigeria

THE FURY of the sun burned in her eyes. Long had he imagined it would warm his heart, but as she stood there firing bolts of lightning from those blue eyes, he felt they had a sort of acid to them. She hated him. Hated him for being one of the villains in this story of hers. Hated him for finding the boy.

There had been no choice. If she had been on that bus, complied with the evacuation order sent by Command at his tip, she would not be in danger. Neither would the boy. She only had herself to blame, and for the first time, he found himself disappointed in a Metcalfe.

Irritation crept along his shoulders as they stood in the open courtyard of the compound, the two Americans staying too close. The man seemed to believe he could protect her. Chiji must relieve him of that misconception.

Fire consumed the buildings, eating through plaster like candy. Chiji blinked against the gritty air choked with smoke as he put the boy with the other children they'd found.

"No! You beast. Leave them alone!" the woman shouted and

lunged toward him, but the American man wisely stopped her. "Ife—"

"Mama Willow!" the boy cried as Debare, one of Ahmet's men, manhandled the boy into the back of the truck.

A thump nailed him in the back and Chiji pivoted. As he rounded, he saw several things at once—her wild, frenzied face framed in a current of straw-colored hair as she screamed and struck his chest; flames viciously eating through the building directly behind the Americans and on the verge of collapse; the American man rushing to intercept Yemi, who had aimed his weapon at the woman; and Ahmet ... watching. Watching very intently.

Chiji snatched up a nearby broom, snapped it in two over his leg, and glided forward, his makeshift kali sticks striking swift and fast, neutralizing not only the American male, but also Yemi. He whirled around and searched for another assailant, but the remaining mafiosos shuffled away, eventually climbing into the trucks to leave.

Jaw tight and both sticks in one hand, Chiji drove his gaze to Ahmet's as he caught the woman's upper arm. Though she cried out, his twitch of the sticks silenced her, made her draw back. "We should leave." Before anyone else got hurt. He guided her to the truck.

"Matt!" she screamed over his shoulder, scrambling for the American. "Matt!" Her white shoes skidded and scraped on the dirt as she fought to get free. "Release me, you beast!" She drew in a breath and all but howled the man's name.

Her words stabbed his conscience, but he could not let her direct the course of events here. "Silence," Chiji hissed, yanking her to his chest, "or you will get him killed."

At first, her blue eyes met his and she cowered. Then, as if fear ignited something rebellious, she drew up. Jutted her chin. Eyes blazed. She shoved him.

Prepared for her fury, he was immovable, implacable. She was, after all, a Metcalfe.

Again, her hands beat his chest like a drum, writhing against his vise grip. He did his best not to injure her, but neither could he allow her to get loose. To run back to the man.

"Stop," he gritted out. "You endan—"

Crack!

The lone shot in the crackling air jolted her into silence. Her hand latched into his biceps a split second before she stilled. Her eyes bulged as she stared at him, frozen in the terror of what that gunshot had meant. Who the bullet had struck.

Chiji did not have to look toward the sound to know what happened.

She sucked in a breath, looking around him. And the shriek of her grief split the air. "No! Nooo!" Her back arched away, as she tried to break free of him and the scene—the killing that had just happened. "Matt! Matt, *noooo!*"

Not wanting to manhandle her, he knew he must restrain her. Keep her from throwing herself into the attention of Ahmet or the spray of bullets likely to come. He turned her into himself, holding her tight even as he saw her strength crumbling.

"No." It was the softest of words, a mere breath, but it bellowed against the chaos and violence of the day. Her fingers curled against his sleeve, tightening it, a move that seemed to mirror the breath that never came. An agonized sob struggled past her restraint, trembling her frame. "No, no, no, no," she wailed, crumbling against his shoulder as he held her in place.Silently, he begged her not to fight him anymore. Not to draw any more attention to herself, or it'd likely have terrible repercussions. To his relief, she submitted to his guidance into the rear passenger seat of the king cab truck.

Shock glazed her expression as pain wracked her. She glanced out the side window to the center of the compound.

Holding the truck frame, Chiji allowed himself to look there, too. Saw the fallen American adult male. The man she had called Matt laid out in a pool of his own blood, the mafioso picking over his clothes and pockets for anything valuable.

With a groan, she sobbed.

The sound, seeing her in such pain, fisted a hand around his throat. He met the gaze of the one responsible as the boss strode toward them with Yemi. The carnage had been expected, but nothing had prepared Chiji to find her still here. To see her so terribly impacted. To give witness to her grief and shock.

"Let's go," Ahmet gruffed.

Chiji nodded to the boss, then folded himself into the truck next to her. She drew in a sharp breath, pulling herself more to the middle as if repulsed by him.

"*Don't*. Touch. Me."

The truck shifted as the boss and his men loaded up and they got under way. "Jachike waits with what's left of the bus," Ahmet said.

Chiji's gut tightened at the idea of what they'd find there— the children, women …

Ahmet glanced in the mirror to the woman, then to Chiji. "She should be easier to manage now that the American is out of the way. But I still think we should share." His laughter could not drown Chiji's conscience over his hand in what had happened.

Repulsed, yet shaking from the shock of her boyfriend killed, she dropped her gaze to her lap.

Needing to divert Ahmet's thoughts from her, he asked, "How many are left from the bus?"

"Why would you ask that?" Ahmet challenged.

"Because I see in these raids that this cell lacks restraint and has bloodlust."

"You sound like the Americans."

"You sound defensive," Chiji challenged, but then put the

31

man in remembrance of the mafia's direction, their need to connect with Boko Haram. "The general wants cells that can operate swiftly, move merchandise *without* drawing attention." He deliberately glanced back toward the compound, now several miles behind them and marked by a thick black cloud of smoke. "That is a mistake."

"Do not question me!" Ahmet's words cut sharp. "We want the general's help, but we were doing fine before you came."

"And will you ruin the name you developed by being overzealous and foolish?"

Ahmet sneered. "Watch yourself, Adigwe. You are here as a guest, not an overseer. Besides, Yemi is not happy with you attacking him—"

"I stopped a waste of time. The smoke draws attention and authorities. If they came while we were still there, then your entire operation will be dismantled."

"You think you know so much about how things work here."

"I know we must move the children to the warehouse by nightfall." Chiji felt Ms. Metcalfe's gaze on him then. No doubt deciding to add "monster" to the "beast" she had called him. "Also, Kalu will not strike a deal without the name of your boss, and he has been nowhere so far."

Ahmet met his gaze in the rearview mirror, but said nothing. Then his gaze shifted to the woman, and something flickered through the empty eyes that warned Chiji of what was to come. What he would be forced to do. His days of playing advocate may be over. The villain she believed him to be? If he was to protect her—and yes, he must—he had to become fully that monster.

MiLE Safehouse, Imo State, Nigeria

"Bad news."

Cord Taggart looked up from his phone and did not like the expression Lowell had on his face. He pocketed his phone and braced himself.

"The bus didn't make it out. Mafia ran it down and took them hostage. Killed the staff."

Hissing a curse, Cord swiped a hand over his beard. Leaned on the table. Felt his gut roil. "How many dead?"

"Ten at last count."

"Missing?

"Twenty—oh, we do have two MIAs, including Willow."

Cord lifted his eyes to his buddy. "Say again?"

Low glanced at a piece of paper. "You heard me. Willow's MIA along with that major working onsite. Team's there, combing through the wreckage."

Wreckage. Cord sighed. It had been the MO of this particular mafia cell to burn places to the ground, leaving no way for the people to recover or regroup. Force control and power into their territory and hands.

"Three bodies need DNA to be identified."

Biting back yet another curse, Cord shook his head.

"Team suggested one could be Willow."

"It's not." No way. Can't be.

"How do you know?"

"Because—" he barked, then reined in his anger. "Because I'm not going to tell Canyon Metcalfe I let his sister die." Holy crud that'd be a bloody encounter. "Ain't happening." He stuffed his hands on his tactical belt. Brooke would never talk to him again. And it was hard enough to get the brunette beauty to take his calls. He dragged his hand over his beard again. And again. "We need to find them."

"How?"

Cord tucked his arms under his armpits. "I'll call Canyon. Update him. See if they can't pull some strings to get us some unofficial satellite traces on the movement of that cell."

"Then I suggest you put on a containment suit because he's going to go nuclear."

CHAPTER
FIVE

HE DIDN'T WANT *to be here, and now he's dead because of me.*

The rawness of that truth scraped against any hope she had of getting out of this alive. They'd shot Matt in cold blood. She had loved him—maybe not in the romantic, gushy way, but ... like a brother. Even if she took a scrub brush to her mind, she could never wash the image of him dead, lying face down in the dirt, an ever-widening dark stain spreading around his head like a twisted, dark halo.

These men were animals. And she could not fathom a way to escape without being brutalized or killed.

Oh, Matt ...

Eyelids sliding closed, she remembered his laugh. Tried to memorize it. His silly, almost corny romanticism. His blue eyes—so like the Metcalfe family trademark, but a little grayer—and the handsome set of his jaw. The most beautiful thing about Matt was his commitment to helping people. Seeing the best in them.

And he was gone.

Because of these ... monsters.

She felt her grief quickly fanning into rage. So senseless, the killings, the brutalizing … She'd never understood violence for the sake of violence—or any kind of violence. It only bred more violence.

Why couldn't people just get along? Help each other. And—

The truck bounced and Adigwe's arm and leg pressed into hers.

Teeth gritted, she twitched away. Didn't want the men on either side touching any part of her. She'd been taught very basic self-defense, but she wished she'd let Canyon teach her more. He'd wanted to. Encouraged her, especially when she went into the Peace Corps and he'd been worried about the places she'd visit and people she'd encounter. But she'd never wanted those skills. Until now. The tall one on her left had beat two men with sticks as if he'd been whipping meringue. That'd be a handy skill to have.

Especially after the leering glances from the two in the front seat. Who would defend her now? She'd never really worried about it before. Even in previous incidents when she'd been threatened or beaten. Matt had been killed, Mr. Abara … Who knew what other deaths these men had caused? And now they were on to the intercepted bus.

"There." Adigwe shifted forward, catching the headrest of the driver's seat, and thrust his arm toward the windshield. "The bus."

Engine gunned, Ahmet veered off road and down a slight ravine.

That's when Willow saw it. Her heart lurched at the sight of the burned-out hulk of the bus. Smoke was still rising and clogging the air. To the side, a half dozen armed men stood over a huddle of people—the Obioma staff and children.

Were Nkechi, Adesina, and Ginika okay? What about Paul?

Willow's heart raced as the truck tore over the rugged terrain toward the scene. The mafia members broke away from the hostages and started moving toward the vehicles, blocking her view, preventing her from seeing her friends and the children.

Please, God ... please please please ...

Before the truck had fully stopped, the men were flinging open doors and hopping out. All except the tall one.

His dark eyes were on the bus. "Stay here." He exited the cab and rounded the front of the truck. He towered over the others, who offered him clear deference. The monster of these beasts. She could not despise a person more, hearing him talk about moving *merchandise* and property. Talking about profits—made off the skin trade. It was repulsive!

Matt ... Matt ... She again looked toward the Obioma huddle, heart jammed over what might've happened and to whom. She did not want anyone else to end up like Matt. Which meant she could not sit here and idly watch them murder more of her friends.

But he'd said to stay. And she didn't dare cross him or any of them. He'd growled for her to be quiet, to stop shouting or they'd kill Matt, and she'd ignored him ... Now Matt was dead.

She swallowed. Felt nauseated as she again looked ...

Blood. She saw blood on the clothing of some of the children. Willow slid across the bench seat and pushed open the truck door. Went around the back side of the truck, moving straight for her friends and the kids. Fingers tipped to her temple, she blocked the sun, searching for Nkechi and the girls. Paul and his assistant ... But she couldn't see them.

As she threaded her way toward them, she had an acute awareness of Adigwe's position. Knew the moment he'd noticed her. Felt the air swirl as he started in her direction.

Heart racing, she hurried forward.

"Hey!" Adigwe's shout made her heart jam.

Among the hostages, a familiar round face turned to her— and gave her back her breath. Did she know where the others were? Willow kept moving, determined not to be stopped before she found everyone.

"Nkechi, where's Ife—" The boy's name caught in her throat as the woman's torn clothes, split lip, bloodied shirt registered.

"No …" Choked up, Willow faltered. Realized what must have happened. When the tall man appeared in front of her, she swatted at him and stumbled back. "Get away from me!"

But Adigwe was not one to be easily deterred. "I told you to stay—"

Rage erupted. Willow shoved him. "You evil, perverted beasts! Monsters!" She leapt backward out of his grasp. "Is this all you people know how to do? Hurt? Maim? Rape? Murder?"

The man had a speed and deftness she hadn't anticipated. He caught her shoulders, spun her around, and pulled her back against his chest. His long, muscular arms encircled her, hands framing her face.

She was … pinned. Feeling powerless, threatened, she thrashed and screamed.

"Silence," he hissed against her ear. "Or they will—"

"Get off me! I won't make it easy for you. I don't care what you do to me!"

His bicep curled around her throat. He applied a firm, steady pressure. Squeezing off her air. Though she slapped at his arm and tried to lift her legs to drop out of his vise, nothing worked. Even attempted to bite. All failed. She couldn't breathe. He'd strangle her. She'd die. Like Matt. Panic lit through her. She bucked, tears blurring her vision as the edges of her vision folded in on her.

"It is for your own good." His deep voice chased her into a void.

IMO STATE, NIGERIA

He held his heart in his arms and felt it breaking.

Aggrieved at what he'd had to do, Chiji lifted her into his arms, pivoted, and started back to the truck. Mutterings of the mafiosos as he strode past warned that his intervention aroused their curiosity and suspicion. Exactly what he feared. He started working up a plausible explanation to give Ahmet for why he paid so much attention to her. Protected her.

O Chi ne cherem, give me the words …

The door sat ajar, and he slid her onto the seat, a little roughly—not so much that he hurt her, but enough to appear as if he was angry with her. He buckled her in, his gaze tracking over her creamy complexion and peach lips. The same face from that picture, the one that told him he would marry her one day. A crazy thought that had dug into his heart and ricocheted off his convictions when he'd first seen her in the compound.

But after this, she probably would never talk to him again. Just past her serene expression and through the back window, he spotted a rope in the truck bed. Knew he had to make this convincing. He backed out and reached over the side of the bed to retrieve—

A weight plowed into him. Shoved him inside the truck. The impact knocked the breath from his lungs, but he was wheeling around before he could be struck again. Fell into a fighting stance, itching for his sticks.

"What is this?" demanded Ahmet, motioning wildly to the cab, where Miss Metcalfe was still unconscious. "What are you doing with her?"

Chiji straightened, mind racing for a justification. Nothing came. *Chineke,* please*!* On the heels of his cry out to his Creator, he reached into the back and retrieved the rope. "Am I to explain everything I do?" Deftly, he moved around the man and pressed his knee onto the seat. Braced, he tied her hands, then secured it to the roll bar inside.

When he exited, he was again shoved back.

Ahmet bared his teeth. Thumped his fingertips against Chiji's chest. "You disrespect me and I will kill this woman myself!"

Something hot and vicious spiraled through his gut. "That would be a mistake."

His near-black eyes widened. "Oh yeah? Why is that?" He motioned wildly with his hands. "I do not care. You are not the boss. I am. And I will make this woman"—he drew a pistol from his belt—"understand what she is good for."

"Do that and you will answer to General Agu himself."

"Man." Ahmet twisted his lips to the side and clicked his tongue. "The general does not care about one white woman."

"He does," Chiji argued, recalling intelligence reports from their last briefing. "Did you hear he is building a high-end brothel in Italy? This one will be a prize for sure." Air whooshed from his lungs at the lie and its audacity. But it was very believable.

"Italy." Ahmet's thick brows furrowed as he considered him.

That he said that as a statement, not a question worried Chiji. He would need to update Cord and Command on this new information he'd injected into the mission. "The general is looking for another woman—a favorite. He said she was his first." If he did not vomit, it would be a miracle. "Her name is Chiasoka. Have you heard of this one?"

"What do I care about names?" Ahmet scoffed. "I only care about how good they are"—his grin was lecherous and toothy—"and the money they make me." He jutted his jaw to the cab. "Do you not think we should sample the merchandise to be sure the general gets the very best?"

"You know virgins get more money."

His lip curled. "She is too old to be a virgin!"

If he did not kill this man that would be a miracle as well.

"She is a Christian and they do not believe in that until marriage."

Ahmet barked a laugh, then his expression went serious. "You know a lot about this woman."

"I do not," Chiji countered. At least in this one he could be truthful. "She wears a cross. And the artwork in the compound."

Ahmet frowned and drew back, his gaze tracking over Chiji's face. "What art?"

"In the classroom—printed pages from a Bible study with depictions of their Jesus."

Though the boss did not say anything, he hesitated.

Yemi didn't, though. "That could have been given by anyone, even the other woman, who we taught a lesson." He thrust his chin at the cab. "Maybe I need to teach this American her place."

It was as much a challenge of Chiji's authority as it was a true threat against Miss Metcalfe, so Chiji drew up and stepped toward the man. "She is for the general," he said slow and low, daring the guy to argue.

Yemi sniffed. "Who is to know?"

Furious at the thought of this man touching her, Chiji inched closer and tucked his chin. "I will."

"Yeah? I—"

"Enough." Ahmet moved between them, pushing Chiji and Yemi apart, as he made his way to the driver's door. "We must go. Get in—both of you."

The trucks now packed with people, including injured. A woman whose right eye was swollen shut hugged two teen girls. Four boys no older than twelve tried to look brave, but the panic in their faces ... Chiji looked away ... The bodies strewn across the harsh land were already drawing vultures. He ran a hand over his face, then rested it on his heart, which ached over those he had not been soon enough to save. At the pure fact that they were dead, their lives wasted.

O Chineke … I know it grieves You, too.

Burdened with the loss, Chiji folded himself into the cab and took in Miss Metcalfe. Blond hair fringed her forehead and accented her strong cheekbones. He prayed she would not wake until they reached the warehouse, because he could not be sure how long he could keep putting off these monsters.

Ahmet eyed him from the rearview mirror.

Did the boss? Had he seen Chiji's grief over the women, the bodies? Did he see through his tough façade to see his protective instinct regarding Miss Metcalfe?

"You notice a lot."

"It is why I am where I am." Chiji lifted a shoulder in a shrug. "I want to make my boss happy." Not the boss Ahmet would assume, but the illusion of words worked well for Chiji.

"The general is lucky to have you."

He cocked his head in lieu of speaking. Took a moment to pray, to process the tragedy happening here. The people—his own people—tearing the country apart from within. He must stop them. Would stop them.

Nigeria was so much better than this. It infuriated him that men would be weak, wicked, cruel to their own people. He was here to make sure Nigeria found its way back to strength and the potential so thickly woven into its fabric.

But first—he must find a way to keep Canyon's sister alive. And, he hoped, somehow he could convince her that he was not the monster she believed. He could still hear her growled accusations of being a beast, a monster. Having to sleeper hold her would not help his case. Not with her anyway.

It should, however, alleviate any concern Ahmet or Yemi might have about his loyalty. Because if that was an issue, then there would be little he could do to keep Canyon's sister alive.

CHAPTER SIX

SOMEWHERE IN NIGERIA

THUNDER HAD nothing on the pounding in her head.

Groaning, Willow shifted and tried to drag herself past the heaviness weighting her limbs. She shifted and levered up—only to collapse, her mind struggling to understand why she'd fallen. Shaking off the confusion, she squinted at her hands. It was too dark. Why was it dark? Where was she?

She grunted—and fell into a coughing fit against a dry, sore throat. Coughing made her head hammer. When she covered her mouth and hit herself with both hands, her brain finally made sense of her clumsiness—her hands were tied!

Amid the drumming in her thick skull, it all came rushing back—watching through the truck window and seeing the women, the injuries ... feeling indignation and anger that they'd been beaten and raped. Thinking of them being killed so cold-bloodedly like Matt. Blind rage had driven her across that field. Then the peripheral awareness of Adigwe swooping up behind her. The alarm and panic. The suffocation from his stranglehold.

Matt ... oh Matt ... Vulnerability siphoned her courage. Remembering him, the promises of safety and protection she'd made to the girls ... which had done nothing to stop the mafia from *again* violating the girls.

She'd lied to them. Gotten Matt killed ...

It was too much. *Too much.* Willow stifled a sob. Felt herself collapsing within.

"You're a Metcalfe. We don't do weak." That had been Canyon's admonishment when she was dealing with bullies in high school. *"Take ownership. Stay on mission."* Which, at that point, had been surviving her senior year.

Now, she had a new mission: surviving this.

No. This wasn't about *her.* This was about Ife, Nkechi, Adesina, Ginika, and all the others trapped in this nightmare. She had mastered enough street smarts having four brothers.

Willow hauled herself up, using both hands to shift upright. Her neck hurt. She touched the sore spot. It didn't feel raw, only ached.

A shock of fear hit her system. Nkechi had been violated—had the tall one raped her while she'd been out? Mentally, she probed for pain points in her private areas but, blessedly, felt none. Then she cursed herself for being relieved when her friends had been hurt and Matt killed. Selfish ...

She groaned around the lashing truth that cut through her. Complete darkness invited her into its void with cold, thick dampness.

"You are awake now?" Nkechi's question came from behind and sounded quiet, tired.

Startled at the whisper, Willow shifted and angled toward her friend's voice. "Yeah. How-how are you?" She winced—it hurt to talk—and again felt the humidity, the cooler temps. "Where are we?"

"Shh," Nkechi whispered. "Guards are outside the door. They say we are in Lagos."

"Lagos?" Willow startled. "Wow." How on earth were they in *Lagos* already? The Nigerian mafia operated in the north, and the compound had been in central Nigeria. She frowned into the darkness, trying to work through the information. Why go southwest? "How long was I out?"

"All night," Nkechi said.

All night? It hadn't even been dark when he'd choked her unconscious. So, easily eight hours … Was that long enough to get to the coast? Not that she didn't believe Nkechi, but— "Why did they bring us here?"

"Whatever it is, it cannot be good," Nkechi warned.

"Yeah …" Willow felt a wall nearby and leaned against it— anything to find relief for her throbbing head that made it hard to think.

Why? Why go south? What was here …?

It seemed so obvious: the coast. They were going to put them on a boat. If they did that, they'd never be found. "We have to get out of here."

"Not yet—the girls have … pains—" Nkechi whispered.

Pains. What her friend did not voice hung gaping in the night between them. "And you?"

Nkechi gave a soft grunt. "'…in God I trust; I will not be afraid. What can man do to me?'"

Glad her friend could not see her, Willow shook her head at the Bible verse. Man had apparently done plenty to these women. How could someone who had been so horribly wronged so easily and readily quote from Psalms regarding this situation? "But are *you* okay?"

"Quiet!" a gravelly voice barked from somewhere nearby. "Or you will get another lesson."

Willow slid down on the cement floor and curled onto her side, facing Nkechi. "Where are the others?"

"They took the boys," Nkechi whispered.

Willow's pulse spasmed. "Ife."

Light exploded through the structure. The staccato report of gunfire punctured the near silence.

Willow jerked upward, her eyes straining against the sudden brightness. A shadow blurred toward her. She cringed and lifted an arm to shield herself.

"What were you told?" the man demanded as he scuffled toward her. Struck her.

Head snapped back beneath the blow, Willow fought every instinct to fight back. The one that said to sweep his legs out from under him. She fought that instinct ...

And failed.

Her leg swiveled around. Caught him just behind the ankle. She leapt up, making sure he went down. Saw the weapon that flung from his grip. Heard the eerie silence broken by startled gasps and cries around her. The children, the girls ...

Even as he fell backward, face riddled in shock, she sighted the weapon. Snatched it. Just as she had a dozen times stealing the football in family games with Stone, Canyon, Range, and Leif in the backyard of Mom's house. Played king of the mountain against those much stronger brothers.

She whipped up the rifle at the same time she drove her heel into his face.

Nervous titters snaked around her from the others in the warehouse as she dropped on the man. Her stomach clenched when she heard his head hit the concrete—hard. Bounce. He went still.

Nausea roiled through her. She hadn't meant for that to happen. But ... it worked. It meant they had an opening.

Startled, she stared at the man. "That actually worked." She shoved back, appalled. Thrust her mind away from the violence she'd perpetrated. Violence she'd abhorred, been abhorrently against. Violence that would give her and the others a chance.

Shaking off her surprise, she pivoted. Saw the door. She mentally aligned the direction the unconscious man had come from. Remembered what Nkechi said about guards out there. She scanned the room and spotted another door. "C'mon!"

She raced across the room, only realizing the emptiness of sound. Confused, she glanced back. Saw Nkechi hadn't moved.

"Hurry! We have little time before they come to look for him."

Nkechi motioned to the girls, who swarmed her like bees to honey. "But where will we go?"

"Away from here." It was the only answer Willow had. "Anywhere is better than wherever they're planning to take us."

"But the girls are injured, too slow."

At the door, Willow gently tested it and felt it give. She held it closed as she responded to her friend. "We'll help them."

"But we are eighteen. How will—"

"We'll work it out," Willow grunted. Nodded. All she cared about was escaping. They'd figure it out as they went. That's how she'd always tackled problems. Stone liked a million plans and Canyon liked to have his tactical objectives … Her? Who cared as long as she got started? It always sorted itself out. Eventually.

"Single file," she instructed. "Let's go. Now." Heart hammering, she expelled a long, slow breath. Hoped there wasn't trouble on the other side of the door. "Fast and light," she whispered to the others, remembering how many times Stone had admonished her to do the same while playing Sunday afternoon football games in the backyard.

After one more glance over her shoulder … bolstered to find the girls had complied, gathering the younger ones into their arms, she faced the door. Knew that anything or anyone could be on the other side. Even the tall one. The man who'd confronted them, taken Ife … put her in a choke hold—she yet felt the ache in her throat from that—and knew death could very easily wait on the other side.

But staying here guaranteed death—if not of the body, then of the soul.

His eyes … they swam into her vision. Dark as night. Deep.

Familiar.

No. Not familiar. Except that violence had one look—ugly.

Which he wasn't. In *any* meaning of the word.

Shut up and open the door.

Shifting the rifle into a firmer hold, knowing she'd never use it—but they didn't know that—she again wished for her brothers. They'd taught her how to clear a door, but the girls had no time for her to teach them. It was up to her.

She reached gingerly for the knob again. Slowly … each twist a panged knot in her chest … she opened it. Light shivered out and she drew in a sharp breath at the darkness outside. The light … she was shedding light into a darkened anterior room.

Breath trapped in her throat, she listened past her own thundering heart for any noise. Movement.

She heard breathing that sent an icy finger down her spine.

Until she realized it was the breath of the child Nkechi held.

Willow shuddered and threw the light into the room, following it quickly, weapon up and sweeping. She wasn't an operator. She was probably holding something wrong or breathing wrong or something. Canyon had always said something about breathing right when you lined up a shot. No idea if the safety was on. Did this thing even have a safety?

Halfway across the open room, she suddenly heard them. The whimpers. The slap of feet on concrete. Nervous breathing. She wanted to hiss them to be quiet, but that would only add to the noise.

Focus on the mission.

"Where do we go?"

Willow's spine rippled at the sudden intrusion of Nkechi's voice. "Quiet."

A rumble of voices coming toward them from the other side of the far wall froze Willow. The girls bumped into each other with nervous yips and cries. Increasing their auditory imprint.

"What is that?" a man barked.

Boots rushed toward them.

"Bac—" The command lodged in Willow's throat a mere second before large shapes rounded the corner.

Light exploded again, blinding them for an instant.

Willow cringed toward the girls, trying to shield them. But nothing could shield them from the furious expressions that popped into sight.

The men jolted at finding their hostages in the middle of an escape. Shouts rang and bounced off the metal structure as they lunged toward them.

Willow set the rifle against her shoulder and peered down the muzzle, her heart a pumping, chaotic mess of panic. "Stop! Don't come any closer." Could she fire the weapon? Fire it, yes. But *shoot someone*? No … But what other way was there? Talking wouldn't work—she'd tried that. "Stop or I'll shoot."

The half-dozen men hesitated, wariness in their faces, but then, their sea of bodies parted, and the tall Nigerian strode into the room. A fury stole over his features that she had not seen before. "You foolish girl!"

His remonstration smothered clear thought.

When he started forward, she flinched. A short burst of gunfire crackled through the warehouse, yanking yelps from the girls. Curses from the men. Shocked—she realized her nerves had depressed the trigger. She hadn't meant to do that! With a strangled yelp, she searched for injuries as her stomach wove into a million knots that left her nauseated. The men looked just as shocked as her. "S-stay where you are!"

Somewhere in Nigeria

She would get them all killed. Though she had fire amid that halo of golden hair that spilled over her shoulder and rested so gracefully against the white lacy top, Chiji wished she also had wisdom to know when to throw that fire around. She did not realize the things she played at, the trouble she was violently stirring. Already this mission had gone bad. He had anticipated traveling north, as most mafia had done, going up through Niger and Libya, then across the sea to Italy to the ancient port city they had overtaken and turned into on massive brothel. As it had always been. If they reached that shore ... the girls would have been as good as lost. Never recovered like so many before them.

Instead, this time, the mafia went southwest. Which gave Chiji time to reach Command. And thankfully, bought time for the hostages. For Miss Metcalfe.

Who was holding the men at bay with an M4.

Tucking aside his shock that somehow she had disabled a man, taken his weapon, and nearly made it out of the warehouse, he lifted his palms to her. Inched forward a step.

"N-no!" she warned, the weapon tucked against her shoulder as she firmed her stance.

She was willing to defend these women and girls, but she was also terrified. Her hands shook, and he believed—hoped— that was what caused the first shot—a misfire. Mercifully, nobody had been injured, including her. But now the men would view her as a danger, a threat.

"Be careful," he warned, "it would be very easy to shoot the wrong person."

"I have the weapon aimed in the right direction. Now. We're walking out of here—"

"That I cannot allow," Chiji said, advancing. Keeping her here was the only way he knew to make sure she stayed alive. Besides, at this point, her escaping was an impossibility. She could not see the men with a higher advantage and their sights on her. He could.

"*Stop!*"

He stopped. Almost within arm's reach. "We cannot let you leave, so what compromise can we come to?"

"You monsters have done enough," she growled. "Stay where you are. I don't want to hurt anyone, but I will. I-if I have to."

He had to appeal to her nature, which was protective yet sensitive. Somehow let her know he was not the enemy she believed. "Nobody must get hurt."

"*You* already did that—you and your men raped these—"

"I would come to an agreement with you."

"I don't need your agreement. I have the weapon. You have soft flesh."

Chiji let a smile ease into his face. "As do you, and I fear if you fire that again, these men may rush you and the ones above may fire."

Wariness crouched at the edges of her blue eyes. "I won't go down without a fight."

He took another inch. "There does not need to be a fight," Chiji said, proud of her. Knowing Canyon would be proud.

That. That was how he could reach her.

"I know it would seem there is a ... *canyon* between us ..."

Recognition flickered in her eyes. She glanced at the men. Then back to him, probably shrugging off the possibility that he meant her brother.

He must convince her. Quickly. "But it is clear you are not so easily dissuaded. You are not like a"—he inclined his head and lifted his eyebrows—"*leaf* tossed on the wind."

Her gaze locked onto his, hungry for hope. Desperate for rescue. He could see thoughts churning through her beautiful face as hesitation warred with her dogged determination.

She had not realized he had all but erased the distance. Like the strike of an adder, Chiji slammed against the weapon, flipping it from her hands at the same time he hooked an arm around her waist, pulling her away and to the side.

Screaming, she was a tornado of moves, grunts, strikes, but

he was skilled. Lethally fast. Took her to ground as gently but firmly as possible. Pinned her to the concrete, the rifle stock against her throat.

His height gave him an advantage that helped control her legs and arms. "Cease!" he hissed near her ear, pulling her head up and back against his chest. "Stop fighting if you want them to live."

She slowed. The fight drained from her thrashing body as wariness perched at the corners of her eyes.

"Get the others back in the room," he ordered the men. "Hurry, before Ahmet returns." Hating to do it, but knowing the others would question if he did not, Chiji zip-tied her wrists. Watching the retreating forms, he drew her upright, then onto her feet.

Please, Chineke, let her listen. And if I am worthy of it, let her forgive me … one day.

"What is this?" Ahmet demanded, stalking toward them.

Holding her firmly, praying she did not choose now to make another statement, Chiji angled around to cut off her line of sight on the mafia boss. Maybe show Ahmet a little possessiveness of his own. "I thought I would keep this one out for a while." He tugged her close to him—and she stumbled against him.

Ahmet cast a suspicious glance between them. "There were shots."

"Nothing I could not handle." Even as he spoke, Chiji caught her fragrance, amazed she still smelled so sweet after all she'd been through and the days that had passed since she'd likely showered. And her eyes were as blue as the sky that held the sun and nourished those flowers. It was as he had imagined when he'd first seen their family photo. She was sunshine and flowers in a desert of darkness. And Chineke had seen fit to place her in Chiji's hands for protection.

"You said General Agu did not want this one spoiled."

Only at those words did Chiji realize he was staring down into her eyes. Without breaking eye contact, praying she did not fight him, Chiji spoke to the boss. "There are more ways than one to spoil a woman, yes?"

Fear made her search his face, taking in every feature. Desperation crouched there, desperate for his words not to be true, that he would spoil her.

And perhaps he read too much of his own will into this. He would have her believe him. Trust him. She must or the damage would be unfathomable. That pushed his attention back to the men he must convince as well. Where did he begin?

Ahmet sniggered and shook his head. "Your pleasure will have to wait. The boat—"

"Did he tell you?" Debare strode in from where he'd taken the others and flung a hand at Miss Metcalfe. "This one knocked out Jachike, stole his weapon, and tried to escape."

Rage swung Ahmet around. He glowered, his pistol sliding free of his holster. "If she is that much trouble—"

He heard her suck in a breath and shifted between her and the line of sight. "As you can see, Ahmet, no trouble. I have her well in hand. Recall that I said I would keep this one out." Chiji remained calm, knowing if he showed that he had not lied, then perhaps the anger would abate.

Ahmet narrowed his eyes, his nostrils flaring as he considered them both. "Teach her a lesson and keep her separate until she learns how to behave. We don't need her inspiring the others to get stupid, too."

These men did not tolerate weakness; they eliminated it. "You doubt me?" Chiji pushed to his full height as he edged Miss Metcalfe behind him, still holding the ties, and squared off. "Who was it, Debare, that discovered this siren as she tried to lead our profits from escaping this building? Who knocked her to the ground and subdued her? Was it any of your men who stopped her from escaping?"

The thick-shouldered man shifted.

"Did you do this, bring this under control?" Chiji demanded.

"I ... No."

"That is right. *I* took her to ground," Chiji growled, baring his teeth. "*I* stopped a loss that could have hemorrhaged this business from within. I protected you against the wrath of General Agu and the Viper." Drawing her with him, he shouldered toward Ahmet. "And you want to question me? Stop me?"

Anger writhed through his pocked face as Ahmet remained unbending. "Remember your place, Adigwe. This is my operation. *My* men. *I* let you be here."

"Kalu—"

"Forget Kalu," Ahmet spat. "Until we are there, until we have delivered them, the general is not our problem."

Dismissing the specter of Kalu Agu removed what little control and hope of staying alive Chiji wielded. He could not let that happen. He towered over him, using his height as a psychological threat. "Shall I call him and tell him that?"

Though he faltered for a moment, Ahmet shoved past him. "Ready the women. The boat is docking."

Chiji hid his surprise and confusion. "What boat?"

Ahmet smirked as he stalked out of view.

Boat ... Why were they putting them on a boat? They were already far south—which was more accurately southwest. They diverged already from the trek to the Mediterranean, and ultimately, Italy. It needled him that they were not moving northward? It did no good ... To reach Italy, this route would take weeks to navigate.

Was there another destination? He'd taken this mission counting on the predictability of the Nigerian mafia, their lust for power and money, believing he could use that to find his sister. Instead, he'd encountered randomness and another man's sister.

He must notify Command. Even as he turned to his ruck, where he'd hastily stowed his sat phone when he had discovered Miss Metcalfe sneaking out, Chiji paled. His ruck ... He took in the warehouse. Where was it? He probed the dark corners and shadows to no avail. Without that phone, he was even more powerless than Ahmet threatened. No chance to contact the team, let them know what was happening. And he was already past his check-in time. As he turned, he caught sight of it. Slung across Yemi's shoulder. Who exited with Ahmet.

His gut sank. It did not matter why they were getting on a boat. It mattered that he had no way to communicate the change of location to Command. That meant if they boarded that boat, they could be taken anywhere. Nobody would know. They could vanish without a trace into the ocean's unforgiving maw.

CHAPTER
SEVEN

MiLE Safe House, Nigeria

"WHAT DO you mean my sister was kidnapped?" Canyon Metcalfe barked into the satellite feed.

Cord had put it off as long as he could, but they hadn't heard from Chiji in days, and GPS off his phone showed them in Lagos … two days ago. "A Nigerian mafia cell hit MiLE's Obioma compound where she was working. They burned it to the ground, killed some, but—"

"Taggart." Warning sailed through the way Canyon said his name. "I swear on all that's holy, if anything happens—"

"Easy, Midas. I have a man on the inside. Chijioke Okorie."

Hesitation crackled through the line. "I know him." His angry tone dropped one notch below apocalyptic. "What're you doing to recover her and the others?"

Cord pinched the bridge of his nose. "Everything I can. Calling in favors—"

"I'll get on the horn."

"Appreciate it."

"Do you have a bead on their destination?"

Cord tucked his hand under his armpit as he considered the

radar map. "Last ping was about fifty nautical miles off the coast of Ghana. Left port in Lagos."

"So, boat. Not the most efficient means of travel. This … doesn't make sense. Why aren't they headed north? That's the mafia's usual MO."

"Unknown."

Canyon grunted. "Leaves a lot of room for … marine animals."

He didn't mean the slick ones clogging the San Francisco docks. He meant the slick ones in San Diego—more specifically, the Naval Amphibious Base at Coronado where Navy SEALs beached, implying that he might know some guys who could help track down this boat.

Cord waited for the help he knew would come.

"I know someone."

Of course he did. "No back doors," Cord warned, knowing the Metcalfes were notorious for getting things done. However necessary.

Another grunt. "I'll call you back."

"Canyon," he growled, but only silence answered. Blowing out a breath, he tossed his phone down. Rubbed his forehead, then again studied the map.

"Anything from Chiji?" Low stepped into the room, his shoulders brushing the jambs on either side.

Cord shook his head. "If they're on a boat—"

"What do you mean 'if'?" He pointed to the grease board where coordinates and timestamps had been logged, locations that were clearly in the Atlantic. "Unless they're Jesus, they're on a boat."

Glowering through his brows, Cord tried to wrestle his irritation into line. "*Assuming* his phone wasn't dumped out there … while still in his pocket."

Low grimaced. "You don't think—"

"Yes!" he barked. "I do think—of everything. Have to. It's

the only way to be prepared." Fist to his mouth, he strained to think of some option, some chance that would help them. "And even if he's alive, I have no way to get word to Chiji that we might have a lead on his sister's location."

"Yeah, but, boss … Sicily. He isn't going to want to know that because that place—"

"He's a warrior—he'll want to know. Someone says they saw her there, we tell him."

"But—"

"It's a place to look. He'll want to know."

Low gave a grave shake of his head. "What if the scum who took Willow are going there, too? If they head there—"

"They're not." Cord straightened, scratched the back of his head, and folded his arms. "Least, best we can tell they aren't. If they were"—he rapped his knuckles on the map—"they would've pushed north through Niger and Libya." As Canyon had insinuated.

"But Libya is a mess with Boko Haram. Maybe they're heading out to sea to avoid having these women snatched from them by authorities." He jutted his jaw. "I'll get Mari looking into the coastal hot spots."

Nodding, Cord considered the input, thought about Willow ending up with Boko Haram or worse—Sicily. A blond-haired beauty like her? She'd be a favorite, a prize … He cursed and swiped a hand over his scruff. "Holy mother, I've never wanted to kill someone so bad."

"You talk to *her* lately?"

"How? She's a host—"

"Brooke."

"Oh." Cord glowered at his friend.

"Thought so," Low said with a sniff. "Call her."

"Why?"

"Cuz this thing happens"—he motioned around his head with a hand—"to your face that is hard to explain."

No idea what his buddy meant, Cord scowled. *"What?"*

"Yeah. It's weird—your mouth changes from this flat line to a semi-curve."

Semi-curve. In other words, a smile. "Son of—" He picked up an empty plastic cup and pitched it at Low. "Get out of here."

"Just saying, you're nicer when you talk to her."

"I don't need to be nicer. I need to be smarter."

"The two aren't mutually exclusive, ya know."

Cord studied the intel wall again. "Gotta figure out where they're headed and how to interdict."

"They in international waters?"

He shook his head again. "Hugging the coast enough not to be."

"Smart buggers." Low huffed, pointed to the table—to a phone. "I'm going to grab some rack time. Do us all a favor and call her."

Cord snorted as Low moved into one of the bedrooms. Talking to her was easier said than done. Always had to be on her terms. When *he* called, she didn't answer. Somehow he always felt like he was flirting with a cobra, who could strike at any moment. He hadn't given up on her—doubted that'd ever happen—but he had to stay mission focused.

But man, the sound of her voice was like a luxurious massage that seemed to knead out all his frustrations, even when she was adding to them.

No. He couldn't call her and get distracted. Things were too tricky and fluid. Though he knew this could come back to bite him, he also knew the bite Brooke would have if he told her too soon with too little intel. Or that she'd go all Rambo on him. Definitely didn't need that.

Buzzing drew his attention to his phone, and he snatched it off the table. "Go for Taggart."

"Sounds like someone didn't get his Starbucks quad-shot this morning."

He felt his lips split into that semi-curve Low had mentioned. Curse the man. "Yeah, couldn't afford the delivery fees out here." He should tell her about Willow. But … bad idea. Situation was too new, too in flux. Brooke was like a firecracker—no rhyme or reason to where they'd go when lit, even though they were mesmerizing to watch.

"So, you're far from home." Thankfully, she didn't ask for his location.

She should know about her sister.

But not from him. "What can I do for you, Beautiful?"

She gave an exasperated sigh

"You're fogging up my glasses with that huff."

Her sigh filtered through the phone. "What do you know about Thailand?"

"Ancient ruins, tropical beaches, palace—"

"In terms of trafficking," she clarified tersely.

Cord tensed. Hated that she'd ask about this topic in that country, of all places. "Ranked one of the worst-offending countries." Dare he ask? "Why?"

"What other countries rank up there with them?"

"Besides the U.S.? India, Bangladesh, Pakistan, China … Why?" He wouldn't stop asking until she answered.

"Have you ever … been there?"

"Sure. Not my top vacation spot, though. I prefer Hawaii. Or New York." Was he being too obvious? "Wanted to ask this woman I'm trying to get to know—"

"Have you ever operated in those countries?" She sounded irritated. Probably because his flirting was getting in the way of her answers. "That's what you call it, right—operating?"

"Ask your brothers."

"Have you been there?" She hadn't missed a beat.

Her tenacity was like Ghost's MWD, Trinity—once she sank her teeth into some juicy intel, she didn't let go. "Where? Which country? I mentioned several." It bugged him that these questions seemed to be narrowing in on a point. It wasn't that she asked them, but the why. "Brooke, what—"

"Any of them," she snapped. "Why are you making it so difficult?"

Me? "Been to all at least once, a couple multiple times." He angled around, focusing on her voice and what he heard that she didn't speak. "I'm being difficult because of your questions. They're leading somewhere. And it worries me."

"Don't think a grown woman can be curious? Or do you think—"

"*I think* you have a reason for asking, and that reason is cause for concern."

"Why?" A challenge burrowed into her question, but probably not as much as she wanted, because now her voice somehow sounded small and pulled something feral through his chest.

"Because I don't think you understand the industry you're asking about. What it's like. How majorly muffed up it is. And if you're asking—and you are—then it means you know something. Or think you know. And it ticks me off that you're dancing around some pretty freakin' serious trouble that means *someone* is in trouble. Lives are at risk and you're playing games." He planted a hand on the table. "Now, either read me in on whatever this is about or stop wasting my time, because unlike you, I *am* trying to save those lives."

There was no answer. No response.

"Hello?" He checked the phone.

Home screen. He bit back a curse—she'd hung up. He slammed his phone down. "Augh!" That woman drove him nuts!

"See? Told you to call her."

"She called *me!*" he barked at Lowell. "Thought you were napping."

"What'd she call about?"

"Trafficking. Again! Her questions are too pointed, too

focused." He eyed his buddy. "Asked what I knew about Thailand."

Head cocked, Low drew closer. "Think she knows something?"

"I *know* she does, but about what, whom"—he shook his head—"I don't know. And I'm trying not to make logic leaps." But the hottie was just too tightly wound in her own head to let anyone in. "I tried to nudge her into telling me what's going on but she hung up."

His buddy snorted. "Yeah, but your *nudge* is more like shoving people off a cliff." He clicked his tongue. "You need to go more gently into that dark night."

Cord huffed. "This *dark night* needs warriors, not cowards. We run to it, not cower in its shadows."

"I meant her."

"I know what you meant," he groused, running a hand down the back of his neck.

Low was right—he'd pushed too hard and driven Brooke away. And while it made him crazy that she might be mad at him, he was more worried about whoever it was that had her asking questions. Because those questions had a point of origin that thrust her directly into this nightmare he battled on a daily basis.

As a business exec living in New York City, she likely had a lot of opportunity to see trouble on the sidewalks as she headed to her latest high-powered lunch. Though trafficking was no respecter of persons or affluence, it most often kept to its own playgrounds. He doubted she associated with people likely to find themselves on those playgrounds—bars, clubs, large parties. Granted, there were exceptions to the rules.

What was going on that pushed her to research trafficking? Because it wasn't like researching for a college paper. If you dug into this sickeningly lucrative industry, you either ended up like him or you ended up like Brighton. And he sure as heck wasn't going to let Brooke end up in either vein.

Who on God's green earth did she know that was involved in this ghoulish life?

A sickening thought stilled him—was it her?

No ... she seemed to have too much freedom. Contacting him would be a dead giveaway and get her in trouble because his name had become synonymous with the fight against trafficking. He had bounties on his head that would get her killed if she was trapped in it and contacted him.

So, not in it herself.

Then who did she know that was?

Okay. "Done asking questions and getting nowhere," he muttered. Time to find out who and where. While Canyon might be better connected than an NIA server room, Cord had weight he could pull, too. Including hacker friends.

If she found out he'd dug into her personal life, she'd be some kind of ticked.

When is she not?

What if she had a lead on something? Like a victim or, heck-fire, maybe she knew something about the man in the castle—the guy at the top of the org that had trafficked Brighton and hundreds of others. The man known only as Viper.

Okay. Yeah ... If that's the sit-rep, then he had an obligation to dig, right?

If he did this, she would never speak to him again.

Hand on his phone, he hesitated.

Crap. Who was he kidding? He might be into her like nobody's business, but he wasn't made for marriage and family anyway.

Time to make some calls.

BEXAR-WOLFE LODGE, NORTHERN VIRGINIA

Stone Metcalfe didn't know how to tell her. Leaning against the fence that guarded the more inner part of the property around the lodge, he folded his arms. Sighed. Glanced up to his cabin where his black Belgian Malinois, Grief, was again sniffing out some critter around the shrubs. Saw a shape pass in front of the window. The door opened, and hugging herself against the morning chill, Brighton started down the lawn to him.

Man, she was a beautiful woman. Even with the messy bun perched atop her head, she had a commanding elegance that made guys pay attention. Sweatpants sat casually on nicely rounded hips, and his hoodie—the one she'd "borrowed" two weeks ago—drowned her.

She angled her head as she closed the gap. "You okay?"

He unfolded his arms to lean back against the fence, but she came into them. He wrapped her close and kissed her forehead. "Got some bad news."

"Yeah?" She buried her face against his chest, apparently perfectly content to stay there and not worry about his bad news. But she would soon enough.

"The marriage license."

She shifted and looked up into his eyes, frowning. "What?"

He huffed. "I don't know what to do—to apply for a marriage license, we have to provide our vital information."

Her gaze swam in confusion.

"Your full, real name."

Understanding washed over her face. "Oh."

"Yeah, it'd be on public record."

"Which means Ladomer Horvath … could find me." She sagged, then eased from his hold and dropped back against the fence in much the same pose he'd assumed.

"We can't do it."

She started. Looked at him. "We can't … get married?"

Stone grunted. "I don't think we should risk drawing Horvath's attention."

"But ... I ... we can't—" With a sad noise that gutted him, she sagged. "It just won't leave us alone." Her eyes glossed. "He wins. He *always* wins."

Those words sliced his heart like a thousand tiny daggers. What happened to her—she hadn't deserved it. He swung around to her and cupped her face. "Wrong. No. He won't win."

Brighton held onto his forearms, fighting back tears. "I want to believe—"

"Then do." He kissed her. Though she'd endured a lot—way too much—she had stayed strong. Fought. Now, it was time to fight for her. "I told you before I don't give up what's mine, and that rock on your finger says you're mine. I plan to complete that circle and keep my word."

"Stone—"

His phone belted out the rock version of the National Anthem. Canyon. "Hold on." He answered the call. "Hey—"

"We got trouble."

"We're Metcalfes," he said, eying Brighton and stroking her arm in reassurance. "When don't we?"

"It's Willow."

Stone stilled, turned away without meaning to. "What about her?" His kid sister long had a special connection with him ... and trouble. "Tell me."

"I'll read you in, but right now, I need Range's number."

Stone stilled, his shock rolling into anger. His brothers hadn't been on speaking terms in years. Range resented Canyon, who loved their younger brother. Even his relationship with the middle brother had been tenuous, but as family "patriarch," Stone had his contact info—with one condition: he was to never share it with Canyon. The distance between the two was in everyone's best interest—and Canyon agreed.

Stone doffed his hat and used his arm to wipe his forehead. "What's going on? You swore you'd never ask—"

"Just give me—"

"Tell me or you get nothing."

"You know I have contacts."

"If that's true, then you would've used them rather than call me." He squinted out over the Shenandoah mountains. "Now, I've had a really bad week, and I'm not in any mood for the games, so spill it, Midas."

Canyon huffed a sigh. "She's been taken by the Nigerian mafia. We think … it's trafficking."

Stone cursed. His gaze drifted to Brighton, a knot growing in his gut at the thought of his little sister being caught in the industry that had nearly destroyed her. "What's Range got to do with this?"

"Cord thinks he could help get her back."

"How?"

"His Coastie connections. We think she's on a boat. I've got some SEAL buddies ready to interdict, but this can't go through official channels. We need a boat and hope Range could pull some strings."

Would their brother help? "If I send his vitals, he won't talk to me again." Getting this info from Stone might just kill their relationship. Then again, though Range had held a familial grudge, he'd always been a champion to those who couldn't help themselves.

"A price worth paying to rescue Willow."

Stone nodded to himself and sent Range's info. "Keep me posted. If I'm needed, I'm there."

"Just keep that wedding on track. And maybe keep that lodge open."

"That's the plan." Gut tight as the call ended, he swiped a hand over his face and worried. Would the family hothead, who was a master at holding grudges, set it aside long enough to help their sister?

Stone would knock that thick block off Range's shoulders if he didn't. And him? He'd get to sit here and—

"What's wrong?" Brighton touched his arm.

He flinched and cleared his thoughts. "My sister's been taken." He met her caramel eyes. "They think it's the Nigerian mafia and connected to trafficking."

Brighton paled, drew back, shaking her head.

The distance just made him ache, realize more the horrors his sister was facing. "Now to figure out if I should tell my mom or wait until we have more intel."

"She should know." Brighton nodded fiercely. "Now."

He knew she was right, but it'd break Mom's heart. She'd lost so much already. An overwhelming sense of powerlessness soaked into his courage. Sitting here doing nothing while Willow was fighting for her life. Man. If he couldn't keep his family safe, then he had no business marrying Brighton.

No. No, he wasn't going to fail the woman in his arms. Not again. There had to be a way, and he'd find it.

CHAPTER
EIGHT

TRAWLER ON THE ATLANTIC OCEAN

"YOU REALLY KNOW MY BROTHERS?"

Even as steel cuffs bit into the soft flesh of her wrists, Willow searched his fathomless eyes for truth. He'd dropped "canyon" and "leaf," though he clearly meant Canyon and Leif—right?—into his conversation at a time when her stubbornness was causing trouble. A trouble she did not necessarily regret, but hearing her brothers' names had rattled her into submission. And she would make this man regret altering her course if he'd just been pulling her chain to bait her into compliance.

But c'mon—their names weren't common. And they were uncommon men. So, how … how could a man like this, one who helped with human trafficking, know Canyon and Leif? Earlier, she'd felt like he was familiar. Had she seen him before? Why couldn't she conjure up where? "Seriously? You know them?"

As he'd threaded the chain of her cuffs into a hook anchored into the wall two days ago, he hadn't met her eyes. Simply gave a single sharp nod.

"How?" she'd begged, but he hadn't answered.

Darkness clung to the damp rusty walls and deck of the ship as that conversation from two days ago haunted her. They hadn't been fed or released from their bonds since, forced to humiliate themselves when bodily functions demanded release.

Steel bit into her wrists as Willow slumped against the interior hull. Behind and to the right, she heard one of the twins vomit again, the room flooded once more with a fresh wave of that acidic odor.

Willow pressed her nose into the crook of her arm to protect herself from the smell. If she weren't cuffed, she'd go to the girl. Hold her. Encourage her. Yet, even as she sat there, she smelled her own stench. She'd spent six months on the *Augusta*, the Doctors Without Borders ship, so she was used to the swells and falls of the ship. Still, even her stomach protested at the motion and the reek drowning their senses. She groaned and fought the urge to wretch.

"Peace, peace." Nkechi's warm words wormed through the chilled air and caressed her wounded soul. "Trust Him, Willow."

Surprised at how much those words warded off the icy finger that'd traced her spine only moments before, Willow sniffled. Here she was, comforted by a woman who had already been raped at least once by these monsters. And *she* was encouraging Willow?

You're a Metcalfe. Get it together. "We need water," she whispered to herself.

"They do this to wear us down," Nkechi spoke into the darkness. "We get desperate enough to do whatever they want as long as they give us food and water."

"And a bath," someone bemoaned nearby, followed by several halfhearted laughs.

She glanced in the direction where her friend's voice had come, realizing the truth of the words. "I will never be that desperate."

"It will happen," another girl spoke. "This is what they are good at."

"But Adigwe," Nkechi said softly, "will protect you."

Willow frowned. Was she talking to her? "Me?"

"Yes, you. We all see the way he looks at you and stops the others from touching you."

"He … he said they're saving me for the general." She swallowed hard around those words.

"That would not stop them. Who could prove who raped you? No, this Adigwe protects you."

"That's not true." Can't be. "I … there's no reason for him to. I'm nobody—"

"With that golden hair and blue eyes, you are definitely not a nobody," a girl said from the dark corner. "Stay close to him, Mama Willow, or they will—"

With a threatening groan, the door lurched open and thrust the light of the gangway into the room. The girls yelped and whimpered, likely cowering from the visitors.

Yemi recoiled and cursed. "My god—the stench!"

What did they expect, locking them in here for days? "Yes—we need food, water, baths! Please." Willow struggled to her feet, the surface slick from waste and vomit. The ship canted left, and she gripped her chains to steady herself. "Please, I beg—"

The man rushed at her, his eyes filled with evil intent. "You beg? Of me?" He sneered as he pressed her against the hull. "Do it, and maybe I will be gentle."

Willow shoved him back, and his boots lost purchase. He slid and went down hard.

Laughter radiated from the gangway, their other captors mocking him. Which only served to infuriate the man, who lunged at her.

"Stand aside, Yemi." Ahmet entered, his disgust at the odor and their state clear as he covered his nose. "Bring in the others."

Willow faltered. Others? What—

A dozen more girls stumbled into the room. They were clean

and smelled of fresh air. However, the bruises and cuts across their bodies betrayed their captivity had been long enough to be taught those infamous lessons.

"What is this?" Willow demanded as the newcomers were cuffed and chained up with them.

Ahmet leveled a gun at her. "Sit down, American whore."

Insulted, humiliated, she drew up. "Why—"

He slammed the weapon against her temple, dropping her to the soiled deck.

Pain exploding through her skull, Willow cupped her cheek. Felt the rush of blood against her fingers and palm. Tasted blood—she'd bit her tongue when he'd coldcocked her.

"Do as you are told or we will throw you overboard."

"Please—we need water."

"Is that your way of asking to be thrown over first?" Venom in his words matched the fire in his eyes. He meant it.

Willow knew she should be quiet. Subservient. It'd be less painful. "If we dock and most of these girls are sick of dysentery or pneumonia or die of starvation, how much will you make?"

The fire swelled to a fury, but he did not move. Or answer. "You will not have time to die of starvation."

The average person could starve to death in ten days. So, they wouldn't be on this ship that long? Her heart pounded as she pushed her luck once more. "We can go in groups—clean up and use the facilities." She glanced to Nkechi, who watched her with wide dark eyes. "She is a cook." She looked at the other captors. "Are your men not hungry?"

"It makes sense," the one they called Debare said. "Make them work for us. In more ways than one."

Though Willow wanted to object, she kept her silence, hoping—praying—Ahmet would relent. Anything would be more humane than being locked in darkness without end.

"If the general shows up and finds *this* …" It was Adigwe. He manifested like a cool rain cloud on a miserable humid day. "He will want to sample the merchandise and this would disgust him. He will be furious."

Recoiling at his words, she faltered. Which side was he on? He said he knew her brothers. But her brothers would never associate with a man who sold women and children for sex, so who was he? At least she knew better than to think him an ally.

"Fine," Ahmet snapped. "Just keep them below. No more than two or three at a time. With two men."

As she stood in her own filth, Willow felt the cumulative relief that rushed through the room. The new girls were shaken and stared at them with abject horror, realizing how their fates had changed.

"American, Hag," Yemi said, picking out three then pointing to the smaller twin. "You. Let's go. You first." He jutted his jaw to Adigwe. "Release them."

The tall Nigerian moved toward Nkechi and knelt, freeing her bonds as Yemi went for the twin, then turned toward Willow. Her heart skipped a beat, not wanting this man to touch her. Something about his eyes, the darkness lurking beneath his knotted brow …

Hands caught her wrist.

Willow startled. Shifted back, half expecting Yemi to be there. But it wasn't. Adigwe—his touch gentle. Yet firm.

Like his eyes.

The realization startled her. She liked his eyes.

No! She couldn't. Wouldn't. Not one of these monsters.

Yet, something about him drew her gaze back to his. And there she found … no violence in his eyes. Only … resolution? Conviction? Determination? Yes. Without a doubt. He meant what he said. Did what he said. And in those eyes now, she saw …

"No trouble," he said, his accent thick, flavored with intonation of a local dialect that was raw, emotional, but confident.

She nodded before she even understood that it was not a command but a question, a pleading. He wanted her to cooperate.

Of course he did. Most men did.

Hands freed, she restrained herself from being confrontational. Reached for Nkechi and Adesina.

Adigwe guided Nkechi behind Yemi and the twin, then indicated for Willow to follow as he brought up the rear. Through the first hatch, he closed and secured it. She couldn't say why, but she waited for him, glancing to the others, then back to him. In the gangway, he seemed as towering and solid as an oak. Presence eating up all the remaining space in the confined passage, he was forced to duck to avoid hitting his head. His shoulders were broad, his arms well-muscled.

All the better to beat you with, my dear.

She shook herself and started walking again, but felt his cool grip on her forearm. She tensed, not sure what it meant. What he intended to do. Kindness in his eyes—what if it'd been longing? Intent?

As they wound their way around a corner and then another, Yemi went left with the other two women. Adigwe took her to the right.

"W-where are we going?" she asked, her heart tripping over being alone with him. Had she been wrong about him?

Of course you were. He's a trafficker! There's no right way about them.

She was beautiful, an angel sent from God for his weary, dry soul.

He let her into his bunkroom, glanced back down the passage to where he spotted Yemi taking the others to a bathroom. A gnawing in his gut told him what would happen to those women. What he could not prevent. Logic said there was nothing he could do. His heart screamed to find a way.

Yemi met his gaze. Gave a prurient grin, then stepped into the room. The hatch closing echoed through the passage and punched Chiji.

"What is this?" she whispered.

Her nervous question drew him into the room and he shut the door.

She shifted to the side, putting distance between them. "What—" Her eyes widened and she pulled away from him.

He motioned to the bathroom, which was smaller than a closet room with a sink no bigger than a serving bowl on the right, the toilet crammed against it on the left. A drain built into the floor and a showerhead above. "There. Go on."

Uncertainty flickered through her blue eyes. She eyed the head, then the door.

"You are safe here. Out there"—he shrugged—"I am limited. Shower. Change." He handed her a pair of shorts and a tactical shirt.

"But they'll think you ... raped me. That you favor me."

"We are long past that." And it was not a lie. He *did* favor her—more than was healthy for him ... or her. "Let us hope their whispers are the worst you will suffer."

Something soft and vulnerable swam in her blue eyes that seemed like molten puddles. When her lips parted to speak, he urged her. "Go." It was harsher than he'd meant it, but he was weary. Weary of seeing her in pain. Hearing the screams from the other girls who were raped and he could do nothing.

It seemed his Creator asked too much of him. But that was the way of it—God pushed mankind so they would seek Him for strength. Realizing the war they fought was not theirs alone. As he'd told Tox many times—the Lord will fight for you; you only need to be still.

Help me, Chineke ... You put her in my heart and life. Show me how to protect her and my mission to find Chiasoka.

He heard the shower spring on and lowered himself to the edge of the bed. Buried his face in his hands. He still had not figured out how to get his phone from Yemi, and he must. Because it was not just his phone in that ruck that could cause problems.

A hand over his other fist, he stared at the deck. Tried to work through how to keep her out of trouble without his interference. She was smart—he'd had no doubt even when he'd had only that photo to know her by. If they discovered that ... it would not be good.

What would he do—he knew the time would come if they stayed on this boat where tempers and clothes were fouled—when the men would look to relieve their boredom with her? He feared what he would do to anyone who harmed her. And yet, he feared destroying his mission to find his sister. Why must his mission be complicated with the Metcalfe beauty?

"Are you okay?"

Snapping to his feet, he nearly hit his head on the ceiling as he locked onto her standing just outside the bathroom in the tactical shirt, which hung past her hips where his too-big shorts peeked out and sat cockeyed on her hips in a way that—

Chineke, help me!

Pants. She needed pants. Those long creamy legs would only cause trouble for her. Why hadn't he thought of that? He glanced around, desperate for a solution.

"Thank you," she said softly, "for ... everything."

He ran a hand over his bald head. "It is the least I can do."

She came closer and extended his shirt, the one he'd given her at the warehouse. "I'm afraid I've soiled it."

He took it, their fingers brushing. "That is something you could never do."

Confusion rippled through her delicate brows. "You *do* favor me."

Swallowing, Chiji could not look away from her, from those blue eyes.

"Don't you?"

Mute, he nodded. Just wanted to leave the room. And yet, he didn't. He wanted to talk with her. Tell her everything. Hear her voice. He'd wondered ever since Leif dropped that photo what her laugh sounded like.

"Adigwe—"

"Chiji."

More confusion.

He should not have told her. "My name is Chijioke."

She drew in a sharp breath. Confusion shifted and slipped aside, making way for something more greedy—hope. "No wonder you looked familiar—you were in the photo with Leif! And you know Canyon?"

He nodded. "Not as much as I would like."

Those pale eyes searched his. "But how … how did you know I was their sister? We've never met."

He should be ashamed. "There was a photo Leif … dropped." He was glad with his dark skin she probably could not see his blush.

"Of me?"

"Your family. All of you at some event."

Understanding softened her ivory features. "Stone's victory dinner." She smiled. "So … if you were with Leif … that means you're—"

He touched a finger to her lips and felt the electricity of that connection. "Secrets must stay secrets. For now." It amazed him she was able to slide right past the fact he hadn't returned the photo to Leif. Thank Chineke she did not ask. "In time, Miss Metcalfe."

"Willow."

He rotated his hand and brushed her wet hair from her face, a touch he did not deserve. A touch that made her shudder.

So she had felt it, too.

Worried he had overstepped, he removed his hand. "Willow."

Shouts sounded in the passage.

He glanced at her, freshly showered—legs! She needed pants. He snatched a pair of sweat cutoffs he normally wore for workouts and handed them to her. "Hurry." Chiji started.

Another voice—a familiar, darker one—stormed the passage. "Ahmet's coming." What would he think to find them here talking? Civil. It was *too* civil, nice. This would anger the boss.

She must've realized the same, because before he could argue, she dropped against the bed and yanked him forward. His legs clipped the edge, sending daggers of pain that collapsed him on top of her with a grunt. Awareness of her beneath him, his soap scent clinging to her blond hair, her curves, her nervous breath dashing his cheek, Chiji stiffened. Realized his hand rested on the gentle curve of her bare hip.

Shame! "N—"

The door slammed open.

Willow cried out and turned her face away from the door.

Shocked and trying to regain his bearings and control, Chiji levered off of her, glancing at the door.

Ahmet stood there staring, scowling. Then laughed hard. "I knew you could not resist her." He sniffed and turned into the passage, giving one more appreciative glance to her. "Come topside when you're done." He turned away, then glanced back. "And save some for the rest of us."

When the door shut, Chiji growled and pushed off the bed. Went to do the door. Hadn't he locked it? This time, he made sure before turning to her. "That was stupid!"

"Everyone on this boat knows you're being nice to me," she said, tugging down her shirt and scooting to the side of the bed.

"You're the only thing standing between me and violation, or death. So I can't lose you."

Chiji faltered.

"I mean, I can't lose *that*." She tucked her chin, too late to hide the blush. "If they don't think you're willing to rape me, it will cause questions. And as we've already seen, someone else will try."

"But I told them you were to be saved for the general. If they think I sullied you, then they will not hesitate to try you, too."

Willow slowed. Paused as she sat on the bed, adjusting a shirt that didn't need adjusting.

He crouched beside her, resting a hand on her knee, only it alerted him to the silkiness of her skin … the bareness of her legs … And he noticed that she stared at his hand on her. "I will never violate you. Never fear that of me."

She looked at him, her gaze seeming to caress his cheek as viscerally as her fingers, and with an intensity that spread heat through his gut. "I don't."

He frowned. "You speak those words too quickly."

"But I don't."

He shoved away, more to put distance between himself and her than out of anger. He pivoted back to her, glad for the four feet that separated them now. "How? How can you know this thing when I have been rough with you, struck you, taken you down? I have been anything but kind."

"Wrong." Serenity kissed her fair features as she stood and erased that distance he'd so expertly established. "Even Nkechi said you favor me, that you are kind to me. All the women see it. And I know … I know, Chiji, because there is no violence in your eyes."

Could she truly see into his soul?

"Only kindness, cleverly hidden behind a warrior ethos. I know it well because it's the same shield my brothers wear."

"And I will use that to protect you the best I can. But you

must know, Willow. My mission, the real reason I am here—it's not you or even these women. It is my sister. She is my mission, why I returned to Nigeria. She was taken by mafia one day when she left the family compound. Now, I search for *her*."

Uncertainty returned. Shifted aside and let fear back into the playground of her mind. She swallowed.

"But you won't lose me." He should not have said that either. Because Chiasoka was his priority. Yet he felt himself falling into a riptide of this woman's making. "I promise. But now, I need you to promise me one thing."

Confidence rattled, she nodded, as if she did not trust herself to speak.

"No matter what you see or hear me do from now on, remember this moment." He held fast to her gaze, for her to once more look into his soul. "Remember that you saw kindness in my eyes." He cupped her face to keep her focus on his, so she would understand the importance. "Promise me this. Yes? I need you."

She blinked. "You do?"

"I need you there, reminding me, pulling me back from the darkness that so desperately wants to devour my soul. This world, these men … it is darkness. Evil. Too easily in America is evil written off or prescribed medicine. Here, the only medicine for wickedness is the Bible. God. And I need you because I believe He sent you to me."

"God sent me here?" Her voice pitched. "To see Matt killed? To see girls raped?"

Watching her sink into her despair, he firmed his grip on her face, gave a gentle twitch for emphasis. "Do not let anger and bitterness steal from you the peace and power found in Him. We stand on a battlefield that is far greater than you or I. Do you think I like this? Treating people badly? Pretending to be one of *them*?"

She caught his wrists, panic flooding into her eyes. She

tugged free, her breath heaving through her chest as she stumbled back. Stared at him.

"I need you, Willow. Please—promise me that you will pray for me."

"I ... I can't."

CHAPTER NINE

TRAWLER ON THE ATLANTIC OCEAN

"CAN'T. OR WON'T?"

The kindness was still in his eyes but now lay shrouded in ferocity.

Just as she'd feared. Willow had been right—Chiji was just like her brothers. That warrior ethos was brilliant in war, shrewd in dealing with bad guys, but not so great—or compassionate—when it came to situations like this. Their track was single-minded determination to see the mission done. No matter the cost. And that ... that she couldn't condone.

But that wasn't what stopped her from agreeing. It was his tacked-on request to pray for him. It was hard to pray for anything when she questioned why God would allow this terror to roam the earth.

"Won't." She firmed her voice. "Violence breeds violence, and God seems content to let it happen."

"And ignorance breeds ignorance."

Willow started. "Excuse me?"

He shook his head, disappointed. "I believed better of you than this."

Indignation rose through her. She balled her fists. "Same."

"We must go." Stretching his jaw, he opened the door. Motioned her out of the room, back to the hold. "Remember," he whispered as they moved through the passage, "this is your choice. When the darkness overshadows you ... be thankful God does not let your silence determine the right course. His love is pure, unconditional, and steadfast. Unlike us."

Rolling her eyes, Willow stepped over the hatch into the hold. She turned back. "I—"

The hatch closed in her face, dropping her into darkness. Faltering, she recalled a switch nearby. Flipped it, only then glancing at her wrists. The welts from being chained up glared back at her. But also pointed out that he hadn't secured her this time.

She turned to Nkechi, only to find the spot still empty. Willow sought out the twins ... only Ginika. Facing the door again, she tried the handle but it wouldn't give. She tried again. Again. Then grunted. Slapped it.

"He did not chain you," one of the girls said.

Willow started to return to her spot, but the filth of the room permeated her senses. She again turned to the door and banged on it. "Open up! Hey!" She banged. "We need mops!"

Unbelievably, the hatch swung back, nearly knocking her on her backside. Willow braced herself against a wall as two bodies were shoved into the room. Nkechi tripped over the lip of the hatch and collapsed to her knees. Willow helped her up, only to notice her torn clothes. Bruises over her neck and arms ... blood on her dress ...

She whipped toward the man at the door. Yemi's mocking laugh tore through Willow. Ripped away her restraint. She lunged at him with a feral shout. Dug her fingernails into his face, going for the eyes as Canyon had taught her. She whirled around and drove her elbow into his gut.

A blur surged at her. Slammed her backward. Her head hit

the steel hull hard. She collapsed, her ears ringing. On all fours like Nkechi now, she squeezed her eyes shut. Tried to push past the pain and dizziness.

"Get her inside. Chain her."

Even as she was wrangled back into the room and chained, Willow struggled to make sense of who had broadsided her. She glanced back to the open hatch, convinced she'd been wrong. But there he stood. Chiji. Jaw up, shoulders back, nostrils flared.

Angry. With her.

"We need a mop," she said, suddenly feeling miserable for what she'd lost in him.

Yemi started easing the hatch to. "Use your hands."

"Stupid girl."

Something in Chiji tightened as he followed Yemi up to the galley. He must respond, but he could only manage a grunt.

"Guess the lesson you gave her was not enough." Yemi used the back of his hand to mockingly slap Chiji's chest. "I guess it must take a real man to teach her."

Chiji reached past Yemi, grabbed the shoulder of his shirt and yanked it across his throat, pinning it to the other side, and shoved his forearm into his throat as well. Almost nose to nose with the man, he flared his nostrils. "Touch her and I will teach *you* a lesson."

Scratches raw, Yemi was too startled to argue. But that didn't last long. With a shout, he shoved all his weight at him.

Though he lost an inch, Chiji didn't yield. He hooked the man's leg and swiped it out from under him, sending him to the deck. His knee dropped hard against his ribs. And if Chiji wasn't wrong, he heard a crack.

Yemi howled.

"What is this?" Ahmet demanded.

"A battle of territories," Debare said as he casually stepped over Yemi and entered the galley. "Seems Yemi wants a taste of Adigwe's American whore."

Chiji straightened, all too aware that his head was skimming the ceiling. "She is my responsibility to deliver to General Agu." He turned his anger on Yemi again. "And I want my ruck back."

"What ruck?" Yemi grunted and held his side and a bruised, if not broken, rib as he came to his feet. "I don't know what—"

Like lightning, Chiji drove a knifehand into the man's side.

Raging, Yemi crumpled, agonized shouts prowling the interior hull.

"This must be a very important pack, yes?" Ahmet lifted his eyebrows at him. "What is so important about this pack that you would attack one of your own?"

"The importance," Chiji snarled, "is that it is *mine*."

"Like the American?"

Understanding the challenge for what it was, Chiji slowly folded his anger into his tactical shirt. "She is not *mine*. She belongs to the general. For Italy." He skewered Yemi, who whimpered on the deck, trying to get to his feet. "As for attacking one of my own? I see none of Kalu's men here."

"What are we?" Ahmet spat.

Again flaring his nostrils, Chiji shouldered into the galley. "Candidates. Potential business partners. But do you really think the general will work with you when you cannot even keep the women from smelling like horse dung? I doubt this ... alliance to which you strive." He poured himself a cup of coffee.

Ahmet straightened like a puffed peacock and moved to the head of the galley table. "Explain to me what happened in the warehouse again. Why you had the girl on the ground?"

Chiji took a gulp of the semi-warm brew as he leaned against the counter. Eyed the boss and these devils. "I could lie about it if it would make you feel better."

Ahmet's jaw shifted.

A little subservience might go a long way. "The story is as told—she escaped, tried to take the women with her. I stopped them."

"And you say all this time she is for Kalu, yet I find you raping her."

The putrid thought nearly made him spit out the coffee. He slammed the cup down. Wiped his mouth. "I am *weak*. Is that what you want to hear?"

Ahmet adjusted on his chair. "I want you to stop prancing around here like *you* are in charge. You came to inspect me, spy on me." The boss's chest rose and fell unevenly. "I hate it, but okay. Yet—enough! *I* am in charge here. *My* men obey *me*. On my boat, you will respect me, obey me. You are no different than them. You are equals."

"Not quite." He would never accept that. At one time that had been true. But these men had caved to depravity. They were what was wrong with Nigeria. What he fought. It angered him that they did not honor the strength and courage of their people. That they only fed the negative views of their country, made true the depravity that Hollywood depicted. Though a lecture danced on the tip of his tongue, he could not. Would not. To them, he must be equal. Corrupt. Wicked.

After ten days with them, he felt the weight of their filth clinging to him.

"You think you are better than us?" Debare challenged.

"My obedience," Chiji said, choosing his words so very carefully, "is to only one." Let them believe he meant General Agu. Chineke knew his heart.

The boss's lips thinned and he reached behind him and grabbed something. Jerked it onto the table between them.

Chiji's ruck. He tried not to react. But what was in there could upend all he had worked for. Expose not only him but *her*.

Chineke, please …

Ahmet stomped to his feet as he hoisted the ruck upright

and a wall of muscle gathered around the boss, the others anxious, too, about what was in the ruck. "This seems important to you."

"Do you like men going through your underwear?" Chiji tried to make a joke of it, but his heart was ramming into his ribs.

Respect, Chijioke. He wants respect.

"I hear you, Ahmet." Chiji faltered for the right words. He would not lie if he could avoid it, but neither could he show respect to this monster. "If you would search it, then search it. My ruck is important to me because it is mine. When you live on the move, personal belongings have more value. Would you agree?"

After opening it, Ahmet looked at Chiji.

His thrashing pulse threatened to betray him.

Please, Chineke ...

Ahmet lifted the bag and upended it, dumping the contents over the metal table. Clanging and thunking mirrored what was happening in Chiji's chest.

The phone was the first thing he noticed, his mind pinging around the contents, searching for the—

There. Peeking out from under a protein bar.

With a sigh of frustration loud enough for all to hear, he bent toward them, spotting one of the collapsible kali sticks that had been a gift from Tox. Turning toward that, he snagged it and used his other hand to surreptitiously pick up the photo and bar at the same time. Slide them into his pocket. He snapped out the kali stick dramatically and grinned when a couple of the men shuffled backward.

Chiji spotted the other and snapped it up, deploying that one, too. "Now you see why I wanted my ruck?"

Ahmet rounded the table, not amused. Not smiling. He sauntered over, his jaw leading the way. "What did you put in your pocket, Adigwe?"

The picture in his tactical pocket felt as a ball of fire, searing through the fabric. Bulky as a brick. But it was neither hot nor large. He must stay his nerves. Distract the boss, who was shorter by at least five inches. Chiji stretched himself to his six-four height. "I do not answer to you," he growled even as he pulled the bar from his pocket, where it had nestled with the photo, and held it under the boss's nose. "Am I to now ask you before I eat, too?"

Anger writhed against Ahmet's composure as he faced off. "If I say ask, *you ask*."

"I do not ask of any man here—"

Two men caught Chiji. He was swift, accurate in his response, using the kali sticks to thump both men on their temples without breaking eye contact with Ahmet. "You want respect, but you do this thing to me. Yet *I* eliminate threats to your business and to those around you. What respect have you shown me but to question my honor, cast those beady eyes on me with suspicions and malice? Treat me like a dog or one of those women."

Ahmet glowered, sliding his gaze up to Chiji's. "I treat as one deserves. Want to be treated better? Then act better."

If you fill your mouth with a razor, you will spit blood.

It was one of his father's favorite proverbs, an admonishment to guard one's words because what he spoke could injure *him*. The warning whispered across his soul like a cool mountain breeze, calming him. He would yield.

For now.

He retrieved the ruck, stuffed the items back in it, then turned to the boss. "My phone." Remember, yield. "Please."

The boss met his gaze. Glanced at the device. Pressed a button. "Let us see who you last called."

CHAPTER
TEN

"INCOMING CALL FROM CHIJI."

"Thank, God!" Cord came up off the chair and turned to the comms specialist with a nod, giving her the all-clear to answer. "Put it on the wall, Mira."

"'bout time," Lowell muttered as he joined them. "He's only sixteen hours late."

Cord held up a fist, silencing chatter in the room.

Adjusting the headset, Mira flipped a switch. A red light glowed above a speaker mounted on the array. "*Salve, Signor Adigwe,*" she said in a sing-song voice with her best Italian, playing the role of a desk clerk at a hotel. "*Grazie per aver chiamato il Sogno Veneziano. Come possiamo aiutalra questa volta, signore?*"

A hum of noise creaked through the line.

"*Signore?*" Mira repeated, a frown flickering through her Latina features. "*Sei qui?*"

Through the bad connection came murmurs that had Cord leaning in closer to hear.

"*Signore? Are you there?*" she asked, this time in Italian-accented English.

A scruff of interference, but among it rose the unmistakable voice of Chiji.

"*What did you expect?*" he asked someone.

"*I expected General Kalu, not some ... Italian ... whatever it was.*"

"*It was a hotel. Where the general and his team stay when he has worked on this place I have told you—*"

"*I do not care! Prove to me you speak to him!*"

Their guy was in trouble. Cord glanced at Low, and over the burly man's shoulder saw the leaner build of Range Metcalfe entering the deck. Attention back on the call, he nodded for Mira to prompt the caller.

"Signore? Hello? Are you there still?"

"*Call the next number,*" instructed Chiji's voice. He was being put through the paces.

Though he remained calm, Cord felt his gut cinching as the call cut. Good thing they'd prepared for this contingency.

"It's him. Calling General Agu." Mira glanced at Cord. "Likely on speaker again."

The only other number on Chiji's phone.

"We can't answer that," Low said. "Ahmet will expect an Arabic speaker. And while we can both speak and understand it, we won't pass as native, not with that dialect. Not by a long shot."

Cord tightened his jaw. "And Chiji will die." His gaze shifted to Metcalfe. "Along with your sister."

Expression unaltered, Range unfolded his arms. Lifted a headset. Nodded to Mira. "Key the mic. Put it through."

Mira's wide eyes shifted to Cord. "Sir?"

A lot of this Metcalfe's sheet over the last two years had been blacked out. But his reputation as a Class-A jerk wasn't. Still, he needed to understand the consequences. "Her life is in your hands."

A sliver of a smirk pinched the blue eyes. "Don't ever tell her that." His gaze again hit Mira. Another nod.

Following a series of clicks came a barked voice, "Hello?"

"*Min hadha?*" Range's voice was deeper than normal and much more in control as he asked who was calling. "'*ayn Aydjiwi?*"

"Who is this?" Ahmet insisted.

"*Daeah ealaa alhatif.*"

"I won't put anyone on the phone until you tell me who this is."

"*Airtadih wa'iilaa falan yaemal hadha alraqm maratan 'ukhraa.*"

Holy mother of pearl, those words flew from Range's tongue as effortlessly as a river over a waterfall. Cord had no idea what he'd just said, but the silence on the other end made his gut cinch another notch. Maybe he shouldn't have trusted Range. The guy was a wild card. Driven by vengeance and unpredictability.

"General?"

At the sound of Chiji's voice, Cord let out a relieved breath and hung his head.

Range continued the dialogue, unaffected—but angry sounding. "'*ant taelam 'ala tueti hadha alraqm li'ayi shakhsin.*"

"I did not give them my phone. They took it and would not believe I worked for you."

"*La tajealha tahdith mujadada.*"

"No, General. It will not happen again."

Cord snorted. He could just see the leer Chiji was likely giving the general right now.

"I have a special girl for you, General. Very pretty. Blond. Pure."

Watching Metcalfe's expression was mighty interesting. The man exuded a ticked persona but that was his sister Chiji just mentioned, and there was no hiding the guy had a soft spot for her.

"Naqi?" Metcalfe asked.

"Yes, General."

"*Aibqaha ealaa hadha alnahw.*" Range flipped the switch, severing the call.

"Merciful twisted tongues," Lowell said with a grin. "That wasn't on your dossier."

"There's a lot not on my dossier."

Cord wasn't sure if he liked this or not. "I got the gist, but we can't afford to miss anything, so walk us through that conversation."

Metcalfe cut his gaze to him. "Knowing Chiji was being challenged and they didn't believe him, I told them to put him on the line or the number would never work again. Once he was there, I asked him why he'd given the phone to someone else, said he knew better. Told him not to let it happen again."

"He mentioned your sister."

Range's eyes iced over. "He did."

"There at the end you used one word—nahky. What's that?" Lowell asked.

"Naqi—it means 'pure.' Chiji said she was as yet untouched. I told him to keep it that way."

"Smart." Cord nodded. "Very smart. You might've bought him time and maybe even saved this op."

"Only worried about your op because my sister is involved. I bought time, that's for sure, but those men don't trust him. That's not going to change because of some invisible voice. They're going to want to see Kalu."

With a huff, Cord shook his head. "Yeah, been afraid it was going that way. We just have to head that off before—"

"I have an idea."

He paused, gauging this guy. Midas hadn't talked much about this brother and what little he'd said hadn't been good. And Stone—

"Look." His word had a lot of bite. "You brought me in

because I have a skillset. Likely got my number from one of my brothers—and I don't care who because I'm not ever talking to them again anyway. But you wanted me bad enough to go outside normal channels. I'm here. Use my skills."

"What exactly are those skills?" Cord asked.

"Whatever I need them to be."

This guy was definitely a Metcalfe. "So, what's the plan?"

"We need to take a trip. Pick up someone I worked with once. Then we take him to the trawler."

"Do *what*?"

"They need to see the general. With Chiji. So, we give them Kalu."

"And nobody knows what Kalu looks like ..."

"Not recently anyway. Last photo of him was ten years ago, before the slaughter that left half his face marred."

"Sir," Mira cut in, "the trawler they're on isn't new by any stretch of the imagination, but it clearly has state of the art tech that prevents us from getting a lock on their position. If they can do that, who knows what other capabilities they have that we're not aware of."

Metcalfe tucked his chin and deepened his scowl. "Doesn't change the plan."

"It does if we can't get to the boat."

"My brother—"

"Which one?"

Metcalfe hesitated. "Canyon." He didn't seem to like that Cord asked that. "He knows some SEALs, and by the look of those logs you're carrying around, you probably know some, too. We need help, we can get help. Besides, we both know if you tell a SEAL he can't do something, he'll do it even if it kills him just to prove he can."

Cord considered him. "It's a crap plan."

"More than you had two minutes ago."

He roughed a hand over his bald head, then his beard. "Work

on that, Mira. Recruit help to get as close as you can and lock their location." Pivoting, he looked at the guy's brown hair. "Your hair's not blond."

He had that danged Metcalfe smirk. "So they do grow brains in the Army."

Cord cocked his head. "Did you just—"

"I think he did just," Low said, rolling up his sleeves.

Metcalfe eyed Lowell. "Guess I was wrong."

CHAPTER
ELEVEN

TRAWLER ON THE ATLANTIC OCEAN

"ON YOUR FEET. AGAINST THE WALL."

Feeling the weakness of nutrition deprivation, Willow stood and did as instructed. Nausea swirling, she wondered who would be taken this time. The girls had been allowed to bathe, but they'd returned with bruises and walking strange, crying. Getting baths meant the girls were open to violation. She had to find a way to make these girls valuable for something other than sex.

A large man, a bit wider in the girth, trudged into the room and glanced around. Debare was one of the nicer ones, if you could call him that. His gaze settled on Nkechi, who was slumped against the wall.

Something akin to compassion rippled through the man's face. He liked her friend, too much, it seemed.

"Could you take me to the boss?" Willow said, breaking his line of sight. "Please, Debare?"

He sneered at her. "You want his bed now, too? Adigwe wasn't enough for you?" Determination marked every step as he moved toward Nkechi, who was literally shaking as he unshackled her.

Her friend's eyes were a watery hole as she sought help from Willow, her chin trembling.

It had to stop. Somehow. How did she stop him from taking her friend? Abusing her? "I-I had an idea I think the boss will want to hear," she said to Debare. "We are all hungry, and I have a solution—Nkechi and I could work in the galley to prepare meals. For everyone."

"You would cook for us?" Debare asked, continuing toward Nkechi.

Heart thudding so hard she was sure it could be used for sonar, Willow struggled to breathe and think clearly.

"P-please … Ask the boss."

Debare saw her glance at Nkechi again and scowled.

"She's not well." There was a grain of truth in Willow's words.

"Then maybe she should lie down …"

Oh God, please … Please make this stop.

Distract him.

"Please. Ask the boss. About me, us"—she nodded to Nkechi—"cooking. We did it at the compound." She reached for her friend's arm. "She should save her strength, in case the boss says yes. Wouldn't you agree?"

Debare's scowl deepened. "Back! Against the wall," he shouted at Willow. "Or I will beat you senseless."

She faltered and saw Nkechi shaking her head frantically, telling her to stop.

"What is this?"

Hope ballooned at the sound of Chiji's voice. Willow turned and found him ducking through the hatch.

Debare shuffled his feet and looked in Chiji's direction but would not meet his gaze. Something … something had changed somehow. This was at least the third time she'd seen men avoid him in the last couple of days.

"Debare!" A third man appeared in the gangway. "Boss said put them to work. The American and your favorite—take them to the galley."

Chiji's head swiveled from the man in the passage then to her and finally, Debare. His lips, which had a nice, full shape to them, flattened as his gaze raked her. Uncertainty churned through his mahogany skin.

How had the boss known she'd offered to cook?

"It is good for everyone if you work in the kitchen," Chiji said. "You can cook, yes?"

"Y-yes." She nodded and reached for Nkechi.

Nkechi's grip on her was like iron as she leaned into Willow's shoulder.

Realizing he had lost his prize—at least for now—Debare growled. "Go. Move!"

Chiji shifted aside, allowing them to pass, then he fell into step behind them.

"I do not need your help," Debare grumbled.

Walking behind them, Chiji said nothing.

Amazing how she felt infinitely safer just knowing he was there. Seeing his eyes. Hearing his voice. It was a dangerous illusion, believing herself safe because he was here. Dangerous because it took only his absence for that security to vanish.

But somehow she knew he was like her brothers—Stone, Canyon, Leif … Maybe Range, if he could ever let go of the bitterness rotting his soul. They were all heroes. Warriors. A unique breed of men that most people did not understand. In her psychology courses she'd taken to help her work with the Peace Corps, she learned about personality types. Simply put, he was a Messiah type. He saw the big picture, pushed people hard to be better versions of themselves. Just as Canyon had done with Dani.

He's so much like Canyon.

That realization ignited a strange, startling fluttering.

And that word alone made her repeatedly glance at him, sitting on a barrel of rice, as she and Nkechi hunted through the galley for foodstuffs. In the smelly freezer, they found cassava, rice, beans, spices. Following Nkechi's lead, she worked over the course of the hour making a soup that would feed everyone.

As she rolled the dough to make bread cakes, Willow was startled when Nkechi reached from her dough to Willow's arm. Touched it. "Thank you," she whispered. "I could not even bear the thought of ..." Her lower lip quavered. "Not again. I ... hurt."

Willow chewed the inside of her lip. "I couldn't stand you being taken again." She hooked an arm around her friend's shoulder. Pressed her cheek against hers. "We will make it." Her gaze slid past the pots and shelves to the fortress of a man learning against the wall, watching them. Her heart tripped as their gazes met. "I promise you," she whispered to Nkechi. "God watches."

"And He is not the only one, eh?" Nkechi teased, waggling her eyebrows toward Chiji.

"He's kind to stand guard."

"Mm, except he's sitting, staring at you like you are the rain itself in a desert."

"Oh, psh." Willow laughed, but the words made her look at Chiji again. It wasn't possible that he ...

I need you.

His words fluttered through her thoughts and belly.

Nobody had ever needed her. Not her mother, brothers, or lone sister. They'd all been strong and independent. Warriors, even Brooke, though her battleground had been the man's world of law in New York City. With her soft heart and obvious emotions, Willow had never fit in. Canyon had made her take martial arts, and while she loved the forms and learning weapon forms, she *hated* sparring. Being forced to hit someone had clenched her belly every time. On nights where they focused only on sparring, she went home with a stomachache.

"I heard the men say he had his way with you …"

If it ever got back that he hadn't, what would happen to Chiji? That thought, too, made her sick. The very idea of getting someone hurt, hurt her.

"I know they lie," Nkechi said, scrubbing pots. "That look in his eye? It is not a hungry one. It is … protection."

Protection. Willow glanced at him again. Was that all this was? Him protecting her because of what he'd said—that he was saving her for the general? But … no. If he knew her brothers, where did his mission or work with these men end and his life that intersected with her brothers begin? Could she trust him?

Well, she hoped so, because she did. "Someone took his sister. He wants to find her."

Nkechi grunted. "Maybe. But that has nothing to do with you. That look of protection—it is personal. He is protecting what is his."

"I'm not anyone's!"

"Then why are you staring at him?"

Willow ducked, the image of him on that stool seared into her mind's eyes. The memory of the fleeting second in his bunkroom when she'd pulled him on top of her. It'd been to erase any doubt in the boss's mind about him, but now she had … an awareness of him. Seeing him over her. His breath gusting out, skating along her cheek. She'd braced his arms—the feel of the muscular curves … Remembering how angry he'd been at her. He had gorgeous mahogany skin, but she was sure she'd seen it darken. Anger? A … blush?

After serving the men and returning to the kitchen to clean, Willow found herself constantly aware of Chiji's presence. The way he straddled a stool, his legs struck out to the sides, his large arms crossed over his chest, was terribly distracting. She needed to thank him … for everything. Gratitude swelled even now, thinking of all he had done for her.

Returning the cassava sack to the shelf—which was right next to his pec—she paused. Slid her gaze to the right, his bicep in view. "Thank you," she said quietly, then pushed her gaze to his.

Those deep dark eyes were locked onto her.

"For staying here, for … being you."

Tenderness smoothed the angles and creases of his face as he offered a small, firm nod.

Only as he sat there, like a king on his throne, did Willow realize how very beautiful he was. And not just the muscles or sculpted torso or the way his neck was buried in shoulders that could bear the weight of the world. It was his eyes. They were dark and true to his Nigerian heritage, but they were also open, honest. Kind. Inviting.

Yet … they also had a sense of being forbidding. Dangerous.

"Mama Willow!"

Breath snatched at the sound of Ife's voice, Willow spun. "Ife!" She saw him in the gangway with some other boys. He'd grabbed the hatch lip. In a heartbeat, she was there, gathering him into her arms and lifting him from the deck. "Oh, Ife! I was so worri—"

He cried out and jerked from her touch.

She froze, confused as she peered at the boy who'd wormed into her heart. Then … *Oh Father in Heaven* … She saw. No—not just saw, but *felt* the bruises. Welts. Cuts. All over his young body. Vision blurring beneath the tears, the rage that rattled through her made it hard to breathe. Made her want to … She dropped to her knees, cradling him to her. "What happened? Who did this?"

He put his arms around her and hugged her, sniffling. "I cried for you every night." His legs wrapped about her waist like a monkey. "And they got mad and beat me."

She squeezed her eyes shut against the mental images. She set him down and framed his sweet face. "I am so—"

"What are you doing? Get away from him!"

Willow spun upward and wheeled around. Saw the man, Yemi. "You animal!" She lunged—

Something caught her waist. Lifted her from her feet and away from her target.

She writhed and beat the arm, wanting to unleash her fury on the man who herded the boys up the stairs. "You beast! What are you that beat helpless boys and—"

A hand covered her mouth. Hauled her around and back into the kitchen. Livid, she bit into the soft flesh smothering her words and fury.

"Augh!"

She was released and whipped around—and faltered.

Chiji stood over her, shaking out his bleeding hand.

"Oh!" She covered her mouth, aware of the blood she tasted, of her mistake, even then seeing he had the boy held firmly by his other hand. "I'm sorry. I'm so sorry." She felt herself pale, eyed Yemi disappearing down the passage. Took Chiji's hand. Led him to the galley sink. Poured water over it. Pressed a towel. "I didn't ..." She swallowed. "I didn't realize it was you."

"And would it have done any good if you had?"

"No—I mean, yes. I just ..." She buried her face in her hands, Ife's wounds searing her conscience once more. "His body ... his little body ..." The tears came unbidden. Rushed over her composure and restraint. Barreled past what little control she had. Turned into sobs.

An arm came around her, wrapping her completely into his safety net. She let him hold her. Let herself cry. Let herself grieve. It had been so much. All these days—how long had they been on the boat? Every day felt like a hundred.

And these monsters ...

Yet ... only because of this man, this protector, had she not been raped. Violated. Like Nkechi. "It isn't fair." Her whispered words hit his chest and bounced back at her, carrying with it his scent.

"I know."

She huffed and dropped her hands. Looked up at him. "No, it's not fair that you protect me and my friends are brutalized. *Children* are brutalized."

Something seemed to awaken in his eyes, which darted over her face, taking her in. He brushed hair from her face and cheek, trilling the butterflies in her stomach, like fireflies in her belly.

"Why did you stop me from hitting that guard? I would have returned every blow he put on Ife's body."

Amusement danced across his expression. "I know you would have." His large hand cupped her face. "But it would have only made the boy his target all the more."

She wilted and shifted around and slumped against the stool. "I can't … I can't do this … being afraid every second you're not there that one of them will take me out of the hold … seeing my friend come back limping and bleeding … seeing Ife bea—" A sob choked off her words.

"I am afraid you do not have a choice."

She looked up at him. His eyes, a lighthouse guiding her to safety, met hers, and she saw them change, and with it, tightness rolled in like a storm and crossed his arms. "Wha—"

"What do you think you're doing sitting there? There is work!"

As if fire blasted the back of her head, Willow had an acute awareness someone stood behind her. It would explain his change. She rose. "I … I'm sorry." She tucked her chin.

Chiji's large hand circled her arm. "Let's go." Though he gave one push, his grip was not tight or painful.

But she played into it. Whimpered as he shoved her out of the galley. Straight past Yemi. She prayed her red eyes and damp face from crying over Ife and Nkechi would be telling enough for Yemi to believe she was being a problem.

As he led her toward the hold again, Willow thought of being in that room with the women. The hatch shut. The darkness. Her skin crawled, feeling as if she would come unglued. It felt like she was trying to crawl out of her own skin. As they rounded a corner, she turned into Chiji's path. "Take me to your room." She met his gaze, saw the shock there. "Please. I can't go back in there yet. I'll just cry. Nkechi needs someone strong, and I can't be that. I can't ... I just need ..."

He was moving her beyond the hold without a word. Down the corridor. Around the junction. Into his bunkroom. He shut and locked the hatch.

She dropped onto the bed and sagged, roughing her hands over her face, fighting off more tears. Honest to God, she couldn't do this anymore.

And yet, she felt spoiled. A brat. For being here, having an escape. When Nkechi and the others didn't. She stood. "Take me back. I can't sit in here while they—"

He held her shoulders and urged her to sit back down.

"I can't, Chiji. It's not right that you protect me and I can find peace with you when they—"

"That is the highest compliment anyone has given me."

She startled—that someone like him could be so easily moved by words. Though she wanted to say it wasn't meant as a compliment, she guessed it was. Right? Confusion weakened her exhausted resolve.

"Sit." He indicated to the bed as he planted himself in the chair that almost seemed like a kid's chair because of his height and long legs. "Find peace, Olamma."

She let out a long exhale, which plied a yawn from her. "What does that mean?"

Bent forward, elbows on his knees, he fisted one hand and rested the other over it. He gave her a tired smile. "When this is over, when we are out of here—and on dry land—I will tell you. As long as you tell me one thing."

Around another yawn, she asked, "What?"

"What are you doing in my country?" He leaned back in the chair and considered her. "Why Nigeria? Of all the countries—"

"I thought it was obvious—working with MiLE as an Aftercare Specialist, helping survivors. I go where I am needed."

"Your face tells me there is more."

She lifted her eyebrows. "My ... face."

"Those blue eyes speak to me."

Her heart raced a little. "They do?"

Again, he came forward but now with an intensity to his posture and words. "When you hugged the boy, in your eyes I saw that this was more than a job."

What did that mean? "I ... no, there's not more. I mean, Ife is special to me, but—"

"And the woman working the kitchen with you the last two days? You risk your life and virtue to interdict, save her from Debare's *favor*."

"I couldn't watch it happen anymore, not to her. She's too sweet. A beautiful soul. It's what friends do. Besides, nobody needs favor like that."

He studied her for a while, to the point that she started growing uncomfortable. Feeling scrutinized, and that pushed her thoughts back to his belief that there was more.

Was there? What ...?

"The last time you were here, you said it was unfair. You wanted to leave, return to your friends."

Chewing the inside of her lower lip, Willow nodded. "I felt guilty." Actually— "*Feel* guilty," she corrected herself. "Even sitting here with you, knowing she's out there ..." And yet ...

"And you struggle because you are relieved to have been saved, even though they have not been."

She caught her lower lip again, hating herself for these

feelings. "I'm terrible, aren't I? I mean—I sat in this room and told you it was unfair, yet, every time you bring me here, I am relieved all over again. I lay in that hold thinking how selfish I am, to leave my friend there, to come and sit with you … time and again."

"You are not terrible. This feeling is normal. It is called survivor's guilt—and I have felt it when my friends die in combat and I do not."

"It's not the same. In combat, you're both fighting. You signed up for it. We didn't—Nkechi didn't."

Chiji steepled his fingers. "Granted."

"Do … do they hassle you?" She hunched her shoulders in question. "About bringing me here?"

"Some."

"Does it bother you?"

"The only thing that bothers me is what is happening here. That I have not found my sister." He cocked his head and studied her, something nearly palpable in his expression.

"What?"

"Will you tell me something? Honestly?"

"I have been said to be honest to a fault."

He bobbed his head. "Your purpose here, the reason you are here … Why? Why are you here, Olamma? Is it because …"

When he did not go on, she angled her head. Wondered what was going on in his. "You can ask me anything."

He shifted to the edge of his seat and reached over—hesitated, then completed the move, taking her hand. Placed it in his and smoothed the other over the back of her hand and knuckles.

She had no idea why that was evocative. Daring, almost … sensual.

"I must know this thing. But you must know it is not an easy thing to ask."

When his gaze lifted to hers, Willow realized how close they were. A breath separated them in distance, but it seemed as if nothing separated them. There was a closeness, a connection, a united sense of purpose in protecting those on the trawler. She had hated him at first, despised what he did—what she thought he had done. Then she'd discovered he was undercover. That had only been a week ago, but the stress and trauma of those days made it feel like a lifetime. It was hard to remember not being around him.

It was hard to think around him. Especially now as their gazes seemed to search each other's for something … something hidden. His cheekbones were strong, and the firm set of his jaw flowed nicely into a corded neck and shoulders. But the eyes … That stern brow.

Wait. He wanted to ask her something. She came back to herself, only then noticing the way he was memorizing her, too. Did he feel that connection?

"Are you here because you see poor Black people? Do you want to feel better about yourself?"

Willow started. Yanked out of her romanticizing. Saw the stern set was perhaps tinged with anger? "I …" She shook herself out of it. "No!" Sadness swept through her. "You know my brothers. I thought you would know me." She stood and moved away, hurt. Angry—no, she wasn't angry. Hurt, perhaps, that he did not know her better. Turning back, she drew up straight at finding him right behind her. Deliberately, she washed her face of any tension. "I—I'm sorry. You can ask. It's your right. But that has nothing to do with why I'm here." Her heart thudded, hating that he'd think that of her. "I just want to help. To be where I'm needed."

He leaned forward, the move not threatening but calm, assured. "Hear me." His expression was so sincere, caring. "You *are* needed. Regardless of what you do or do not do."

It was important to her that he understood. "I am here because of my work with MiLE, to help the survivors—no matter skin color or status or wealth or location. Whether Africa, Europe, Asia—even America!" Why was he so close? So … intense? "I do this because I love people but more than that, I want to help the survivors. At Obioma, Nkechi became a very dear friend, and Ife"—she laughed—"will have you wound around his little finger after five minutes. I'm here because I want to be, because I love the people. Their skin is one facet that makes them beautiful to me. Their hearts make them amazing."

"You do this thing, work with MiLE to serve your own need for affirmation."

"I don't!" The insult seared her conscience, hating that he thought of her like that. That he could believe her so shallow and self-absorbed. So … corrupt. "How dare you insinuate that I don't care about Nkechi or Ife. I love them!"

"I never said you did not."

She pivoted to the door, pulse thundering. "Take me back. The chains hurt less than your accusations!"

He came to her side. "Forgive me. I do not accuse, and I would not have us argue in this time that is made for your peace."

Who was this man, so concerned with her and peace between them? His presence was almost overpowering, and she had this sense that she could fight it … or embrace it. She side-eyed him, wanting peace. Wanting to embrace it, but … the stress of this place, the mafiosos, 24/7 vigilance that left them afraid … always afraid.

"There are those who come to my country to feel better about themselves, bragging about their work on social media—"

"That's not me."

"I know. I know." His fingers caught hers, and nerves trilled in her stomach again. "But they come, brag, and then leave. Go home to their comfortable lives with multiple cars, phones,

TVs ... and my people are left with yet another hole ... a vacancy."

Conscience seared, Willow faltered. "I ... I don't even have a TV or one car. I'm not rich—well, except in terms of family and freedom." She wobbled her neck, head shaking. "Okay, not freedom here, but—"

"Thank you. I wanted to hear it from you."

She hooked her hand on his arm. "Then hear it, Chiji. I'm here because I love the people. Your people. I felt more at home working in the compound with Nkechi than I have anywhere else in a very, very long time. I simply want to help where I can. That's all."

He nodded, his expression unreadable.

"Do you not believe me?"

"I do, but—"

"I think I should leave now."

"Olamma—"

"Please. Now." It was too confusing in this environment. The traitorous feelings she felt toward this man, that he was beautiful yet overwhelming. Yeah, far too confusing.

CHAPTER
TWELVE

TRAWLER ON THE ATLANTIC OCEAN

SCREAMS BLISTERED the air and yanked Chiji from his sleep. He levered up, propped on his elbow, listening to the ship.

Screams came again. Agonized. Terror.

Another girl. She sounded … young.

He swung his legs off the bunk and dropped to his knees. Swiveled to the bed. Folded his hands. Closed his eyes. "Forgive me, Chineke." Amid the continued screams, he recited the Lord's Prayer. Sought forgiveness though he was not sure he could forgive himself for sitting here, doing nothing.

He buried his face in his arms, hooked his hands over his head. Tried to shut out the screams as he recited the prayer again. "Help me stop them. I beg you. Forgive my inaction."

Another scream pierced his protective cover.

Chiji shoved up, nearly whacking his head on a wall-mounted cabinet. He grabbed his kali sticks and spun to the door.

Rushing out there in anger would destroy everything.

He balled his fists. Stared at the catch even as strangled, muffled sobs reached his ears. "Please ... Chineke ..."

Like a balm, Willow's face cut through the fog of anger. He remembered her laugh, her honest words. Somehow, it awakened a powerful realization—he *did* need her. Wanted her.

He must act with honor toward her. Always. Since the picture had come into his possession, he had believed without doubt that she would one day be his wife. Now that she was here, that she was in his life and had been in his arms, he realized ... understood ...

It is not the way for me.

The path before him was too treacherous. He did not want her harmed. After seeing what Tox and Haven had been through, the damage his career and warrior ethos had done to her and their relationship ... Chiji did not want to do that to anyone, especially not Willow. It would be egregious to knowingly put anyone through that kind of life. And that was the life Chineke had called him to. Provided a way for training, for connections, for brotherhood. All so he could find Chiasoka. That was his mission and purpose here. Not wooing the sister of the Metcalfes.

His protecting Willow succeeded by a narrow margin. It would not last. Not if they remained on this boat. *How can you protect your people when you cannot even protect Chiasoka?*

His sister being snatched happened because he was away. Helping the Americans. Now, he was back. To find her and make a difference. Deliver justice to those who had taken her.

Time to stop being distracted. He climbed the stairs to the bridge deck and made his way to the galley where the men were gathered. There, he poured himself a cup of black coffee that was lukewarm and bitter. Glanced around, unsettled at the strange quiet lingering on the trawler.

"Where is everyone?" Chiji straddled a chair at the table.

Debare barely looked up from his bowl of stew—apparently

the women were cooking again. A smart thing Willow had done. He had intended to find a way to give her value, but she had done that herself. Impressive.

Debare glared at him over the rim of his bowl. "Inspecting the new girls."

Inspecting. Another word for raping.

Appetite spoiled, Chiji realized that's who had been screaming—the new ones. And this man across from him ate without problem.

"Too young for me," Debare said, shaking his head.

Chiji slowed, recalling the girls brought on board. "They did not seem so young."

Debare grunted. "Not the first batch. While you were snoring, a second group was brought aboard. Taken to the other hold." His lip curled. "Children. Some not even old enough for school."

Sit. Stay. Do not—

He punched to his feet. Stalked out of the galley.

Feet thudded behind him. "No, no! Adigwe, wait."

Chiji toed the rails of the stairs and slid down to the next deck. Pitched himself forward, pulling the kali sticks from the holster at his back.

"Ahmet will kill you if you—"

The hatch to the room was shut but did not stop the screams crawling along the hull. Those shrieks were young, too young. Chineke forgive him for not intervening sooner. There was no excuse. It took everything in him to contain the rising rage. Fury drove him into the hatch. Shouldering into it, he pushed the heavy barrier out of the way.

"What're you doing?"

Chiji spun to the right where a scream became a wail. A sob. He saw one of the men zipping his pants. A boy—

Creator, help me!

It was Willow's boy, the one she had protected.

Unholy furor drove him at the man, his arms a bombardment of pain. The man tried to shield himself. Chiji struck his temple. Ribs—a sickening crunch told of the perfect aim.

Howling in pain, the man stumbled to the side.

Planting his boot in his chest, Chiji kicked hard. Sent him spiraling backwards. "Do not get up if you want to live." Breathing hard past his onslaught of anger, he retracted the sticks and stowed them. Turned to the boy now curled into a ball, wailing. His wary eyes watched Chiji from a shield of fingers.

"Come." Chiji motioned to him, but the boy just curled tighter. Going to a knee, he glowered at the man protecting his side as he struggled to sit. Not waiting for the boy to comply or the brigand to interfere, Chiji scooped the boy into his arms.

The kid came alive, shrieking. "No! Leave me! Don't!"

Rolling the boy into his chest, he pinned him tight. "Quiet. Quiet. I will not hurt you."

Shuddering through his cries, the boy couldn't move … and wasn't trying to. He kept his face to Chiji's chest.

"What are you doing?"

In the far corner stood Yemi, making no effort to hide his undone pants and what he had been doing to a girl. No more than ten, she slowly drew herself away from him, huddling against the wall. Two other men moved toward Yemi, dressing themselves.

"You are sick! Evil! All of you!" he roared. *Chineke, help me, or I will kill them all!*

"Are you crazy?" Yemi stalked forward.

"They are *children!*"

"Yes. And this is what they are for. We are just preparing them—"

"Not them!" he bellowed, grieving the whimpers skittering

around the room, the little ones afraid of his rage and evidence of the innocence destroyed. "Not. Them."

"Ahmet will throw you overboard for this."

"Let him try," Chiji hissed as he motioned the girl away from Yemi. Took her hand. Shot the wicked men one last glower, then made his way out. He guided them down into the hold with the older girls and women.

When he flooded the room with light, he scanned the twitching forms and finally spotted Willow. Confusion careened through her expression but fell away as she looked at the boy. "Ife!"

Chiji hurried the girl toward Nkechi, then three long strides delivered him to Willow, in whose arms he laid the shuddering boy.

With a strangled cry, she hugged the boy tight. "Wh-what happened? What're you doing?" The last question was but a whispered. "They will kill you for—"

"I have made a mistake," Chiji said solemnly, grievously. "But my conscience would allow no other decision." Taking the boy's hand where a metal cuff was still dangling, he knew he must salvage what he could of his cover here. He linked Willow's chain to the boy's. "I may not be back." His gaze hit hers. "Stay strong. And ... I know you could not before, but I beg you—pray for me. Please." He stood.

"What? Why?" She hooked a hand over his arm. "Wait. What's going on?"

"It must stop." Misery churned through him. "I thought I could do this, be here, play the role so I could find my sister. But I cannot let it continue. Chineke will make me answer for the children I did not protect."

"Chi—Adigwe," she said in a calm, firm voice, the boy tucked against her shoulder. "*Think* about this. They need you. *I* need you."

His gaze struck hers. "I can't ..."

"You're one against what? A dozen?" She shook her head. "Impossible odds. Be smart about this. I beg you!"

"Chineke understands, Adigwe," Nkechi said quietly from nearby. "You feel the pain He feels seeing his children so wounded. But He has put you here."

Willow sniffed a smile. "What she said."

"What if He did not put me here?"

"I'll never believe that," Willow whispered, eyes watery. "I don't want this to have just been about me. There are more lives to save here. Please. Help me save more."

Chiji looked into those oceanic depths and felt her tidal pull. The logic of her words.

No. He had a mission. He shoved to his feet and turned to the door.

"Please—no! Come back. Don't leave me." Her words followed him into the gangway, up the stairs. Chiji stormed to the bridge deck and straight to Ahmet's cabin. He hammered on the door.

It swung open and Ahmet growled. "What do yo—"

"This cannot happen. It is sick," Chiji growled. "Bad business." At the indignation in the boss's face, alarm spoked through him. Shoved a dose of logic into his head. "The general does not allow this. He will be furious!"

Ahmet faltered. "What are you talking about?"

"The men raping children. *Small* children. I will not tolerate it."

"What did I tell you about—"

Chiji snapped out his phone. Made a call.

Ahmet grabbed it from him. "No!"

"I have told you how the general prefers his merchandise. Battered, bloodied because your men are bored is not acceptable."

Irritation squirmed through the man's bearded face.

"I would think with what you stand to lose if the general

rejects brutalized children, that you would take better care of what you ship to him."

"It is *my* business. I will do as I please."

"You will regret this." Chiji pivoted and stormed away.

"Watch your back, Adigwe. You make many enemies here."

In the galley with Nkechi the next day, Willow had brought Ife with them. Kept him tucked in the pantry and gave him a large bowl of mixed grains, five cups, and told him to sort them for her. She worked well through the morning, preparing lunch. Watching the hatch for sign of Chiji. Where was he? His ominous words about making a mistake and stopping this worried her, especially now that so much time had passed with things unchanged. And no sign of him.

Their captor was the thick-bellied Debare, who was too fond of Nkechi.

Her friend stayed on the opposite side of the room, moving around the galley and preparing jhorri rice. There was no meat, but it was still something besides broth and yams.

"Where is Adigwe?" Willow asked their guard casually as she set bowls for the men.

"Do not worry about him," Debare sneered. "Save your pretty neck and get that food done."

Nervous, worried something had happened to him, Willow slipped into the pantry. She retrieved maize for cakes and whispered to Ife, "Stay out of sight. It is bad now. Understand?"

He nodded, looking at her around bruised and swollen eyes from where he sat sorting the grains, three-fourths of the mixture divided up. A task that kept him busy and quiet, but also helped them divvy up the food servings.

"Good job," she said, indicating his sorting.

Meal in hand, she rounded the corner—and plowed right

into a solid mass. Even as Yemi's face registered and she sucked in a breath, Willow heard Ife scramble to a corner in the pantry. "Sorry. I—" She ducked and shifted to move around him.

He grabbed her arm and yanked her around. "Where is the boy?"

Heart drumming, Willow frowned at him. Scowled. "How would I know? I've been here cooking."

"They said Adigwe brought him to you in the hold."

"He did, but I left the hold this morning, as you can tell, and I've been cooking—"

With a violent shove against her chest, he stormed into the pantry.

Willow froze. Couldn't bring herself to look, to speak. Trusted the boy to hide as she'd instructed. Hoped he had hidden well enough not to be found.

"Don't you destroy that food," Nkechi yelled from the ovens. "You do that and Boss will kill us both!"

Yemi charged back out. "I want that boy."

"Maybe Adigwe has him," Willow said.

His fist struck hard and true, spinning her around and slamming her face into the wall.

She cried out, but his vise grip on her hair felt like daggers pricking her skull. She tried to grab his hand to lessen the pain.

"Maybe I will take you," he hissed in her ear, his hands going where none should. "Adigwe should not be the only one to test you."

"Yemi."

His grip remained tight as he swiveled toward the door and voice. "*What?*"

Ezuedo looked at Willow apathetically, then to him. "Boss wants to know what's holding up the food."

With another shove, he rammed her into the wall—hard— and let go.

Head spinning from the impact, Willow braced herself

against the wall and choked back tears. Like a feather, a touch came to her leg. She glanced down and saw Ife's hand reaching from around the corner. She covered his fingers. Leaned around and smiled a smile she did not feel. After making sure Yemi was gone, she smiled at Ife. "You were brave. So very brave."

"If I had my brother's knife, I would kill him!"

Willow gave him a hug, wanting to tell him violence wasn't the answer. But it would be a hollow reply considering all he had endured. "Okay, hide in there again. Stay out of sight, yes?"

Back in the kitchen, she tried not to look at Nkechi. It was like this, every day. Worrying which man would take a piece of their souls. Unbelievably, Willow had escaped physical assault so far, but with Chiji not around, and Yemi in such a rage … it was just a matter of time.

"I know you do not pray, but maybe this is a good time?"

"We'll be fine."

"In Chineke's hands, yes."

She bit back the vitriol she felt bubbling up. The hatred that tumbled through her gut and made her want to rail at the woman. Chineke had done nothing to stop Ife from being hurt. Had not protected even Nkechi, who sang his praises.

Willow tucked her chin and focused on making maize cakes. She was angry—that they were in this mess, on this boat, that Chiji was … gone. What had happened to him? If he had been killed, then she would be raped like the rest of them. With him gone, hope was gone, too.

And God … where was He? Why had He let this happen? Why could He not send Canyon or Leif to rescue them? What good was it to have brothers with violence skills when they could do nothing for her? They were on a boat in the middle of the ocean. How would anyone find them?

Hair slipped into her eyes and she batted it back.

It dripped again.

She growled her frustration.

"He is okay," Nkechi said. "They listen to him."

"But he's not in charge. You heard him—he'd made a mistake." She moved around the kitchen, whispering to her friend.

"Caring too much is never a mistake."

"Until it is," Willow bit back, hair again dashing into her eyes. She huffed. Slapped the strand, plastering it to her head, demanding it obey. As she went back to kneading, the bowl slipped across the counter. "No!" she shouted as it careened to the deck. She growl-screamed, suffocating the noise so she didn't draw attention.

"American."

She startled at the man's voice. The same one who'd been there before, asking about the food—Ezuedo.

"Boss wants food. He's not patient."

"It is done," Nkechi said, scooping into the bowls. "He can come when—"

"He said you"—he pointed at Willow—"bring it to him."

Willow faltered. Glanced at her friend. Then back to the guard, Ezuedo. "I ... I'm making bread." And Ife was in the food closet. Going up there, to the boss, was trouble. Chiji must be dead if the boss was demanding her already. The boss did not just want food.

"Do it," he ordered. "Now. Boss say you do it."

Again, she looked to Nkechi, who lowered her gaze, her expression mirroring the panic and defeat spiraling through Willow's veins. Heart trembling, she grabbed a bowl of food and spoon. Refused to look at her friend again, did not want the panic drumming in her chest to leap out. "Watch for the mice in the closet, Nkechi."

"Vigilantly."

With Ezuedo at her back, Willow left the galley and climbed the stairs. Hesitated on the upper deck, but he nudged her forward. Led her to a cabin door. Flung it open and jutted his jaw for her to enter.

After a moment's hesitation—*please, God, where is Chiji?*—she entered and set the bowl on the nearest flat surface. Pivoting, she aimed back out the hatch.

"Stop!"

At the command from Ahmet, she closed her eyes even as the hatch closed in front of her. Steeling herself, she felt a wave of warmth rush across her chest and shoulders. Fear. It was not the first time she had been in a situation like this. Glancing over her shoulder at him, she blandly offered her only hope that he would not be interested in her. "I am not a virgin."

He laughed. "Yes, we are aware Adigwe fixed that."

He thought … that's right. Chiji said they would assume it.

But it did not presume that this man didn't want her anyway. "I left the maize cakes baking. I should get back."

"The other woman can ensure that. Yes?" He was at her side. Took her hand in his and pulled, directing her toward his bed.

Willow resisted, jaw set.

"He is not here to save you this time."

Suddenly, her panic wasn't for herself. "What did you do to him?"

The boss laughed. "Do to him? Nothing. He showed such concern over the children, I tasked him with seeing to their care." His eyes took her in. "I can see why he wanted to keep you to himself."

CHAPTER
THIRTEEN

TRAWLER ON THE ATLANTIC OCEAN

CHIJI GOT the children settled with their food, then walked them one at a time to the head. Each visit up the gangway, he strained to hear what was happening in the kitchen. When he took the third set of kids to the bathroom, he bumped into Debare leading Willow's friend away from the galley.

Chiji frowned. "Debare, I need your help."

The man hesitated, other intentions clearly on his mind.

"The children are in the room while I take these to the head. Go make sure none have escaped."

Debare wasn't too happy about the idea but he nodded to Nkechi. "Stay here."

The woman gave him a sidelong look, then watched him move to the other room. "The boss has her," she said flatly.

Chiji stopped cold. Her ... Willow. His brain jarred violently. "Ahmet?"

She nodded. "Ordered she bring his food, but he was clearly not hungry for jhorri."

Rubbing the back of his neck, Chiji glanced back toward the

children. To the head, where one was now emerging. "We *have* to get off this boat."

"Mm, agreed." She took the little boy's hand and jutted her jaw at him. "Go. I will take him back."

Chiji glanced again toward the room, knowing Debare was there. But watching the children, he would not be able to take liberties with the woman. He hoped.

"I can take care of them. And him."

Grateful for her help, he touched her shoulder. "I will be back."

"I would expect so, unless you plan to swim for the next month."

He almost smiled at her teasing words as he hauled himself up to the bridge deck and pulled out his phone. Made a call. "I need the general again." He rapped on the door.

Nobody answered.

In his ear, he heard the voice of the man who played Kalu.

Chiji pounded on the door again. Again. He would not go away.

"Enter."

For a fraction of a section, he hesitated at the casualness of Ahmet's voice. Almost … taunting.

Chiji shoved open the door. Faltered and jerked his gaze down, but not before the scene seared into his cortex the sight of Willow standing in nothing but her underwear and bra … a bra whose center strip had been cut, a line of blood down her sternum. The shorts he'd loaned her were piled at her feet, along with the shirt.

"You were right," Ahmet said merrily. "There *is* more than one way to spoil a woman."

Trembling, skin pebbled, Willow moved to cover herself.

"Ah ah." Ahmet shook a finger at her. "Remember, you can't hide a body that beautiful anymore."

Rage, the only thing he had felt since getting on this boat, fired through Chiji's veins. The squawking of his phone reminded him of the call. He shoved the phone toward Ahmet. "Kalu."

The boss glowered, then snatched it. "Yes?"

Chiji moved toward Willow and felt a stinging sensation across his bicep. He thought to ignore it, but Willow sucked in a breath, eyes puddling with tears. He glanced to the spot and saw a thin crimson line across his arm.

Ahmet held a dagger to Chiji's bicep, its point chomping into his skin. "Get back," he said. "No, not you. This little pest who thinks he runs my operation."

Stunned, Chiji considered taking the man. Killing him. But if he attacked, he'd have a dozen other men to contend with.

"Yes, it is protected … no," Ahmet continued the conversation. "I don't know how to turn the jammer off, and why would I?"

Shocked, furious he hadn't seen this coming, Chiji looked at Willow, who stared straight ahead, hands fisted at her side.

Ahmet set down the dagger.

Chiji started for her again.

A pistol swung into his face. Ahmet aimed it at Chiji with equal parts apathy and bloodthirst. Which shifted sharply. His gaze flickered. "What do you mean you're coming?" He turned to the side.

Willow's eyes refused to come to his, and Chiji ached to her let her know he would pay this man blood for blood. He had failed her. Failed to protect her. Though he had thought it before, now he vowed to get them off the boat. Everyone. Somehow. He would find a way.

Sniggers came from the gangway, and he spotted men gathering outside, staring at Willow. One took a photo of her with his phone.

Chiji shoved the door closed, blocking their view, bringing Ahmet round with a grin, pleased that he had wrested some of the control back from Chiji. This situation made the sadistic pig happy.

"I cannot stop the boat. Yours is faster anyway, and time is critical to meet the trucks. One change." Ahmet somehow had the dagger again and turned to Willow. Slid the tip of the blade along her thigh, up beneath her underwear, cutting both the material and her thigh.

She hissed and recoiled, but Ahmet darted forward and thrust the edge against her throat.

With a whimper, Willow flung out her hands to avoid falling back onto his bed.

"Enough!" Chiji stepped forward.

But Ahmet must've anticipated him—he thrust the dagger at Willow's throat, drawing them both up short. He bared his teeth and gave a low, feral growl. *"You* are not in control. No more. Get back or I will make the others hold you here to watch while I rape her."

Chiji drew up, balling his fists. Rage pummeling him with adrenaline. Praying His Creator would steady him, help him find a way to get them out. He met Willow's blue gaze, but she pried it away as a tear slipped down her flushed cheek, fringe sweaty and plastered to her forehead.

Ahmet slapped the phone to his ear again. "Yes, what?" Listening, he skipped a look to Willow, then away. "Why does this American whore mean so much to you? Your man has already had his way. Her virtue is gone."

More angry squawking.

Ahmet's expression grew pale and stony. "Yes," he bit out. "Fine." Eyes wild with the panic of a man who knew he had lost control, he threw the phone at Chiji. "Get her out of here."

Released from his frozen state, Chiji lifted the blanket and started for her.

"No," Ahmet barked. "That's mine. It stays. A little humiliation will do her good. Go!"

Furious she was forced to leave almost naked, Chiji snatched his phone from the floor. "You will answer for this."

"Apparently so," Ahmet growled in resignation. "Kalu is en route. He'll be here by sunrise."

Stunned by the words, Chiji stepped out of the room. But the sight of a half dozen men gawking released his pent-up rage. "Move! Clear out!" As they surged away, he drew off his shirt and handed it to her.

She stuffed her arms into it, and he was glad for his tall height since his shirt reached her lower thigh, just where the blood had stopped. They walked quietly, silently down the hall, then the stairs. When she started for the stairs to the lower hold, he offered his bunkroom for some privacy and so he could dig up more clothes for her.

"No." Her answer was as sharp as Ahmet's dagger, and she pivoted to return to the hold. Then hesitated. Took a step, but her posture sagged. It was clear she did not want to return to the dark isolation of that room.

"Please." He did not want her to go back there either, did not want her out of his sight again. Couldn't just send her back into that to sit with women and cry. If she would cry. This woman was made of steel. "Come, we will talk. You can—"

"Just leave me alone," she snapped, turning toward him. And away. Faltering no matter which way she turned. "I just ..." She gripped the sides of her head, her face reddening. She was fighting the tears, the collapse of the adrenaline.

"Olamma." He touched her shoulder, ached for her to trust him once more.

"Stop!" She shoved him back and stepped into a fighting stance, surprising him. Her brow, a tangle of anger was also bound up in grief. "Don'ttouchme." Her chest rose and fell raggedly. "I thought you were dead. That you gave up fighting and got yourself killed."

Chiji held up his palms. "I am sorry. This is impossible, untenable ..."

Her wet, red-rimmed eyes rose to his. "Yes ..." She touched her forehead and pulled in another shaky breath. "Sorry."

"You owe no apology, Olamma."

"*Stop* calling me that," she said, then shook her head. "I don't know if you're calling me camel dung or what."

Telling her its meaning would not help. "Okay." He inclined his head. "Please, come. I want to talk."

"I don't," she pouted, but started toward his bunkroom without another word.

Inside, he locked the door, then dug in his pack and found a T-shirt for himself. For her ... all he had left were the tactical pants he hadn't yet laundered. "They're not clean, but ..."

She took them. "If you keep giving me your clothes, you won't have anything left."

"They are my last pair."

Willow gave a hollow laugh. "I can't take them."

"You are borrowing them." He cocked his head toward the shower closet. "Go on. Take your time."

In the bathroom barely wide enough to angle her elbows out to put on the pants, Willow winced at the stinging line down her breastbone. It wasn't deep. More like a paper cut. With lemon juice on it. The pants didn't fit—they had an extra four inches in length and almost as much in the waistline—and man, they were itchy. She'd need a rope to keep them up.

But they covered her. That's all she cared about right now.

The cold memory of the blade slicing off her shirt, cutting a line between her breasts ripped through Willow again. With each piece of clothing he'd shredded, her dignity went with it. The last vestige of hope that she could avoid being raped. Even now, remembering the boss's breath, his stink, the way he looked at her, touched her ...

Tears stung as she braced herself against the lavatory wall. It wasn't like she'd never been felt up before. She'd worked some of the darkest parts of their world over the last decade, seen things she wished she could forget. Really, when she thought about it, avoiding rape this long was unfathomable. Unrealistic. And it made her feel terrible because all the others—male and female alike—were being violated.

Why? Why save her? It wasn't right.

I deserve it just as much—maybe more!

She pressed the heel of her hand to her forehead, like that could hold back the violent images, memories. The tears.

No. She would not cry. Instead, she pushed herself back into the room and to Chiji, the sharp contrast to the darkness and despair on this boat. Steady, calm. His riveting dark eyes held her, offered assurance. Comfort.

Haunted that he had seen her practically naked, she crossed her arms involuntarily. When he'd suggested coming to his bunkroom, she had just wanted to run back to the hold. Hide in the darkness because the thought of being here, being cold and alone—she hadn't wanted to face him and let awkward silence wedge between them. Didn't want to see his—

"Don't pity me."

Chiji inclined his head.

"I'm lucky." Willow heaved words that felt like an anchor in her throat. "Everyone on this ship has been raped. Except me." She hated it, yet was grateful for it. The conflicting messages in her brain were making her crazy. *"Why?"* She scowled at him and felt her lower lip quivering. "Why, day after day, do you protect me? It's jeopardizing everything. If you hadn't, they would've ..."

Her anger and words weren't logical. She was angry ... but not at him. Not really. He'd mentioned survivor's guilt the other night, and man, was it thick now. She dropped onto the edge of the bed and shuddered a breath.

He crouched at her side. "I will get you off this boat."

The words were likely meant well, but entirely unrealistic and kind of disappointed her. She didn't think he was the type to offer glib promises. "We are in the ocean. *Where* would we go if we got off this boat?"

"When we were in the cabin, you heard him speaking to Kalu. Yes?" His voice went very low.

She had no idea what his point was. "I doubt I'll ever forget *anything* that happened in that room." Her exhausted self shifted back on the bed, putting her spine against the headboard. Drew her legs up and hugged her knees. Still working to shut out what happened in the boss's cabin, she worried with the Velcro pocket of the tac pants.

Chiji's strong brow furrowed. "I am sorry I was too slow to stop—"

"No. Don't." She hugged herself tighter, not wanting to have this conversation. "I'm not going to talk about it, except to say you *did* stop it." Her own words pushed her gaze to his, and it seemed as if something hooked into her soul—a lure that drew her into the warm pools of his presence. "Again."

"Not soon enough, and I regret my naivete. They deliberately assigned me to help the new children. I thought it was a way to protect them, but clever Ahmet"—he shook his head—"wanted you … alone." His brow furrowed and darkened into his features. "It will not happen again." He shifted on the chair. "But my point in asking is to explain that he was not speaking to Kalu."

She frowned. "No, he was. I heard him—"

Chiji held up a hand with a small smile.

Willow wanted to argue. After all, she'd seen the boss talking on the phone, how he had blanched, then grew so angry he threw the phone at Chiji.

"He only thought it was the general. I believe it was your brother."

"My brother—why? How would you know—"

"I cannot know for certain as I lost contact with MiLE, but last I heard, they were engaging your brother. Since I know the men cannot speak the dialect well, and I know they definitely did not have the general with them, only one possibility is left— your brother."

"Wow." Lowering her legs, Willow came off the wall. Sat cross-legged, feeling hope thread itself through the darkness on this trawler. "Canyon, huh? He talked—"

"No, the other one."

She smiled. "Leif." Of course. Her little brother—

"Ah, sorry. Not him either." Looking abashed, Chiji swung his head.

She blinked. "Stone?" How did that make sense?

Now he quietly laughed. "Forgive me, no. I forget you have so many brothers."

"I don't understand. I only have—" She sucked in a breath and raised her eyebrows. *"Range?"* Her voice pitched, mirroring her acute disbelief. "Not possible. He hates us."

"I think it is better said that he hates himself."

She considered him. "Are you—" She shook her head. "No way. Range is Coast … Guard." She paused. "Okay, that actually makes sense since we're on the ocean, but—he's *U.S.* Coast Guard. American waters. We're very far from those waters, so he'd have no jurisdiction here."

"The American Coast Guard often advises and instructs the African Navy on ways to better patrol our coast."

"But …" She squinted. "Are you sure?"

He nodded.

Willow shoved her bangs off her forehead, frowning. "I never would've expected this. It's been so long since he's talked to anyone in our family that I wasn't even sure he was still alive."

"He is. Very much so. And determined to interdict."

Struggling to understand that the one brother who wasn't the walking-talking hardcore warrior like her other brothers was the one helping ... "This doesn't make sense."

Chiji lifted those broad shoulders in a shrug. "I only know that he is your brother and was somehow drawn into this circle."

"If you'd said any of my other brothers, I would have believed you. But ... Range ..." Was it terrible that she felt the earlier hope dim? She hated herself for it, but ... it was Range!

"I don't know this brother, but I do know Cord. If he let Range help, then there is good reason."

Weary, she fought back the tears again as a swell of relief—and worry—chugged through her. The point—Range was coming. With help. "I'm glad the girls will be safe. And—" She nearly choked on a breath and shoved to her feet. "Ife!"

Chiji stood and gently stilled her. "Nkechi has taken care of him."

"You are sure. He's safe?"

"I would not lie to you, Olamma."

There was that name again. "No. of course not ..." She smiled, feeling weird. Realized she was holding him, bracing herself. Lord forgive her, but she also noticed how his bicep was corded and flexed beneath her fingers. "G-good." She didn't want to let go. "Thank you. Again." She remembered the immense succor of his presence when he'd interrupted the boss's mental games. "I really thought ... I mean, you weren't there and he was cutting off my clothes, cutting me ... I just knew ..."

That memory, the chill against her bared skin ... the door opening and Chiji standing there. The shock that assaulted his features, quickly followed by a feral rage ... It had done her so good. So very good.

Yet, even now she didn't want to look into his eyes and see

that he, too, remembered her standing there, undressed. Why did she feel shameful? It was illogical yet so powerful a feeling. She'd counseled many a girl that it wasn't their fault, they weren't to blame. She said the words over and over, yet their eyes still held the lie.

One she now felt was very real and understood on a new, deep level. And for that, she was glad.

Anxious for a place to set her gaze that didn't force her to look into those eyes, she settled on his shirt. But her mind registered the mahogany skin peeking from between the two buttons that weren't fastened—likely couldn't be, since the shirt was *very* snug across his chest and shoulders.

How are you so beautiful?

She jarred at the question, half afraid she'd asked it out loud. Heat crept up her neck, adding to her shame. These thoughts weren't appropriate.

Yet the chastisement had no effect on her swirling stomach at his touch and gaze. She couldn't help it. He was tall, heroic, good-hearted, kind, handsome ... His eyes were this rich shade of dark chocolate that made her probe for the line between iris and pupil. And the way the light waxed and waned over his mahogany skin ... Lips that were the envy of many a botoxed influencer. "Women would kill for lips like that."

"Excuse me?"

Willow jolted. "S-sorry. I mean ..." Major fumble on the one-yard line! "Never meant what I mind." She twitched. "I mean—"

His laugh was nice and deep.

Mesmerizing. Flustering. Embarrassing. Made her smile. At least it was better than being humiliated and exposed. She turned away, moving to the other side of the bed to put a barrier between them. She didn't like feeling this way about a man, not right now. Not after Matt had died. But she did feel it, didn't she?

"Willow."

His whisper of her name shot warmth through her belly. She glanced over her shoulder and found him sitting again. Visually, he may have shrunk, but psychologically, he had to realize that seated position did absolutely nothing to diminish his powerful presence that ate up every square inch of breathing space.

"You have nothing to fear from me."

Oh yes, she did. She most definitely did. She had everything to fear—mostly she feared losing her heart to him.

Too weird, too soon, Wills.

More than once, she'd walked out of a movie theater over the love-at-first-sight trope. She hated it. It was unrealistic. Granted, this wasn't first sight. They'd been stuck with each other for the last ten days. And those ten days felt like ten weeks because they were together all day long. So, it was natural to grow ... comfortable with him.

Yes, but women around you are being raped, and you're getting googly-eyed over a hot Nigerian and thinking about kissing him?

Okay, true—she had thought about his lips. Impossible not to when they looked that good. Nice, full, but not in a feminine way. Lord, nothing about this man was feminine.

Stop stop stop.

She spun and put her back to him and chewed her lower lip. "I ... I should go ..."

"I think you should stay."

"No, I'm ... I'm pretty sure I shouldn't." She tried to laugh, but it came out as a hollow squeak. "I should go back to the hold."

"It is not safe for you. You will sleep in my bed."

"What?"

Palms up, he rose, chuckling. His presence doing that devouring thing again. But not in a threatening way. It was actually ... calming. "Poor choice of words."

Weirdly, she secretly hoped he would hold her shoulders again. Hold her. Tell her it was going to be okay. Merciful heavens, how badly she needed to hear that because everything on this boat was only getting worse. She had the cuts to prove it.

"The men," he said, his voice a low rumble, "what they saw in Ahmet's cabin ..."

Me, unclothed. Thankyouverymuchforthereminder.

"It will breed problems."

Her mind twisted and knotted, trudging past her shame and fear. Having seen her undressed would not be something they'd soon forget either. She understood how it could fuel their more lecherous thoughts. "Right ..."

"I will tell them I am keeping you here." He motioned to the bed. "You sleep there, and I will take the floor."

"What? No."

"I grew up sleeping on the floor. It is—"

"No, I mean I can't leave Ife. Not after what Yemi did to him. He's more vulnerable now than ever."

Chiji paused and stared down at her. "After what happened to you, still you think of others first."

She met his gaze, saw the admiration. And shoved it away. "It's nothing heroic. Just common sense. He needs me."

He hooked his finger under her chin and brought her gaze back to his. "It is heroic." He nodded. "I will bring Ife here, too."

Okay, Wills. Just slide right past the admiration and attraction thing again, okay? "But won't the boss get mad that you're keeping us here?"

"After the call and promise of Kalu's arrival, he has greater things to worry about than where you sleep this night."

"Arrival?" Willow startled. "Range is coming. Not just helping?"

"That is what I hope, but communication is limited, so I must trust the team."

"Yeah. Sure."

131

"I will go retrieve Ife. Wait here—lock the door. But ..." His smile was beautiful, like a warm hug. "Let me in when I return. Yes?"

Willow considered him for a long, taunting moment. "I ... I'm not sure I'll remember how to undo the lock. I mean, a night alone with a warm bed and no threats of harm ..." She winced. "Sorry—sarcasm is an old habit I learned from Canyon to deflect emotion and fear."

Two strides delivered him to her. His hand slid along her neck and cradled her nape. "I hate that you know this fear, Olamma. Hear me when I say I would do anything for that to be removed from your mind and life."

Heroic. Sweet. Again, unrealistic. Yet ... his eyes ... something she had known before in a distant manner she now understood in an intimate, powerful way—he would do violence to protect her. "Why?"

"After what happened with Ahmet, I realized ... I need you."

She sniffed. "Nobody *needs* me."

"Words are power. Do not speak these words again. Not in front of me."

"Behind you?" When his eyebrow arched, she shrugged. Shifted from his touch. "Of course, I will let you back in."

Tenderness flickered through his features, and he ducked out.

Willow quickly secured the hatch, then glanced back around the room. Sat in the chair he'd vacated. Smoothed her hands down the tactical pants. Felt something crinkle against her leg. She looked at the pocket and rubbed the spot. There was something in it. Willow tore back the patch and opened it. Her fingers caught a paper and she drew it out. And stilled ...

A tattered photo—of her family. At Stone's victory dinner at the lodge when he'd won the nomination. Edges were worn. It'd been folded ... around her image.

Thunk. Thunk.

She jolted. Jumped to the hatch. Then hesitated. What if it wasn't Chiji? What if someone had seen him leave? Hand hovering over the mechanism, she thought to ask who it was, but that'd give away that she was inside. Of course, they'd figure that out once they tried to open it.

"It is me."

Consoled at his voice, she freed it and tugged it back. A ball of energy bolted to her and clamped onto her legs. "Ife!" She bent and wrapped her arms around him in an awkward hug, since he wouldn't release her. When he did, she picked him up and moved to the bed. Sitting, she hugged him and peripherally saw Chiji take up that chair again. "I am so glad you came, Ife."

"I was scared, Mama Willow," he muffled into her shoulder. "When they took you and you did not come back, I was afraid the bad men would get me again."

Biting her lower lip to keep her emotion in check, she ached that this child knew this fear. Her gaze skidded into Chiji. He hated that she had known the fear of being raped. She understood that feeling of his a little better now. This precious boy ... "Oh, I love you, little one, and will make sure we are always together." She cupped the back of his head, kissed his crown, then pressed her cheek there, her gaze connecting with Chiji's.

He angled to the side, head cocked, watching her as he rubbed his lower lip in deep thought. What was he thinking? He seemed ... content.

A swell of gratitude for his protection, his wisdom, for ... *him* washed over her. "Thankfully, we have a protector who will help me keep my word."

Chiji leaned forward, intensity radiating through his dark features. He gave a slow nod, but there was something else there. Some hidden meaning or question. She wasn't sure what. It was as if he'd realized something.

Which would be quite the coincidence since she did, too. She realized she trusted him. Believed him. Liked him. A lot. His character reminded Willow of her brothers. Of her father. Real men. Godly men. Men of character, passion, and patriotism. Men ... heroes.

Yes. Chiji was a hero.

Her hero. The thought sent a crimson blush through her cheeks. He wasn't hers. They'd only known each other two weeks.

Yeah, she'd have totally walked out of this movie.

CHAPTER
FOURTEEN

Southern Syria

"THOUGHT YOU SAID this guy would help?"

Tac gear on, Range cleared his weapon and checked his ammo. "He will."

"Then why in the blue lagoon do we need all this?" For Cord, there was something almost religious about gearing up. Something about the way his M4 fit against his shoulder and the nuzzling of the grip in against his palm. See? There was a reason he didn't need a wife, not when weapons and killing bad guys made him this happy.

"It's the others around him who won't help."

Cord paused and looked at the pretty boy. "And you didn't think to warn us?"

"It's Syria—kinda figured that gave away the guarantee of opposition."

With a snort, Cord went back to his prep work. Within the hour, they were loaded up and trouncing across crater-laden roads to a backwater village that had more back than water.

Lowell tilted his head back and closed his eyes. The guy was as at home here as most men were tucked into their down comforters with the remote and their stupid Smart TVs.

"If we face unfriendlies, it won't be until we get inside the gate," Range spoke over the comms. "They always give us heck, but if I can get the imam to come out, we'll be okay."

"Imam?" Cord balked.

"Trust me."

"Yeah ..." He chuckled, shaking his head. "Already regretting getting in this MRAP with you."

He knew Canyon Metcalfe. And Stone, even did a mission with Leif once. But this guy—the brother with the bad attitude and chip on his shoulder ...? Not so much. He'd heard from more than one source that Range Metcalfe was a hothead. His attitude apparently went hand-in-hand with feeling like life owed him something. At least, that's what his brothers had said.

Besides, when staring down a baddie with him in their RPG crosshairs ... couldn't afford to be too picky about who helped you take down the son-of-a-gun.

Range slowed the MRAP about a klick outside the walled village. "Looks like a nothing of a village, but this place is key to drug and human trafficking."

Cord shot him a double-take. "Skin trade?"

"We've been hitting their trade route hard the last six months, trying to capture the madame, Kasra Jazani. She's ruthless." He pointed down the road to the compound looming in the distance. "Ran an op once to snatch her. Got back to the FOB and our package turned out to be her assistant—a man—dressed up as her." He shook his head. "Still haven't lived that one down."

"You didn't verify her identity?"

"Thought we had. Can't even explain how they switched her. Saw *her* go in. Followed *her* in. Took *her*. Got back. Discovered *him*."

"And you think we won't have trouble getting *this* him?"

"*This* him is one of ours. It's why we go in like this—to protect his cover. Make it look like he's getting arrested."

Cord eyed him, trying to fit this puzzle together. "Last I knew, you were Coast Guard."

Range smirked but stayed eyes out as they approached the village. "Think we already talked about brains in the Army."

"Want to explain how you're here running black ops now?"

"Nope." He straightened in the seat. "Okay, boys. Here we go." Accelerating, he barreled toward the walled compound.

Cord had a sickening realization—the guy was going to ram the gate. Tightening his buns, he braced, one arm on the door, ready to be pitched forward. Dust plumed. The MRAP thrashed the dirt road. Teeth gritted, he mentally counted down. Three …

The truck pitched forward.

Two.

Lowell shouted in anticipation but Cord tightened his shoulders.

One.

Just when the front end nearly kissed the wood barrier, the gate swung inward. They vaulted into the compound and Range nailed the brakes. But the lumbering giant of a vehicle didn't stop on a dime. Or even a silver dollar. This took the whole freakin' Fort Knox.

Eyes out, Cord settled into the familiarity of the role of operator. As best he could in the confines of an armored vehicle, he scanned high and low, shadows and corners. Doors. Windows.

Range climbed out.

Cord did the same, weapon up. Tension up. A curtain shifted to the left. He snapped in that direction, finger against the trigger. Two taps on his shoulder told him Lowell was behind him. He eased forward.

"Contact, your four o'clock," Low rumbled.

Cord swiveled in that direction, scanning. Sighted an adult

male, approximately thirty-five. Armed. "Show me your hands," he demanded in Arabic. He didn't know the various Syrian dialects, so he hoped the people here could decipher the way he butchered their language.

"Easy." Range's voice came from his nine in a fluid dialect stream that Cord didn't know. Incredible. It came off his tongue like butter on a hot biscuit.

The man remained where he was but didn't release his weapon. He pointed to his right.

"What's he saying?" Cord asked.

"Our objective is back here." Range moved a little too easily through this village, a little too unconcerned about his six and eating some lead.

Cord didn't have that level of stupidity. *Slow is smooth, smooth is fast.* Do it right the first time and you didn't have to repeat it. Or end up dead. Dumb Coastie didn't know how to operate with a team and had left them.

"Hands! Show me your hands." Low's words were frantic and repeated, this time with a few more colorful words.

Unnerved by the stress he heard in his buddy's commands, Cord shifted around, keeping his back to the MRAP as they backstepped in the direction Range had gone.

Cord spotted the trouble. Two men with rifles raised had been closing in on their six. Crap. He did not want any extra holes in his body. "Hey, pretty boy," he called over his shoulder, never taking his eyes off the two hostiles. "Range."

Nothing.

Cord muttered an oath. "Stop! Put down the weapon," he said in every language and dialect he'd mastered in his ten years as a Special Forces operator.

"Where the f—"

"Not here," Cord bit out, knowing Low wanted to know just as bad as him where the punk had gone to. "Let's just keep these guys—"

Crack! Pop! Pop!

Cord felt every one of them vibrate across his skin. Felt the electrical shock in his system and peered over his shoulder.

On the upper landing of what looked like apartments, Range darted for cover.

"Crap!" Today was going to Hades in a handbasket. He tried to assess which was a higher value—

"Go!" Low barked to Cord. "I got this."

He hated leaving his buddy to deal with these hostiles. But Cord backed away, moving toward the sound of the shots coming from the apartments, if nothing else, to beat Range Metcalfe to an inch of his life for this snafu.

"Pretty boy!" Hugging the lower perimeter of the building, he ducked and moved past a window. He swung around the stairs, cursing as he did because of the futility. Not quite fish in a barrel, but didn't have a way to protect himself either, since both sides were exposed. If he went straight up, he could take a bullet in the back. Or get shot in the head.

He was going to kill Range Metcalfe.

Up top, the guy was yelling something. A woman yelled back.

Guess he found the madame.

Shots cracked the day.

Cord bolted up the stairs, moving sideways to stay out of crosshairs. At least make the shooters work for their kill. As he neared the top, he slowed, sweeping his muzzle back and forth to check for hostiles. Seeing none, he advanced. Past a curtained door, he saw slippered feet. Beyond them, boots. Range.

Slippers were parallel to the door, so the woman would see if he entered. Could easily anticipate his approach because his body would block the sun. And if she had a gun on Range, spooking her wouldn't be good.

Five feet away, a window. Curtained. If Cord was figuring

right, the woman was directly beyond it. He glanced around for a rock or pebble. Spotted one. Pitched it through the window.

Pop!

A series of grunts and shouts erupted. The meaty sound of punches.

Cord glanced under the curtain again—woman was down. He surged up onto the landing. Shouldered against the door. Eased back the curtain. What he saw seemed like something out of a movie. Back on her feet, the woman was engaged with Range in heavy CQB. Every punch she threw he either countered or reversed. But the woman had some crazy-fast skills. Cord cleared his throat, hoping to distract her.

It worked. She looked away for a fraction—then jerked back to the fight.

Too late.

Range coldcocked her.

She dropped to the matted floor like a rock.

Propped on all fours, Range grunted unintelligible words. Closed his eyes—seemed to be working through something. He lumbered to his feet. Shaking his head, he looked at Cord. "A little late."

Cord felt the glue holding his temper together melting. "Wanna try that again? And what're you doing punching a woman in the face?"

Range's thin nostrils flared. "That? Not a woman." He sneered. "That's a monster in a hijab." He shifted and waved to someone, said something in Arabic.

A man emerged from the corner.

"Holy mother—" Cord snapped his weapon toward the shadowy man.

"No!" Range held out his hand. "We need this one alive."

"And we don't need her alive?" Cord eyeballed the woman. Mid-thirties. Very beautiful, even with the shiner rising across her right cheek and eye. Colorful clothes. Makeup. Bangles. "This her? That madame?"

"That's what he says," Range said, zip-tying the man's wrists. He seemed to hesitate, study the unconscious woman. "But they'll say anything to throw us off."

"Yet you punched her."

"She tried to shoot me."

Cord sniffed. Eyed the target. "Surprised you didn't shoot her."

"If she's Jazani, we'd need her alive."

Skitters crawled over Cord's shoulders. "This sounds a lot like we're bringing her in."

"I wish." Range took her picture with his phone.

"I don't—"

"Let's clear out before reinforcements get here."

"Cord!" Low shouted from the courtyard. "Incoming!"

Prisoner cuffed, they headed down. In the distance, dust plumed angrily, as if it too were offended at their incursion.

"This was messed up," Low muttered. "I mean, I understand you want to show his hottie sister you're all heroic and stuff, but maybe not this much."

He really could kill the guy. Bury him in the sand. Nobody would know. But even as the thought hit him, Cord was yanked around, his tac vest caught on something.

Range's fist. Blue eyes blazed. *"My sister?"*

Somewhere on the Atlantic Ocean

If Chineke would allow, Chiji would marry her. One day. He would. The entire thing with Ahmet and the abuse stirred him from his selfish idleness regarding her plight and ignited the protector passion that lay beneath. He felt fickle for his hastily spoken words but thanked Chineke for opening his eyes.

Restless, he relocated himself to the floor. Eyed her. Prayed for her.

Willow lay on the small bed, curled around Ife. Arm cloistering the boy to her in protection. It was strangely beautiful, her ivory skin contrasting with Ife's darker skin. She loved his people. It was clear. And … surprising. Amazing. It was one thing to come to another country and help poor or displaced people and refugees. It was another to put one's life at risk to protect another. More than once had he had seen her do this thing.

Sitting with his back against the wall, he fisted his hand and rested the other over it. Tucked his head and pressed his hands to his forehead. Prayed. Asked his Creator to keep them safe. Keep *her* safe. Make a way for them to get out of this so he could marry her.

It was assuming a lot. And Tox always said, "You know what assuming does …"

Chiji smiled, remembering his friend, who was back home in Virginia with his wife and their two-year-old son and another babe on the way. It had Tox weighing his options carefully, not quite ready to give up his operational status, but he also did not want to leave his family unprotected or without a father.

A pang struck Chiji—he had done this thing, gone undercover to find Chiasoka, but he had nothing to actually find her. No clue as to her location. Not even a sighting. It was this way. He knew Cord still had not found his sister either. The purpose, the hope, kept them going. Kept them engaged in the fight against this devouring evil.

Westerners were quick to shrug aside spiritual matters. Use "logic" to say there was no such thing as evil or God, but he had seen a demon twist a young girl into a savage. Seen that demon leave and the girl returned to her family. At one church service, hehad heard the howls of another spirit who mocked the churchgoers, told them they could not have the young man who was their mouthpiece. They had said "their" because there were many occupying the young man. The elders prayed for the boy and delivered him. He was now also a pastor, serving their country.

"Penny for your thoughts."

Chiji opened his eyes and looked to the bed.

Still cuddling the child, Willow now had one arm propped under her head, her blond hair a halo around her face.

"You should sleep," he said quietly. "We do not know the trouble that comes."

"Doesn't that go for you, too?"

He almost smiled. "We will take turns. You first."

"Ha," she said with a mocking laugh. "Stone did that to me when I was little and wanted to stay up Christmas Eve to see Santa. Then he let me sleep through it." After extricating herself from Ife and the bed, she slipped into the bathroom. He heard it flush, then she returned.

Except Ife was now sprawled over the whole bed.

She shrugged in surrender. "It's good he's sleeping so soundly."

Chiji shifted over, creating room for her. "It is not as soft …"

Without a word, she joined him on the floor and sat against the wall. "I still can't believe Range is the one coming to our rescue."

He liked hearing about her and her family. They had normal American lives. So different from how he grew up, though it was not bad. Only different. "You are close to your brothers?"

"Mm," she said, her head back, eyes on Ife. "Closer to Stone, my oldest brother, but none of us are really estranged—except Range. He hasn't really spoken to any of us since Canyon married Dani."

Chiji frowned. "It was a bad thing that they married?"

"No, actually, they're made for each other. But Range rescued her from the ocean and pretty much claimed her. Took her to the Coast Guard ball and everything. But … she met Canyon. Not even trying, he stole her right out from under Range. It wasn't pretty." Her light laugh made his heart stir.

"Um …" Knees bent, she reached into the tactical pocket.

Chiji stilled. He had forgotten …

She unfolded the picture and looked at him, their shoulders touching. "Where did you get this?"

"It is the picture I mentioned. The one Leif dropped."

"And you kept it?"

That blush again. Surely it made his face red. "By the time I found it, he had already boarded a jet to return home. So …" He sniffed. He could not lie to her. "I … that is not wholly true."

She gave him an amused look. "What is true, then?"

He grinned. "I had plenty of time to return it"—he tapped the photo with his knuckle—"but I did not want to."

Willow eyed him curiously. "Why?"

He reached across her to the photo she held. Pointed to her likeness. "This woman." Did he dare do this? "She spoke to my heart. I looked at her in this photo and said, 'I will marry her one day.'"

Willow drew in a breath, looking … aghast?

No. Surprised. Amused. "You knew you wanted to marry me just by looking at this picture? My hair was a mess and—"

"Yes."

She stared up into his eyes and searched his face. "Yes, that my hair was a mess?"

"Yes, that it was all that it took for you to set claim to my heart." But she did not seem to believe him. "I would not lie to you."

Laughing, she propped her elbow on her knee and pressed her fist to her temple, looking at him. "I would never have accused you of that, but … it is hard to believe."

"Why?"

She eyed the picture. "Because."

Chiji waited for a better answer.

"How can you look at a picture and know you want to marry someone? That's crazy. You don't even know me."

He tapped the spot over his heart. "I knew here. There was no doubt."

"Your heart? You're saying you knew in your heart?" She shook her head again and traced the photo's edges with her long, delicate fingers. There seemed to be a question in her eyes, one that she was not ready to voice. And somehow, Chiji knew the question—after all they'd been through, the way she'd treated him at first … did he still feel that way?

Should he answer it? Answer her? The longing of his heart was that she would one day want to marry him, too. But that could be a very long time off, if it ever came at all. Still, he would have her know … "Yes, I still feel the same way. Will always feel this way about you, Olamma."

"That's crazy."

"Perhaps, but I will take that kind of crazy. Crazy about you. Crazy to protect you. Crazy to have you fill this hole in my life."

She ducked and her chin pimpled as she fought tears. "Do you want it back?"

"I think it would be best if we kept it out of sight. It would not do well for Ahmet or Yemi to find it and know you are important to me."

Again, those blue eyes found his and questioned the veracity of his words.

He covered her hand and guided it to the pocket.

She nodded and slid it back into the pocket and closed the Velcro tab. Expression winsome, cheeks flushed with a pretty blush, she seemed anxious to redirect the conversation. "Have you found anything out about your sister yet?"

Arrow to the heart. "Nothing. On one hand, the trafficking syndicate seems one small thread in our chaotic world, and on the other, it is so vast that thousands vanish into it every day, never to be seen again." He ran a hand over his jaw, then rested his forearms on his knees. "There is a boy named Gardy who was taken from the churchyard while his parents were inside the church. In a blink—gone." He flicked his fingers. "His father searches relentlessly. For years. To this day. Reports come of a sighting and he hurries to investigate it. Gardy is still out there, waiting for his father to find him. I believe with all my heart"— he placed his palm over the beating organ— "that Chiasoka is waiting for me, staying alive till that moment when Chineke puts me in her path again."

"I hope you are right and find her." She squinted at him. "What does Chineke mean? I hear Nkechi say it, and I know—"

"My Creator," Chiji said with a nod.

"How ... how can you believe God ... that He even cares? You've seen what is happening—what just happened to me. And He is doing nothing."

"Is he?" Chiji said, his voice rising. "You know this, that He does *nothing*? You are there standing beside him and Gabriel?"

She lowered her gaze at the remonstration.

"Let me ask you this—your brother, Range. You said he had not spoken to you in all this time?"

"Years," she confirmed.

"Yet, he is on his way. Had I not told you, you would not know until the moment when you see him. And you would have been surprised. Yes?"

Willow hesitated before answering. "I suppose ..."

"Yet, is it not true that your being unaware of his actions and movement does not change that he is doing, he is acting even as we speak? You simply cannot see it."

"But it's different."

"How?"

"God is omnipotent."

"Ah, yes. Very true, thankfully. But He also"—he took her hand and opened her palm and set his over it, smiling at how

their hands seemed like opposites yet fit together so nicely—
"put in your hand *will*. Choice. Every day we make choices.
Every day, those choices have consequences. We are the little
minions doing all the things, yet somehow, that is God's fault.
We blame him. Accuse him." He motioned with his hands in
surrender.

"But He knows bad things will happen and does nothing to
stop them."

"It is true He knows all things. Your mother—she seems like
she is a very good woman."

Lips parted, she eyed him. "How can you know that? You
haven't met her. And why do I feel this is another verbal trap
you're luring me into?"

He winked. "I know she is a good woman because, I have
met her daughter and some of her *many* sons."

Willow laughed.

"Did she, every day in every way stop you from doing every
little thing that was wrong?"

She almost rolled her eyes. "You're making fun of me,
mocking me."

"Never!" He took her hand again, threaded their fingers. "I
would just have you see that, yes, God see these things. Perhaps
He does not address them as you believe He should. But you see
this one, finite moment. Time does not constrain Him. What he
sees is yesterday, today, tomorrow—all at once. He knows the
timelines, how they must intersect. He sees the whole,
fathomless picture of time and humanity. What we are doing
right now, He has already been here and is here. Determined it
is okay." He angled his head toward her and whispered, "I think
He called it good. Very good." Another wink, then he went on.
"Whatever happens, it will either bring glory to Himself and/or
benefit us or someone else. Sometimes, beautifully, both!" He
glanced at her over his shoulder. "What you do at the compound
for the children—do you do it for yourself alone?"

"Of course not. The children—I love them."

"Mm, yessss."

She laughed. "Okay, okay, I get your point."

"But do you *believe* my point?"

With a sigh, she shifted and rested her head against the wall once more, felt the vibration of the engine through it. "I don't know ... A month ago, I would have said no. Immediately. Seeing so much hurt, so much pain ... fearing daily that bad things will happen ... I confess, I *want* a savior to be real. I want to be rescued—which would shock my brothers as I've never needed or wanted rescue from anything."

Chiji lifted their threaded fingers and cupped them with his other hand. "You are not alone in this, Olamma. I, too, would accept a rescue. My efforts here are failing. Time is coming to an end."

"I guess it's good my brother is coming."

Sitting with her, the comfort of a challenging yet calm conversation stirring his heart more toward this woman. Holding her hand ... it was a dream come true, something he could not fathom would have ever happened.

"I don't know if I fully believe, but ... I think I believe more than I did."

"Then I was right."

She looked at him, waiting for him to clarify. "How?"

"I said God would use this, and already He has."

"Please do not tell me all this was to make me believe differently about Him. I'm not sure I could stomach that."

"Would it be so hard to believe?"

"Yes!" she balked. "It would mean I am causing the pain of Nkechi and the others. The abuse of Ife," she said, her gaze sliding over to the boy curled toward the wall, his soft snores rattling the air.

"You are not that powerful, Olamma." He drew her arm over his knee and hugged it, drawing her attention to him. "And again you ascribe to God things that are not His to be blamed over. He did not cause this, but did He allow it? Clearly. To what end?" He grinned. "Ah, that is the question."

She shook her head at him, smiling. "You enjoy this, don't you?"

More than he could say—but not the way she suspected. Having her here, talking about God, about their beliefs ... knowing that for the moment, in this locked bunkroom, he could keep her safe ... Yes, he enjoyed it *very* much.

"You have a captive audience to whom you present eschatological views."

In her tone there was an edge, a frustration that he felt as much as heard. One that hovered close to anger. And anger—an emotion that hid what was beneath it—meant he was hitting a nerve. But it startled that she had guessed his thoughts so easily. Her tone, her frustration, made him wonder what wound did she carry that made her reject God?

"Did I make you angry?" she asked, her voice sleepy.

"No. But I would readily accept your anger any day over unbelief."

She tugged her hand free and frowned. "You *want* me angry with you?"

"I want you thinking, weighing these things that steal your peace and tie a stone around your heart, threatening to drown your hope."

She wilted. "I ... Hope ..." She shrugged and settled back beside him, head resting on his shoulder. "It is a distant memory." The light haloed around her blond hair. "But not as distant as it once was."

There was a time to talk, a time to challenge ... but he was tired, too. And her admission of thinking over these things was good. Very good. Chiji felt the nudge to let the conversation rest, let her rest. Even himself. For he knew this time of peace would not last.

CHAPTER
FIFTEEN

Trawler on the Atlantic Ocean

WHIMPERS RAKED THE NIGHT, turning into screams that snapped Chiji awake.

He was on his feet, casting about for his kali sticks before he could make sense of the noise.

"Sh-sh-sh." Willow's whispers bathed the strident cries as she climbed onto the bed next to a sweat-drenched Ife. With a sad, empathetic glance to Chiji, she wrapped the boy tighter in her arms. "It's okay. It's okay."

Soul stirred, he stared down at the two. Her, an American with her beauty and blond hair, comforting this Nigerian boy as if he were her own. Showing compassion and love no matter the color of skin or familial bond. Her blond hair was as daylight against the dim cabin, the dark mattress, and Ife's little body. And Ife, a boy of six who had no mother or father, clung to her as if she were his mother. His endearment—Mama Willow—spoke of how he saw her.

Eyes closed, she nestled onto the bunk, and soon the two were fast asleep. Before Chiji could even pull himself from admiring them. Skull pounding from the sudden rush of adrenaline, having believed they were in danger, he lowered himself to the chair. Cradled his forehead and sighed.

How close were Cord and Range? When would the rescue come? How could he get the women and children off? What if there was a firefight? An explosion?

A thought he'd never considered struck him. Ahmet would be furious when he discovered Range wasn't actually Kalu. The mafia boss would be livid. He'd do anything to protect his business and himself.

Would he kill everyone? Blow up the boat?

It would not be the first time Chiji had seen or experienced such extreme measures.

Check the boat, the waters.

Roughing a hand over his face and slick head, he was startled at how loud those words were in his head. Why? And why was his heart thumping harder now? He glanced at the door, listening carefully to the goings on within this trap of a ship. Quiet ... water lapping ... the engine rumbling ... voices down the gangway, but not many.

Knuckles to his lips, he considered Willow and the boy. Could he leave?

He had to.

Chineke, show me ...

The boy rolled onto his back, but Willow did not move. Ife glanced over his shoulder at Chiji, his dark eyes wide. "I have to use the bathroom."

Chiji nodded and stood. Opened the door. "In here."

"I'm stuck." He indicated to Willow's arm around his waist.

Quietly, Chiji shifted closer and gently lifted Willow's arm, which did nothing but elicit a soft moan from her, even though the boy scampered free and hurried to the closet.

And now, he had his answer. He dug into his ruck and grabbed his phone. When Ife came out, Chiji crouched before him. "You must help me. I must go do something. Lock the door behind me, yes?"

Ife's eyes went round as soccer balls.

"I need you to keep Willow safe until I come back. It will be a very short time. Can you do this, little warrior?"

Two fingers in his mouth, Ife looked to her, then back to Chiji and nodded, lowering his hand. "Okay. But only if you promise to come back."

"I promise." After showing Ife how to lock the door, he stepped out, eyes probing the ominously quiet deck. He waited until he heard the *shunk* of the lock.

Moving stealthily down the gangway, he tried to keep his movements as quiet as possible, especially as he neared the stairs. On the bridge deck one level up, he heard chatter. He thought through his route—climb the steps, to the right, and up the short passage to the door that lead to the topmost deck.

Straight ahead, loud voices and thuds clomped toward him.

Chiji ducked around a corner and pressed his spine to the hull, praying they did not come this way. He had no reason to hide except that he did not want the others knowing Willow and Ife were alone.

Ezueda and Yemi stalked past, talking about the boss's anger over the American. Of course, they used another name for her. One Chiji despised. Though he wanted to speak out, he let them and their coarse language pass without comment. Knowing his time was short, he hauled himself up to the bridge deck. Used his long legs to carry him quickly to the right and then toward the passage.

"Should I be jealous?"

Almost to the topside door, Chiji slowed. Considered just continuing on, but Yemi ... He turned to the man and waited for him to complete his question, one most likely intended to arouse anger.

"Taking her to your bunkroom, keeping her all night?"

Ezueda shrugged, palms out as he advanced. "Are you done? Can I have a go?"

Chiji lunged. Drove the heel of his hand into the man's nose. Blood gushed, falling to the ground with the heavy body.

At least, that's what Chiji wanted to do. But it would unleash a storm. "You saw her," he said, the words like acid on his tongue. "If I let every man here have a turn, she would not be fit for General Agu. Then he would deem me unfit." He lifted his palms. "I like my head where it is."

"Hm, something I cannot agree with."

Chiji caught the handle of the door. "Then it is good we will not be stuck together much longer." Quickly, he moved onto the deck and toward the stern, keeping his ears attuned behind him. But he did not hear steps nor did Yemi pursue the conversation. Even as he made a circuitous route stern to portside, he scanned the deck and wheelhouse, making sure he could not be seen or interrupted. He pulled the phone from his pocket. Made the call.

"*Sogno Veneziano.*"

"*I need to check my reservation.*" Voices carried from belowdeck, but he was still in the clear.

"One moment, please," she said in Italian. "We will need your confirmation code, sir."

Chiji coded in and a second later, a gruffer voice assaulted his ear.

"You alone?"

"Yes," he said. "But this is not good. It is a bad idea."

"Yeah, well, we're clean out of good ones right now."

"Nobody will believe him to be Kalu, and then I will be killed."

"That would be why I'm not going to be the general," intruded Range's voice.

A stream of perfectly and rhythmic Syrian Arabic flew through the line, and it was like a balm to Chiji. "Who—" He lifted a hand. "Never mind."

Something glittered in the darkness, interrupting the horizon. Chiji frowned as he moved to the rail, squinting through the heavy shadows. "You are close …"

"Negative," Cord countered. "Least, not as close as we'd like. Had to pick up Mr. Kalu first. We're still a good hundred nautical miles out. Part of the problem is that we can't get a firm fix on your location. Need you to disable the jammer."

How was he to do that? It would be protected, monitored.

"It's probably going to be wherever they have communications."

Chiji looked toward the wheelhouse, recalling new systems up there. "I think I know where."

Light flickered again in the distance. Chiji narrowed his gaze and probed the darkness. Though he found a small source of light, there was … something out there. Like a void that swallowed light. Tricked his eyes. He scanned and felt a hollowing in his core as the shape of whatever he was looking at—or wasn't looking at—seemed to swallow his field of vision. His gut sank as his eyes finally assembled something his mind refused to believe. "We have a problem."

"What?"

"There is a ship, a very big ship—a mega yacht—closing in on this boat."

"You sure?" Cord asked. "We're not showing anything."

Moonlight caressed the oversized yacht, its decks finally taking shape, filling in the void that had consumed his sight. It was more than a few nautical miles out, but the vast size made it seem as if it was even now bearing down on them. "I see it. It's … massive. Closing in fast." His best guess—he had a half hour to do something. At most.

"Well, who—"

"Uh … does the real General Kalu Agu have a superyacht?" Lowell asked. "And I hate to say it, but if that's him—nothing good can come out of him finding you there, Chiji."

He searched the horizon in all directions for options, safe havens to swim to. But there was nothing. Only the glitter of the moon on the inky waters. "Where is the nearest land?"

"Nothing is close," Range said. "You're still too far out. And I don't like being the bearer of bad news, but there's some pretty strong headwinds and storms bearing down on that area."

Chiji laughed, searching the deck as he worked through his plan.

"So, I'm just going to say it—don't take to the waters. Because it will take you. You're too far out, and unless you have a boat, you're going to exhaust yourself. That means muscle cramps and dehydration. Drowning."

Nodding, Chiji started toward the portside and pitched a blue ice chest over the side, along with a couple of otter boards. Moving quickly, he knelt to untie plastic fuel cans and buoys from the side.

"Chiji? You hearing us?" Cord asked.

Something made him turn back and free two more buoys.

"Chiji!"

"*Ebe onye dara ka chi ya kwaturu ya.*" With that, he ended the call and headed to the wheelhouse.

100 Nautical Miles from the Trawler

"What the blue blazes did that mean?" Cord pounded his fist on the table. He didn't need the answer because he knew that tone. "Tell me he's not going into the water."

"He's going into the water," Low said.

"With my sister." Range's eyes sparked with anger and he cursed. "You better get your man back on the line and under control, because if he does this, he's going to kill my sister. And that's something I can't forgive."

"Yeah," Low growled, "let's just act like your sister is the only person on the boat worth saving."

"She is! To me." Brow gnarled and lip curled, Range glowered. "I don't care about anyone but her. She's what you used to bring me in, get my seafaring skills to help this lost cause. But nobody asked why I agreed to come."

"Out of the goodness of your heart," Low challenged.

"You're thinking of the wrong Metcalfe," Range grunted. "Ask Abqari here about me and goodness."

Cord had two strong hands and really wanted to wrap them around this punk's neck. But he shifted his gaze to the scrawny Syrian standing here, hands at his sides, eyes dull. His apathetic expression betrayed nothing, but he spoke around a very thick Arabic accent. "Zalaam cannot have goodness because he does not have a heart."

"Salaam?"

"With a 'z'," Range corrected. "It's means darkness."

"I have no idea why they call you that," Cord grumbled, then shook his head, disappointed with the kid. "You're a Metcalfe."

Range gave a cockeyed nod. "Only on my birth certificate."

"Holy mother …" Cord gritted his teeth, doing everything in his power not to rampage right here and now, not to throttle the guy. "I'm not sure I like you."

"Don't care." Range pointed to the sonar map where Mira was trying to pinpoint the location of the trawler. "*That* is all I care about. Finding Willow before it's too late."

"Then do something! Help us figure out a solution and stop your dang moaning."

"We're close enough to land for a helo to make the trip, but with a storm and high winds coming, no pilot worth his weight would do it. Besides, even if we called one up, we still wouldn't make it before the yacht." He folded his arms, which was really starting to feel like a power move somehow. "And if that superyacht is invisible to radar"—he jutted his jaw to the array again—"once they're captured, we'll never find them."

Lowell huffed and scratched his beard. "And if they go overboard? They'd have a chance, right?"

"D'you miss what I said to your guy?" Range snorted. "If they don't get attacked by marlins, stingrays, or sharks, surviving out there? Impossible. Even if they did stay alive, trying to find them would be like looking for a diamond in a sea of crystals." He lifted his shoulders. "Lost cause, because we can't track that phone. Not without advanced tech y'all are seriously lacking. Not as simple as tracking a cell phone, not on open water."

"Don't need you telling us what we can—"

"It boils down to this." His eyes blazed. "If he takes her overboard, he kills her. And if that happens"—he cocked his head—"you'll see why they call me Zalaam."

CHAPTER
SIXTEEN

HIS LIPS WERE ON HERS, teasing, testing.

She wrapped her arm around his neck and perched on her tiptoes to seal the kiss. Melting into his arms, feeling his fingers entwine with hers. He was beautiful, the kiss was beautiful. His hold so strong, his chest so firm. His resolve so firm.

"We must go."

Mmm. She didn't want to leave the safety of his warm embrace. Instead, she traced the line of his shoulders, muscles arcing toward his neck. Gracefully descending to his taut bicep.

"Willow."

She kissed him again, wanting his words to stop and his heart to speak to her more. Strangely, it was not the kiss that spoke as loud as his fingers entwined with hers. His hands were warm. Strong, exuding that same confidence that radiated from his dark eyes. "Just one more kiss."

A giggle waded through the moment.

Willow blinked, finding herself staring up at Ife and Chiji, one smiling, the other … surprised. "Oh." A dream. She'd been dreaming. Pushing the bangs from her face, she sat up, her head feeling like it weighed a thousand pounds—and clogged with humiliation and sleep. "What …?"

Chiji's hand caught hers, and it speared her stomach with warmth. Thrust her back into the dream. "We must go," he said. "Quickly."

She scooted to the edge of the bed. "Go where? Why?"

"A yacht is coming. Fast. If we get on that—"

She gasped. Alarm spiraling through her, Willow shot to her feet, dregs of sleep cut away and her heart amping. "W-what do we do? Where …?" She looked at Ife, then Chiji with a frown. "What do we do?" she repeated.

"Come. Topside."

What had he said? "A yacht?" Right. "Why is that a bad thing? Couldn't it be my brother?"

"It is not them. I talked to Cord. They are too far out. I think the yacht brings General Agu."

Oh no. "The traffickers. D-do you think the boss found a way to contact him?"

Chiji hesitated, then nodded. "It would make sense."

Coldness spilled through her stomach. "We-we have to tell the others. Get Nkechi."

"First, we must get to the top. Make sure it is safe."

"Right." Willow nodded, her mind still drenched in sleepiness. And that dream. She forbade herself from looking at his lips. That was not what their relationship—friendship—was about. Yes, *friendship*. He was a friend. Who had rescued her so many times, she wasn't sure she could count. "Okay." She nodded at him. "Let's go."

He took her hand and Ife's.

Not romantic. Just practical. But it yet again reminded her of the dream, their fingers entwined as they kissed.

"We go out, up the steps, and up the next steps and out onto the top deck. Do not stop. No matter what." He nodded to both of them, his expression stern. Fierce.

She bobbed her head and glanced at Ife, who looked absolutely stricken. She lifted him into his arms. "We can do this, right?"

"I'm scared."

Willow kept him close, giving Chiji another nod. "And we'll come back for the others."

"First things f—"

"Yes, yes. Check topside." She was ready. More than ready. The thought of getting out of here, taking charge of the situation and their future … it was invigorating.

"Remember," he said, looking into her eyes, "we stop for nothing."

"Nothing," she agreed. Willow worried at his insistence, his urgency. That he feared trouble made her crazy scared.

He held out a knife to her.

Taken aback, she scowled.

"Protection," he said, urging her to take it.

"No." She shook her head, stomaching tightening. "I couldn't … I … violence isn't the answer."

"Sometimes, violence can only be stopped by violence."

"Sometimes," she conceded, then quickly added, "but not always." Besides, she could never do hand-to-hand combat. More than once in sparring with her brothers she had a visceral reaction when she thought she'd hurt them. No way could she plunge a knife into someone, feel their blood oozing over her fingers.

Oh man. She was going to be sick.

Willow shook her head frantically at him. "I'll just have to trust you." Probably wasn't fair to add this, but it's where they were at, wasn't it? "And God."

His eyes darkened. "Even God has an Angel of Death."

"Then let that angel come and deal out some death because I'm not. Won't."

He cupped her face.

And she swore for a heartbeat he was going to kiss her. Like that dream. And her pulse raced a mile a minute in the fraction of a second that he touched her. He was trying to weaken her resolve. And her jellied knees said he was a real threat to her convictions.

"You are—"

"Aren't we supposed to be hurrying?"

Chiji's expression hardened. Turning to the door, he reached back and caught her hand. She held on fast as the door swung open. It was like a tidal wave, the moment rushing over them. A swirling vortex of fear and danger rushing in to grab them and sweep them into its fray.

Holding Chiji's hand and hugging Ife tightly against her, she hurried down the passage. Each thump of her shoes sounded like a cannon blast on the metal grating as they hurried to the steps. He shifted to her and took Ife, motioning for her to ascend. Silently, she obeyed and glanced around, grateful it was the middle of the night, so few were awake.

Chiji rose onto the deck, and they switched Ife back to her arms, the little monkey's legs coiling around her waist and his arms around her neck as he clung on for dear life.

They rounded a corner and started for the last set of stairs, hope surging through her that they would actually make it. Finally, something was going right. They'd get out the door, check things, then gather the women and children. Get off this boat. Swim to freedom.

I'm not the best swimmer …

Didn't matter. She'd do it. Anything to be free. With Chiji, she felt as if she could face the world and know that no matter what, he'd do his best to keep her safe. With him, she had a chance. With him … she dared to hope. With him, she felt the blessed tendrils of belief encircling her, tightening her resolve and focus.

She'd never felt all this with any other man.

Matt.

Not even him. Grief tugged at her, pummeling Willow with guilt. She'd just left him on the side of the road where they'd killed him. What kind of person, girlfriend, did that?

Guilt chased her through the last hatch. Ahead, she could see the door. Excitement raced through her. She hurried, but misjudged the height. Tripped. Metal grating scored her knees. Willow clutched at Ife, not wanting him to get hurt. But she crashed into the wall. The way her shoulder hit, she wasn't alone in getting hurt.

Ife had struck his head on a steel corner. He let out a shout.

She clapped a hand over his mouth and looked to Chiji, who pivoted around to the direction from which they'd come.

Clambering to her feet, Willow glanced back, a move that put her off-balance. Made her stumble right into Chiji.

"Adigwe! What is this?"

Gasping, Willow spun to her savior. Stumbling again, she paused. But then saw the weapon aimed at them.

"Go," he hissed to her, moving her around him. "Do not stop!"

"No," she cried, but remembered the promise she'd made him. Keep moving, no matter what. She whirled, not wanting Ife to get shot. The door ... less than a half dozen feet away. They could make it! With a grunt, she launched toward it. Felt as if she were in a dream where her legs weighed a thousand pounds. Where she ran for hours but only got a few inches farther. Whimpering did no good. She felt as if she ran through oatmeal. Desperation plied a yelp from her. Peering over her shoulder petrified her.

Two more mafia were there. With weapons.

She wheeled around. Reached for the door. Ife's scream pierced her ears. Terrified her. Propelled her toward the door. The cold, wet door struck her palm. She shoved into it, vaulting into the open. She shuffled and slid on the wet deck, the sensation of freeing herself from the tight confines of the passage liberating. Darting forward, she realized she had no idea which way to go. But the thought of stopping proved terrifying. The men were coming after them. "Which way?" A quick glance over he shoulder stopped her cold.

She was alone. "Chiji!" The door slapped closed, him nowhere in sight. "No!" What should she do? He said not to stop. Made her promise.

But were was she supposed to go? What was she to do without him?

Panic overwhelmed her. What if he'd been shot? What if they'd killed him? They'd come for her and Ife next.

No. No no no.

"Chi—" She snapped her mouth shut. Couldn't draw attention to herself. But ... what was she supposed to do?

"Where is he?" Ife whined.

She hugged the boy closer. "It's okay. He'll be here." He'd come, wouldn't he? Hadn't he always? But as time ticked by without him, she fought the panic. They were losing time, so she searched the deck. For ... what? She strangled a cry of futility.

She had to go back for him.

He was dead. Wasn't he?

Which meant ... *I am, too.*

Heart thick with grief and panic, she stood there, unmoving. Paralyzed by fear, the thought of him dead. Her alone.

Cracks and pops peppered the night, blending with the strange and eerie noise of the boat on the near-silent ocean. She faltered, hesitated—maybe he was coming now? Or maybe that was his life coming to an end—then surged forward.

The door flung open.

She cried out and pulled back to avoid getting whacked in the face.

"What are you doing?" His hands were flinging her around. "I said keep moving!"

"I thought you were dead!"

He winced, then inclined his head. "Not quite." He nodded her to the rail. "I had to do something."

He was here. They could check, then get Nkechi and the others. "So, what do we need to check? We should split up to save time, right?" she asked, her throat thick with emotion. "We ... If they know we're here and shoot at us ... How do we get the—"

"Here." He stuffed something into her hand. "Hold Ife."

She frowned. "I am."

"Tight." Chiji was coiling a rope around her and Ife.

"What're you—"

Crack!

Willow flinched, her gaze snapping to the upper part of the ship that towered over the deck. Fire and smoke poured from it. She gaped, even as she felt the constriction of the rope crisscrossing her torso, her hands free. This ... this didn't seem right. She looked into Chiji's eyes as he secured the rope and found a ferocity, a violence ... one that she hadn't seen before.

Pop-pop-pop.

Sparks erupted from the top, followed by a very heavy, ominous groaning that drew her gaze upward. An entire side of the wheelhouse was gone. The rest leaned heavily toward the deck. "Oh no."

"Forgive me."

Her gaze shifted to him. "What?"

He stepped back and vaulted at her. His full weight broadsided her. Sent her over the side. "NO!"

She was airborne ... falling ... ripped by wind and terror. Water rushed up at her. Split-second intelligence struck. She covered Ife's nose and mouth even as her legs impacted the water.

Greedy and powerful, the ocean yanked her into its depths. Terror clawed at her, reminded her she wasn't a good swimmer like Range. She wasn't a warrior like Canyon. She wasn't even clear-minded like Brooke.

She was Willow. A reed bending ... breaking.

Darkness consumed her.

CHAPTER
SEVENTEEN

75 Nautical Miles from the Trawler

"YOU HAVE ACCESS TO SATELLITES?"

Cord glanced at Range, not willing to tell him anything. He was fed up with this Metcalfe. "How else do you think—"

He jutted his jaw at the screen. "Pull it up."

"Pull *what* up? We can't track them. How are we supposed to—"

"You have a triangulated position. From satellites, we should be able to find some semblance of a wake to track, and it should be big or noticeable enough with two ships in the same area."

Cord hesitated, eying the guy. Cursing himself that the blue eyes made him think of Brooke. Which made him wonder what she'd say about all this—her only sister trapped on a ship with traffickers, her rogue brother helping—sort of. "Really think that might work?"

"Only one way to find out."

Cursing himself, again, this time for not thinking of this first, Cord indicated to Mira. "See if you can piggyback that connection again."

She lowered her chin, casting a begrudging look to Range, then did as instructed.

Arms crossed, legs shoulder-width apart—not a power thing, but to keep his balance on the cutter—Range flattened his lips. That clean-shaven jaw jounced a muscle. "Never did answer about my sister."

Cord flicked a hand toward the array. "What do you think—"

"Brooke."

He glanced down before realizing his mistake, which made him look guilty. "How'd you know it wasn't Willow?"

"Because you don't seem especially cut up about her being out there."

"He's not exactly an emotional guy," Lowell put in.

"She's one of the best Aftercare Specialists we have."

"But she's not the sister you're trying to hit."

Cord felt his anger rising. "I'm not trying to *hit* anyone."

"Brooke won't give you the time of day."

Now he was pissed. "Oh yeah?"

"She swore off anyone military after our dad died."

"Huh. So having dinner with her twice …?"

Blue eyes sparked again. "Serious?"

"Dead."

Range grunted. "That's what you'll be if Canyon finds out you're going after her."

"He already knows," Lowell said. "But he said the same thing you did—she'll never go for him."

"Not sure why you'd want that trouble anyway. Brooke—" Range shook his head and winced. "She doesn't play nice. She plays to win, and on her terms."

"And you think I'm not okay with that?" Why was he getting so mad? This punk didn't know anything about him, and he clearly didn't know anything about his own sister. Because Brooke might be sharp edges and hard words, but she was also tough, classy, and—well, hot.

The guy's left brow dipped and curled, then he sniffed. "Whatever, man. Don't say I didn't warn you."

"Yeah, and don't say I asked for your advice."

"Your funeral."

"I—"

"Cord!" Mira's fingers flew over the keyboard. "I did it. He was right."

"About what?"

"I used sat-imaging to find the wakes in the triangulated area." She motioned to the screen on the wall. "Found this."

Cord glowered at Range. "Don't let it go to your head."

"A good idea isn't the same as a good outcome."

They crowded in, hovering around the screen to see the partially grainy image. Just as Chiji had warned, a superyacht was bearing down on a fishing trawler.

"That's them," Cord said.

"What's the timeline on this?" Range edged closer.

"Ten-, fifteen-minute lag," Mira said, punching keys. "At this time, the super was about a half hour from the trawler."

"Can you tighten this up so we can get identifiers?" Cord narrowed his eyes, as if that would help the satellite zoom in.

"On it." Mira made a few more keystrokes, and even as she nodded, the distance between the satellite and North Atlantic waters began vanishing. The trawler zoomed into focus.

"Bigger than I thought," Lowell muttered, bracing against one of the support posts. "What won't these traffickers think of next?"

"Don't encourage them," Cord said as the satellite image enlarged again, the trawler close enough now for them to read the lettering on its hull. "Too bad we can't see inside."

Range grunted. "Thermals would be nice."

"If only," Cord agreed, wondering how they were supposed to figure anything out. "Mira, lock this location and get it to the captain so we can get under way."

"Already done," she said, and as if to confirm her words, the engine's rumbles increased and he felt a tug of his person as they increased speed. It wasn't anything like a car or jet, but it was noticeable. And comforting.

"Whatever's going down, we aren't going to make it in time," Range said.

The guy would relieve himself on a rainbow given the opportunity. "So what? You want us to not go? Not try to help?"

"Never said that. What I—"

"Hold up. Look," Lowell said. "Someone's on that deck."

"Who is—" The question died in his throat. That white-blond hair was unmistakable.

"That's my sister." Range bent forward, squinting. "What's in her—" He cursed. "She's got a kid in her arms. What's going on?"

"Hey. Looks like they've got a lightshow happening," Lowell said.

"Small arms fire." Cord shook his head. "Guess Chiji ran out of time."

"Yeah, but where is he? Why's she topside with that kid when—"

"There he is," Low noted as another shape barreled onto the deck.

Though Cord felt relief at the sight of the Nigerian who had more tricks up his sleeves than a magician, he didn't like where this was going.

"Only place to go on deck is into the water." Range's eyes lit with anger as he met Cord's. "I warned you—"

"Hold your fire, Metcalfe. We don't know—"

"There's nowhere to go—"

A bright flash erupted. Orange-red. "Fire," he breathed.

"An explosion," Range corrected.

They watched, stricken and anxious as the two forms ran to the stern, then around to the side.

"No," Range said, as if warning his sister. As if this were happening right now. As if he could stop it.

Cord covered his mouth as they spotted gunmen spilling out from belowdecks. "Holy mother …"

"He's going to do it. And then I'm going to have to kill him."

"Shut up," Cord bit, not wanting to believe it.

But even as he willed Chiji not to go into the ruthless waters of the Atlantic, not to tempt Mother Ocean's fury, Chiji rushed Willow. They went overboard.

Range cursed. Again. And again. He pivoted and slammed a fist onto the table. "Augh!"

"Okay. Okay. I know—not good. But we have satellite. We can—"

The screen went grainy.

"What—" He looked to Mira, who was scowling at the screen. "Get it back up."

Fingers flying over the keyboard, she shook her head. "I can't."

"What do you mean—"

"It's not there. The feed has been severed."

"By whom?"

"No idea, but …" She lifted her hands. "I'm guessing whoever controls that satellite."

"We do—"

"No, sir," Mira said, face pale as she looked up at him from her station. "Remember, you told me to piggyback—"

"Crap." He'd forgotten. "But we got their location, sent it to the captain, right?"

"Yes, sir."

Okay. Maybe he could breathe.

An annoying buzz sounded over his shoulder. He glanced there and saw a phone mounted on a post … at the same time he detected a noticeable slowing and the quieting of the engines. He frowned, looking around as if they could tell him what was happening. His gaze met Range's. The buzz continued.

"That's the captain's line, sir," Mira said.

"I know," he growled and yanked the phone up. "Go ahead."

"Sorry, Mr. Taggart, but I've been told to stand down."

"By who?" Cord barked. "We're civilian—"

"SOCOM, African Navy … yeah, nice little mess you've gotten us into, Taggart."

CHAPTER EIGHTEEN

SHE COULD STILL FEEL the jetlike propulsion of bullets around her, piercing the waters. Seeking her body. Seeking to kill her. Willow had dived deep, keeping Ife from opening his mouth and sucking in water, drowning, but the buoys Chiji had tied to her fought her. Forced her upward.

Willow kicked hard, trying to put as much distance as possible between her and the boat even as she ascended. Once she'd broken out, she gasped hard, sucking in air and relieving her aching lungs. The ship was chugging away, its engines churning a thick wake and blurring the moonlight on the water. But the mafia were still at the stern, weapons up and firing into the water … in the wrong direction.

Even as she thought that, Willow realized Ife wasn't moving. Or struggling … and she couldn't see Chiji. Panic ignited, firing through her veins. Treading water, she glanced down at Ife, who was limp in the ropes tied to her.

Oh God, please …

She patted his back. "Ife." He didn't move, his head lolling to the side, water like crystals in his ebony hair. "Ife!" Frantically, she pounded his back. "Ife, please. Breathe!"

A swell caught her and thrust her up and backward. She tensed, fighting the wave that pitched her toward the boat. "No, no."

Shouts bounced her gaze to the trawler. The men were firing into the water—but not at her. They were focused on an area closer to the ship. It must be Chiji. She searched the inky waters, overwhelmed with all the emergencies demanding her attention.

Shouts drew her gaze back to the mafia—and found them pointing in her direction. They'd seen her.

No ... they'd seen the buoy. Bright and big, it was a homing beacon to her location.

Willow frantically extracted herself from the tangle of ropes that had saved her life when Chiji had pushed her overboard. Anger dug its claws into her chest as she struggled to keep thumping Ife's back, keep them afloat, and yet free them from the buoy. Crying out, she was sure they were going to die. She wasn't a strong swimmer. But she sure wasn't going to just give up and let them drown.

"Ife!" she screamed, hitting his back, desperate.

He coughed, his head rearing back, then slamming into her breastbone. It hurt—by the angry seas, it hurt—but she welcomed the pain because of its source. Glad because it meant he was alive to do it, and she was alive to feel it.

"Quiet, quiet," she hissed to him. "They'll hear you."

His wails silenced.

Thank God. She felt the rope finally give and leaned backward, kicking hard as she used her hands to keep them afloat, trying to keep her movements small in the hope—

Wind tore at her, thrashing her around in the choppy waters. Losing the buoy was meant to free her from being a target. But it had also enabled the waters to pitch her around like a gnat.

Fire tore across her arm. She hissed and glanced down, seeing a dark line across her upper arm. Blood.

A bullet had grazed her!

She again looked to the boat. Saw the sparks—muzzle flash.

Then she saw it. A large swell, growing … growing …

Oh, come on!

"Hold on," she shouted to Ife. Kicking, she angled into the water and swam as best she could to work with the swell. Cursed herself for not taking more swimming lessons. The water caught her and lifted … lifted … lifted … Even as they were ferried up on the powerful tendrils of Mother Ocean, Willow felt terror she'd never known. They were higher than the boat. As the ocean raged, it tossed her forward. Then collapsed out from under her. She screamed as they plummeted. Saw the water rush up at them. She snapped her mouth shut. Clamped a hand over Ife's nose and mouth—but felt his own hand there.

Water drove them down … down … down …

Hearing gone vacuous and heart pounding, she realized the pressure against her body was building. With no sunlight to guide her back to the surface, Willow had a horrific epiphany: she had no idea which way was up.

They were going to drown.

We are not going to drown.

She kicked, forcing herself to calm. Which was brutally impossible when her chest and lungs felt crushed. *What do I do?*

Exhale. Follow the bubbles.

That's right! Canyon had told her that ages ago. With the darkness, she couldn't see them, but she could feel them. Bubbles swept her right cheek, then ear. She angled and started kicked and pulling them up.

In her arms, Ife started thrashing.

Willow kicked harder. Fought the urge to cry or cry out. It was too far …

What if she wasn't even going in the right direction?

A whimper bubbled through her chest. She felt her tenuous grip on her air slipping ... the pressure thumping in her temples, demanding air.

Ife's thrashing was slowing ... His body jerked.

Willow strangled a sob. Felt her lungs ready to burst. She kicked. Kicked so hard. Desperation wound a tight cord around her throat.

She broke into the open. Gasped. Coughed.

A wave crashed into her. Shoed her back down.

She got a mouthful of water. Coughed—and took in more.

I'm going to drown.

It was too late! Her nostrils flooded. Her throat. Burning.

Something snagged her. Yanked her backwards. Disoriented, panicked, she flailed, her mind struggling to make sense of what was happening.

Then cold air smacked her.

She coughed. Coughed again. Felt a tight band around her waist. Felt ... arms. Flesh. She blinked away the salty water, her eyes burning. Her throat and lungs. Everything burned!

"I have you, Olamma. I have you."

Willow choked out a sob, grateful for Chiji's hot breath against her cheek. Felt them squeezing Ife between them. He, too, sputtered. Vomited up water. She felt the warmth of it, but the ocean quickly washed it away. Another sob. It was coming, hard and fast—her weakness. Her non-warrior-ness.

"Shh, shh, they are moving away."

Right. Right—the mafia.

Swallowing her overwhelming need to have a complete meltdown, she pulled up the dregs of her courage, siphoning some from this incredible man, and nodded. Felt him shift Ife from her chest.

"You okay?" he asked, his arm eased from around her.

She wanted to say no. That she wasn't okay. That she didn't want him to let her go. But she nodded. Realized he wanted to secure Ife to himself. And as he tied the boy to his back, she assisted Chiji in staying afloat.

"We need to find the buoys," he said.

"I … I had to let it go. They could see it and were shooting at us."

"You did the right thing," he said, his accent thick and beautiful. Everything about him was beautiful. "But we are alone on the ocean. We need them. They should be nearby."

"You saved me," she said, an unintended whimper bleeding into her words.

"How can I marry you if you are drowned?" he said with more than a little smile.

She shook her head. "Marry me? I'm not sure that's a good idea. I would be getting the better end of the deal."

"I must disagree. It would be my ultimate victory. A dream come true."

A sob wracked her. She had no idea why. But it did. And it took over her body. Her mind. Her thoughts.

Chiji's arm encircled her waist and pulled her to himself again.

Willow hooked her hands around his shoulders, catching Ife's shoulders, too. There was no propriety here as she buried her face into his shoulder. Her body wracking. Shivers vibrating down her torso and into her limbs. "I'm sorry. I don't know why I'm crying."

"Perhaps because you were shot at, pushed into the ocean—"

"I need to talk to you about that," she murmured into his neck.

"Maybe when we are on dry ground."

"Mm." Water lapped her face and she rolled her head, giving her a perfect view of Chiji's profile. Strong cheekbones. Those full lips she'd dreamed about. Remembering it made her smile.

"Are you okay now? Can we search for the buoys?"

Duh. She lifted her head and paused for a moment as their

eyes connected. Hands on his shoulders, she frowned. His eyes were hooded. But not in romance. Something … "Are you okay?"

"The bu—"

"There, look!" Ife shouted. "I see one."

"You are my hero, Ife. Thank you." Chiji grunted as he turned and caught sight of the buoy. He looked at her again. "Ready?"

She released him and they swam to the yellow bobbing device that looked like a big balloon. It had tangled with another. Though she could not tell time, it seemed as hours, floating in the vast canvas of the ocean. So far, they'd found four, and while they weren't flat, they were sturdy enough for them to take breaks from swimming, hugging them and drifting.

"Shouldn't we be swimming?"

"Yes, but if that is all we did, we would exhaust ourselves and drown."

In every direction as far as she could see, Willow saw only more water. The moon glittered across the choppy surface. As he secured the buoy to Ife with the ropes, Willow saw bobbing in the distance. Not a buoy. It was big, square … "What is that?" A shiver traced her spine from the cold water and the wind over its surface.

Chiji winced. Then glanced over his shoulder. "Ah, the ice chest."

She frowned at him. "Ice chest?" Her mind whipped through the facts. The buoys. The ice chest. He'd known they were all in the water. "You planned this."

"No. But when I knew what was happening, I tried to create a means of survival, if we were forced on this path."

"You pushed me off the boat."

His dark eyes caught hers. "I did."

"Why?"

"The yacht. If he caught up with us—we would have both

been killed." Chiji clung to the buoy, his muscular arms nicely accented in the moonlight. "Going into the water was a risk, but it was a better risk than being taken by the general."

"But … what if your sister was on that yacht?"

"General Agu is not only a trafficker, he is also a murderer. Responsible for the genocide of many villages across Nigeria. He is what is wrong with my country. And I believe he has government officials in his pocket, buying their votes and guiding policy."

"Hm," she said, more as a grunt than agreement. "I think that's happening in my country, too. But your sister …"

"Do not worry, Olamma. I will find her. That is a mission I will never surrender until she is safely home with our mother." He nodded. "Now, we must swim."

Willow scanned their surroundings. Water, water, and more water. "How do you know which direction to go?"

He looked up and pointed to the dark night. "It is easy to check your latitude by the height of Polaris, the North Star visible there in the northern horizon. Or"—he held the buoy and smoothed Ife's head in reassurance, then looked behind him—"in the southern horizon, the Southern Cross. Too, certain stars point very nearly due north or due south. I use them for guidance."

How on earth did he know all this? "Is there anything you don't know or can't do?"

His expression waxed serious. "There is much I cannot do. I could not stop Chiasoka from being taken. Or you from being humiliated."

She touched his arm. "You are not responsible for what happened to me. Not everything rests on your strong shoulders, Chiji. And I am sorry about your sister. I feel terrible—you were looking for her, and you ended up having to abandon that to save me." She sniffed, limbs trembling from the exhaustion.

"I would do it over a thousand times. I came for my sister,

but Chineke knew not only would I need to be here to help you, but you would need to be here for me."

That seemed unfathomable, that she was a necessary component. She had done nothing for him. "That ... that's not ... it's not fair to you." She shook her head. "You got robbed."

He laughed. "Robbery implies stealing, and one—God does not steal, but two—one cannot steal what is gladly given."

Willow wrinkled her nose. "Given?"

"I would give everything to see you saf—" He winced again, then cleared his throat. "Safely returned to your family."

"My family ..." She wrinkled her nose again as they swam, though she was growing frustrated. Where were they swimming to? What direction? Where was land? "I haven't lived with them in ages. Did see Stone before coming to Nigeria, but ..." She shrugged—as much as she could clinging to a buoy-rigged raft. "None of us are close like we used to be. It's ... strange. Sad."

Quiet settled between them as they alternated between swimming and floating, her trusting Chiji with the direction. Hours were falling away and the night seemed as endless as the waters. They'd fallen into a quiet rhythm, one that was almost serene—so much so that Ife fell asleep. Willow felt the exhaustion sinking into her bones.

"We must ..." Chiji grimaced. "The sun ... will bake us."

Willow lifted her head, confused. "We have time." But as her mind struggled awake, she realized it was already daylight. "Did ... I fall asleep?"

"You"—he jerked, eyes clenching shut—"needed it."

"So do you." Noticing beads of sweat on his brow and upper lip, she frowned. But it wasn't hot. Not yet, at least. "Are you okay?"

"I do not think either of us can say yes to that." He looked past her and widened his eyes. "Get on the buoy."

"On it? Why?" She peered in the direction he was looking

now and sucked in a breath. Saw a fin cutting through the water. "A shark?"

"Two dorsals—Marlin."

"A m-marlin? Is that bad?"

"Not as bad as a killer whale, but an apex predator, it is very dangerous." He jutted his jaw. "Use the ice chest. Try to—"

Pain exploded through Willow's calf. She screamed.

CHAPTER
NINETEEN

THE MARLIN LEAPT AWAY, Willow's blood on his spiked nose.

She arched her back, hands coming free of the buoy as agony marred her features. Her scream pierced the day. Immediately she sank into the waters, as if the ocean knew she'd let go and yanked her down.

Chiji lurched for her. "Olamma!" Heart thundering, he caught her arm and strained to stop her descent. Frantic, afraid of other another attack, he scanned the water for the fish that had struck. North of their location, it speared out of the water, a smaller fish flipping up into the air as well.

No doubt the thing had come for him, his injury probably leaving a fragrant trail for the carnivores gliding through the choppy waters.

Sputtering and coughing, Willow grabbed onto the buoy. Hugging it. Her face screwed tight in pain, her lips thinned. Glad the marlin found an alternate food source, Chiji made sure Willow found a rope tether to wrap her hand around.

She groaned and tilted her head, then nodded. "I'm ... okay."

181

"For the effort it took you to say that it would seem you have lost your senses," he teased.

"I think that happened long ago." She gave him a weary look. Apparently, she read the concern pumping through his veins. "I'll be okay." With a smile she clearly did not feel, she touched the boy's head. "It will take more than a fish with a long nose to stop me, eh?"

"Your leg," Chiji insisted. "Is it—"

"Fine." The answer was curt. "A mercy—it didn't penetrate. If it had, I think we'd be swarmed by sharks." She cocked an eyebrow. "Don't get me wrong—it stings like crazy, but hey. At least I don't have to walk on it, right?"

He hated to see in her pain, hurting, but he appreciated her good humor and ability to see positives. Responsibility for her injury rested on his shoulders, since he had pushed her into the water. They could do nothing for her wound—covering it would be ineffective since the water would soak through.

Exhaustion pulled at him. He did not know their exact position, but the distance from land ... he feared they would not make it. That exhaustion or dehydration would claim them. He'd tried ... Chineke had given him the idea to toss the cooler. They had some water, but not as much as they'd need. And with his injury ...

He was tired. So very tired ... He should have ... Chiasoka ... Failed her. Would he ...

"Are you okay?" Willow asked, her blue eyes seeing far more than 20/20 vision.

"As you said, I am okay."

She arched an eyebrow. "Cheater."

That made him smile. "I learn from the best."

"My mom would say I should be ashamed to claim that title, but ..." Another quirk of her eyebrow. "I am what I am."

"Where is your *bamama*?" came Ife's tired but curious voice. "Why are you not with her?"

"She lives back in Virginia. In fact," Willow said, resting her head on her hands, which were coiled in the rope tying the buoys together, "she just moved into the lodge my brother owns. When we are done pretending to be fish"—at this, Ife laughed—"would you like to go there with me and meet them?"

His little nose scrunched. "What's a lodge?"

Willow paused, no doubt looking for a way to explain to a boy who had slept on a straw mat for most of his life the luxury that America experienced. "Well, you know the boys' dorm where you slept at the compound and how it had rooms with beds in it? Well, it's sort of like that." She held her pointer and thumb close together. "A little. Each person or family has their own room they stay in for a short visit, then they go home."

Ife's eyes rounded. "Would I have my own room?"

"I'm sure we could arrange that," Willow said.

As she went on, explaining to the boy about the mountains and horses that were at the lodge, Chiji closed his eyes. Listened to the cadence of her stories, the lilt of her voice. It was soothing, calming. He was glad, so very glad Chineke had allowed him to meet her. He had known that first moment he saw her in the photo that he would marry her. If they survived, he must ask her to marry him.

But ... she lived in America. And he had finally come home. Leaving again was not in his plans. He left the Igbo people years ago, believing he had a greater destiny than to live among them. While he had done great things and seen the miraculous with Tox, he began to notice a hole in his heart. The visit home while Tox battled a vigilante had made that hole grow exponentially greater ... until it threatened to consume him.

Not ready to surrender and go back to Nigeria—as a failure he believed. Because of his work with Tox and saving, well, *the world*, he had been invited to join the Navy and go through BUD/S. When he succeeded, he had been given the Navy Special Warfare rank and granted U.S. citizenship. But when his sister went missing, he realized it was time to return to Nigeria. For good.

"Look, I'm boring him right to sleep," Willow's whisper drifted past his closed eyelids and into his thoughts.

"It is not a bad thing, since we all need sleep," Chiji teased, not opening his eyes. They felt too heavy. His whole body did. The injury …

"Chiji?" Her words sounded blurry, like she was talking underwater. "You okay? You seem … pale."

"Well," he said, every word feeling as thick as lard, "you cannot say I am the milkman's kid … where I come from because that would be the family goat."

"Ha ha. Very funny," Willow said. "I'm serious. You seem—"

"Tell Ife of DisneyWorld."

"I know about DisneyWorld," Ife exclaimed. "Dr. Paul showed us pictures on his tablet. He and his family went last year. Mama Willow, is it true princesses live in castles there?"

"Not quite," Willow answered, but he could still hear the worry in her voice.

"And Dr. Paul said there was a café in the rainforest, too."

Now she laughed. "Yes, I suppose there is. But my favorite place is animal theme park, where there are real tigers and elephants and—"

"I wouldn't want to go there," Ife objected. "We have those right here. Too boring."

"Okay, fair. But I think you would like Tomorrowland," Willow said. "There are roller coasters like space ships and—"

"What's a roller coater?"

Chiji grunted a short laugh, glad his plan had worked. On this topic, she was in an endless loop of conversation and questions. It would let him regain some strength. A rest—just for a moment …

Ife scrunched his nose and drew back. "Why would I want to see a giant mouse?"

Laughing, Willow nodded. "You have a point." She glanced at Chiji, resting on the buoy. Sweat beaded his face. He truly looked ashen. Was he too hot? He'd been right—the sun had been baking them. Crispy-critter material. She was sure her hair would soon ignite.

With a whimper, Ife covered his face. "I'm hot."

He really needed shelter. They all did. Shelter and water. And rest. At least, Chiji was getting some. An idea flickered into her mind. The marlin had struck her leg, tearing Chiji's tactical pants. Slipping her arm through the rope to stay in place, she used that tear in the pant leg to rip off the bottom of the pant leg. Without scissors or a knife, she had no way to get the other one off. For a half second she considered just taking the pants off altogether. He needed protection from the boiling heat, and she was submerged from the waist down anyway. But if—*no, when*—they found land, she didn't want to humiliate herself.

Willow tore the seam out, turning it into a square piece of shade. "Here." She flapped it over his head and covered him.

"I'm too hot for that," Ife whined.

"I know, but the sun will burn your skin if you don't keep it covered. Trust me, it's better this way. We have no way to shelter from—"

With a gasp and wide eyes, Ife popped his head up. "Chiji!"

What ...? She turned her head and saw Chiji slipping into the water. "Hey! Chiji!" Surely, he would wake when the water hit his face, startled him—

But then she saw his eyes. Whites of his eyes. Rolling into his head.

"Chiji!" She thrust herself forward and caught his arm, but

he was below water. Bubbles filtered up to the surface. Willow extricated herself from the rope and slipped into the water, immediately feeling his weight pulling her down.

Oh no. No no no.

Could she even rescue the big guy? He was taller and heavier.

She dove down, kicking hard, praying for mercy from a God she hadn't asked for help from in ages. But please … please please please. Her hands tracked down his arm until she could slip her arm under his and around his chest. Kicking as hard as she could, she aimed upward. A grunt at the level of exertion this required snatched some of her breath.

She did not care what it took, she was not going to let him drown. Or her. Them. Any of them! Above, she saw the shape of their buoy-raft and pushed toward it, his weight something else. Though a lot less than if she were trying to carrying his unconscious body on dry ground. But still …

Breaking the surface, she hauled in greedy gulps of air. Lugged Chiji up, propping him against himself to keep his head above water.

"Is he dead?" Ife asked, his voice small.

Ignoring the question, she struggled to know what do to. The impossibility of the situation rattled her. How on earth was she to do breaths and compressions without them sinking? Chiji wasn't breathing. Wasn't moving. Dead weight.

Okay. Think, Willow. You can do this. You're a Metcalfe.

Yeah, but not that kind.

Pacifist. Tenderhearted. Like all the compassion her brothers and sister didn't have got dumped into her.

But she did have an iron will. Had to with four brothers and a self-righteous sister. She rolled him around and angled him toward the buoy. Somehow, she had to get him over it.

Right. Cuz lifting a six-foot-four, well-muscled sexy Nigerian was easy.

Even if sexy wasn't essential.

Not that she was complaining.

"Ife, can you help me?"

His wide eyes shone with fear and he shook his head.

"You're strong, Ife. I just need you to help me—tie his hand into the buoy. We have to keep him above water." When he didn't move, she panicked over how long Chiji had gone without air. Too long and he'd have brain damage. Assuming she could resuscitate him. "Please!"

Though small, the six-year-old reached over the buoy and caught Chiji's much larger hand. Tiny fingers worked to tie the rope. "Okay."

"You're my hero, Ife! Thank you." She slowly released Chiji, and though he slipped down some, she was able to hook his other wrist through another and let the buoys and current pull him backward. Floating. Yes! It'd worked.

She swam to his side, pressed her head to his chest, his wet shirt almost forming a suction with her ear. Even with the lapping and Ife's questions about whether Chiji was alive, she heard the faintest of thumps. "Okay, c'mon. Breathe!" She tilted his head back, pinched his nose and tipped his chin down, opening his mouth and airway. She hoped. It wasn't solid ground, so who knew how the dynamics would affect this. She pressed her mouth to his, ignoring the awkwardness, the fact she'd seen her mouth on his in that dream. Began mouth-to-mouth. Though she felt them sinking, the water crowding in around his face and nose, she blew her breath into him.

"Why are you kissing him, Mama Willow?"

Lifting her face, she repeated it. Then did her best to thump on his chest, trying to get his lungs to clear. She continued mouth-to-mouth. Saw his chest rise and fall with each attempt. "Please, God. Please. He's Your most faithful servant. You can't let him die. Please. I need him, and I don't need anyone."

Again, she went through the procedure. On TV, they'd give

up about now. Call time of death. But that wasn't realistic, and giving up wasn't Willow. She continued. Didn't care if she did this until they drifted to dry land. She was not giving up on this man who wanted to marry her just because he'd seen her in a picture.

Tired, but vigilant, she lowered her mouth to his. Blew her air into his throat … lungs …

Chiji jerked violently, headbutting Willow. A spray of wet, sticky water and goo plastered her face. Even though she recoiled, Willow realized the problem. With his wrists tied, he couldn't right himself. She fumbled with the ties as he vomited water and bile again.

A sob-laugh choked her. Tears burned. Not caring that he'd thrown up—literally in her face. Touching his chest, she realized she wanted proof he was alive. Tangibility. She submerged, wiping her face clear of his spittle and vomit. Then, she did what she hated seeing girlie women do—she cried.

Chiji groaned and rolled to her, catching the buoy.

Holy wow, he looked terrible. Death warmed over. Without the warmth. Cuz they were in frigid waters.

Then again, he had just come back from the dead.

"What happened?" he breathed, clearing his throat. Coughing. Spitting to the side.

"You drowned," she said around her tears. "You were there one second, submerging with your eyes rolling into the back of your head the next." She drifted closer, offering him physical support of her arm around his waist. It felt … intimate. But she was worried he would pass out again. "What's going on?" she whispered, the space affording no propriety.

Arm around her shoulder, Chiji leaned in and wiped his face. "My injury …"

She frowned. "Injury?"

His eyelids fluttered.

"Don't you dare!" She shouldered in, bracing him. *"What injury?"*

"Sh-shot. Yemi."

It took entirely too long for Willow to make sense of his words. He shot Yemi? What difference would … No. No, that's not what he meant. She reversed the words. "Yemi shot … you." She gasped. "On the trawler?! You've been bleeding out? This whole time?" No wonder he was feverish and lethargic. Falling unconscious. His body wanted to shut itself down to repair vital systems. "Why didn't you tell me?" Not that she could've done much, but …

He cleared his throat again, his body gloriously warm.

Wait. Too warm.

She pressed the back of her hand to his cheek. "You're burning up!"

He nodded … which turned into a head lob, his face hitting the water. He snapped awake again. Groaned.

"Chiji." Fear pounded through Willow. They could not lose him. Could not have him die out here. She would have no hope or chance of making it without him. "Chiji. Please." She touched his face, hating the heat radiating through his ashen skin. "Please stay awake. We need you." But with his condition … "I need you. Do you hear me?" She bobbed her shoulder to nudge him.

A halfhearted nod, his eyelids heavy. Eyes pained.

His head was lolling forward again, and she directed it back to her shoulder. "Chiji, tell me what to do. Land—we have to find land, right? We won't make it just drifting, hoping someone finds us." That had happened with Dani, Canyon's wife, but Willow knew that wasn't how her story would go. It was just too easy. Too convenient.

"The current … flows …" His hot breath skittered along her neck, giving her goosebumps. "Wa … watch … canary."

Why was he talking about birds now? She cupped his head,

fighting tears. Feeling her chin tremble. With her cheek against his, she whispered, "Please don't die on me, Chiji. Please."

"Ca ... n't. Marry ... 'member?"

"My brother will kill you," she taunted him.

He grunted a laugh.

"You need fluids," she whispered. "Let me get you some water."

"No." It was more a grunt than a word. "Save ... you ... Ife."

"I'm going to save all of us. But first, you need water. Your breath is bad."

He huffed a laugh.

She angled and glanced at Ife peeking from under the pant leg. "Can you get water for him?"

He nodded, shifting around, the buoys knocking together as he maneuvered to the ice chest. "It is the last."

She saw the lid lift, then heard it close. A moment later, a half-full water bottle appeared in her line of sight. Grateful, she took it. "Chiji. Here. Drink."

With a labored grunt, he lifted his head—his hands gripping her back and waist for support—and took a sip.

"Good," she said. "More."

"No."

"*More!*"

"You ... sound ... my mother." He took a draught. Then another.

"That's a good thing—she's an amazing person," she said.

"You have not ... met her."

"No, but I've met her son." After forcing him to finish off the water, she let him fall into unconsciousness again, drifting with the buoys, feeling the current pulling them along. When she had asked him what to do or where to go, he'd said something about birds. It was rare to get birds this far out, so she wasn't sure what he meant.

"His eyes are closed. Do you need to kiss him again?" Ife asked.

She laughed, appreciating the innocence of a child. "Well, this time he is breathing, so I do not need to help him breathe."

But ... they could not stay like this forever. As the day wore on, the sun climbed higher. Thrust its brutal power on them. With Chiji's fever, he couldn't afford severe sunburn. Willow did the only thing she could think of. She tugged off the tactical pants and draped them over his face and chest, also shielding herself.

Even as the motion of the water and the buffeting of the current continued, the sun finally surrendering her power, Willow started losing hope. She was tired—exhausted. Was there even a word for this level of exhaustion? Her arms felt leaden and it hurt to move them.

"Mama Willow, does Chiji need to kiss you now?"

She sniffed. "No, though I wouldn't mind if he did."

"Is that ... permission?"

She started, his voice, thought soft, clear—near. "You're awake."

"If you can call it that."

"It's almost dusk."

"Mm. My skin does not feel ... deep fried now. ... What ... my face?"

"A shield, against the sun. Don't ask what I used," she muttered, feeling the urge to cry. The desperate need to sleep. She knew she couldn't give in to that. But neither did she have the strength to swim. Drifting it would have to be. For now.

As sleep tugged her into its embrace, she heard a distant cry. *Chiji?*

But she couldn't open her eyes. Too tired. Every part of her felt like it weighed a ton. Gratefully, it didn't or they'd be on the ocean floor by now.

God ... please. We need help. He'd let them outlive bullets and a marlin strike and two near-drownings. *Land, God. We need land.* "Help me help Chiji. Please. And Ife."

That distant cry came again.

Willow blinked open her eyes, surprised to find dusk had descended. And so had a gull. It alighted onto the buoy where Ife was sleeping. She gasped. A bird.

A bird! That meant land, right?

She strained around Chiji's head to scan their surroundings. The threat of darkness made her panic. He'd talked about the Southern Cross and a north ... something. What if she got them going in the wrong direction? They could be carried farther out to sea.

Kicking, she rotated them, searching and probing the thick veil of night. Her heart was pumping hard and her head throbbing from dehydration. She saw nothing. Just more dark stretches of sky and inky waters.

But there was a bird. Land had to be—

With hard thwaps of its wings, the gull lifted off.

Willow watched the direction it flew. Followed its trajectory. Barring an unusual flight pattern, it was heading that way, away from the sun. Okay ... but she saw nothing there but swaths of blacks and blues.

Her heart jammed. What was she supposed—

But her eyes saw it. Not just an ombre sky. That lower, darker striation was— "Land! Chiji, there's an island!"

CHAPTER
TWENTY

"WHAT'RE YOU DOING ABOUT THIS?"

"Stand down," Cord said in a low voice, frustration fresh that they were basically getting nowhere, dead in the water. "This is political. My hands are tied."

"So, what?" Blue eyes darkened. "You going to do nothing? Tuck tail and run back to your cozy beds while my sister is *lost at sea*?"

Cord glowered at Range. "I called you in—"

"That's right. You called me in. And I'm telling you—"

"I called you in," Cord yelled to regain the conversation, "because I needed your help, and that hasn't changed."

"I have contacts. We can go under the cover of night—"

"That's not how MiLE works." Cord did his best to harness his frustration over the situation and his growing anger toward Range. "We do not go in the back door. I've spent years gaining the trust and cooperation of governments around the world by respecting their rules and working with them, not against them." He shouldered in, letting the anger fall away. Focused on the mission: getting Chiji and Willow out of there. Alive. "I just have to talk to them—"

"Waiting to talk to them, and then talking to them, is costing Willow time she does not have." He lasered those blue eyes around the room to Cord, Lowell, and Mira. "Anyone here ever been stranded at sea?" His mouth and jaw were tight. "I have. Every hour exponentially increases their chances of not surviving. Of never being found. Maybe you can sit on your thumbs and do nothing, but I can't. That's not how I work."

"Yeah. It's not, is it?" Cord shifted around the table and closed the distance. "You go all loose cannon, run up against authority when you don't get your way."

"Step off, man."

"No."

Lips thinned, Range looked ready to blow a stack.

"Now get your head out of your own butt and—"

Range shoved him.

Cord barreled into him, slamming him up against the hull as a right cross connected with his jaw. But Cord didn't let go. He had the guy's shirt and twisted it up across his throat. "Think, you Home-on-the-Range twit! Your sister is out there. Get her home. Lawfully." He thrust his arm into his chest again.

Face red, hands fisted, Range stood there with his nostrils flaring.

With a huff, Cord shook his head. "I told Canyon this was a bad idea."

The revelation that his brother had been involved rolled through the guy's whole body. "You called in my brother."

"Tried."

"And he wouldn't come, so you called second best."

"Third best if you ask me. Maybe fourth," Low mumbled, hissed.

"You would read it that way." Cord had no patience for this. And he could see it had lit the guy's fuse again. "I called Canyon and he said this was your gig. So, I pulled you in because of your knowledge of the sea, of maritime rules. So get to work! Put that thick skull to work and figure out a way around this stand down order by the African government." He ran a hand over his mouth and neck. "I know you want to go get her. So do I. Your sister is a good friend and invaluable asset to MiLE."

Range jutted his jaw. "Talk's cheap."

"No spit." What Cord wouldn't do to pistol whip this guy. "So shut up and get to work."

"Taggart."

Cord glanced over his shoulder and found the captain standing in the gangway. "We free—"

"No, but you've got a VIP on the line for you."

"Told you it was political," Range said.

But the captain wouldn't have come down here just to say that when he could've radioed him. His gaze skidded back to the gangway.

Cap stood there as if debating something. Chewing on whether to say it or not.

Though his hand twitched to take the call, Cord didn't move, afraid he'd trouble the waters and draw the sharks.

"'Sup?" Low whispered.

Holding a hand out to his buddy, Cord cocked his head. "Cap, everything all right?"

This time, he looked to Range.

"I'm all ears," Cord said, "if you have ideas."

Muddy brown eyes came back to his. "Take the call."

Man, the let down was killer. He'd been so sure the captain had found a way to circumvent this. He picked up the handheld and depressed the button. "Taggart."

"Mr. Taggart, this is Ibrahim Haruna of Ministry of Transportation for the Nigerian government. It is our understanding that you have entered African waters with the attempt to interrupt the safe transport of goods by a trawler owned by a Nigerian fisherman. We do not know to what end you are attempting to interfere with his livelihood, but we insist you return to international waters immediately."

"SOLAS," Range muttered, peering over at him. "Tell him you suspect that ship to have migrants. The International Convention for the Safety of Life at Sea of the International Maritime Organization has protocols for the safe transport of migrants. Say you're filing a complaint with the UN against that vessel."

Cord frowned. What good would that do?

"It's political. Bet your life on it—or my sister's, since you're content to let her vanish at sea. Bet you dig and find he's dirty and has his hands in the trafficking pot. He may even know someone on that superyacht or the trawler." Range nodded. "Tell him." He started toward the door. "Now, I quit. I'm outta here."

"What—wait!"

But he stepped through the hatch and climbed the metal steps to the upper deck.

Fighting the urge to curse, Cord returned his focus to the call. "Mr. Haruna, I appreciate your position, but ..." He repeated Range's assertions, then added some of his own concern. Reminding them he'd worked with the Federal Ministry of Justice just last month to rescue the teenage daughter of their prime minister. That it would be a shame to see that cooperation dissolve amidst a misunderstanding.

"A complaint?" Mr. Haruna objected. "Why would you do this?"

"It's what I do, Mr. Haruna. I hunt for survivors. Bring criminals to justice. You've shut down my ability to interdict and verify there are not possible trafficking situations here, so I must lodge this complaint. I know this woman named Rumor who does great exposés to shed light on corruption, and I'm sure she can help me figure out who to talk to about this."

"You are playing a dangerous game, Mr. Taggart." The venom was acid-laced. "You risk the life of an American woman pushing into the business of the Nigerian government."

When the connection died, Cord stared at the table, his mind racing. "He's dirty."

"Yeah," Lowell said. "How'd he know there was an American on that trawler? We haven't told anyone."

"Exactly. Means he's at least in contact with the traffickers." Cord motioned to Mira. "What do we know about Ibrahim Haruna?"

Fingers flying, Mira dug up the dossier on him. "Fifty-seven. Married, five kids. Took office last year. Won by a landslide on a fighting corruption platform."

"Fighting it? Or joining it? Bet you a steak dinner he's getting kickbacks from this Nigerian mafia boss."

"So, you weren't lying. She was with you."

Noticing the hardware manager's gaze once more on Brighton at his side, Stone grinned and picked up their bag of deadbolts and cans of paint. "I wasn't lying."

"She have a sister?"

"Nope." Stone slid his hand around Brighton's waist as they turned toward the front door. "Thanks." Palm on the small of her back, he took a certain kind of pride in claiming her as his own. Publicly. No apologies. No fear.

He tugged open the door, the bell jangling noisily, and held it for her.

Brighton smiled coyly at him—what was that?—and started to exit. Then planted her hands on his chest, tiptoed up, and pressed her lips to his.

His heart chugged hard at the unexpected kiss.

She threw a smile over her shoulder to the hardware manager.

"Not nice, rubbing it in."

Brighton laughed as Stone tucked his head, thought to apologize to the guy, then decided he didn't owe him one. He let the door close behind them and she was there, threading her fingers with his.

"Maybe, but it was perfect." She wrinkled nose at him. "There are not many times I can make you blush."

"I didn't blush."

"Right. Your face is red from too much sun."

"I work in the yard."

"You don't even have a yard."

"Just several hundred acres."

"And you live under a black ten-gallon hat."

"It's a Cattle Baron."

"And you are not."

He smirked. "Woman." He hooked her waist and pulled her closer. Kissed her temple. Wished he could figure out a way to marry her. It was a thorn in his side. Made them both sad. He felt it oozing off her. How long would they have to wait? Not that there was any question about waiting—he would. As long as it took. But he really hoped it wasn't as long as it looked like it would be.

Brighton slowed and turned in to him. "I see it in your eyes. I know you're sad." She encircled his waist with her arms.

Though it felt odd to be public about their affections, he found he didn't care ... as much. "We can't do anything about it, so we trust God. He's already been here. He knows the plan. We don't, so we trust."

She nodded. "Now, I think my sadness needs a donut."

He laughed. "Cream filled."

"The only kind."

He took her hand, kissed the back of it, and started

walking—right into someone else. "Sorry. My bad." He shifted and apologized again, only then registering the face. "Oscar."

"Hey, boss." His day manager adjusted to let another man walk by. "Oh, Uncle Julio. This is them."

Stone frowned as he watched the older man in a suit focus on them.

Peering over the rim of his glasses at Stone and Brighton, the man didn't seem impressed. "That so?"

"I'm sorry?" Brighton asked, looking between them.

"Mr. M—Mulroney, this is my uncle, Judge Julio Santiago."

Judge.

Brighton's hand tightened in his.

All his protective instincts rose to the fore, and Stone angled in front of Brighton shielding her. "And why are you talking about us?"

"Oh, sorry. I told my uncle about your situation."

"Our situation." Anger, an old adversary, climbed the walls of the fence he'd built around it, begging to escape.

"It would seem you are in need of a justice of the peace to perform a certain ritual …"

"Oh." Brighton tucked her chin.

"Yeah, but … we've got some things to work out."

"That's just it," Oscar said. "My uncle has it worked out."

Stone lifted his eyebrows. "Is that right?"

"Yes, you see, marriage licenses are handled through the county."

Not something new. It was the whole reason they couldn't get married yet.

"Yes, there was this couple," the judge said, his manner suddenly jovial and conversational, "I once married on these very steps."

Stone hadn't even realized they were at the foot of the steps to the courthouse.

"And it was a holiday. Then we had the great storm. Snow

everywhere. Froze the pipes in the old building." He clucked his tongue and shook his head. "When we came back to work, it took us forever to sort through the papers to file and log them in the system." Another shake of his head. "So this couple, they show up the following year with their new baby, but there was no record of their marriage because we were still working through to recover the documents!"

"A year," Brighton said, her voice wistful as she turned those brown eyes on his.

"Yes," the judge said. "It would be like you and Mr. Mulroney marrying and then not having any proof of it for a year."

"A year." Stone considered her. His heart pounded at what this man was implying. What he suggested, that he would help them ... Was that what he was saying? It couldn't be ...

He considered the judge. Was he on the up-and-up? Legit? By the sparkle of amusement in his eyes, maybe ... maybe he was.

"It seems we have dumbfounded them, Oscar."

Brighton shifted forward, her auburn hair tossing in the wind. "Are you saying ..."

"That it would be a shame if that happened again?" He craned his neck forward conspiratorially. "I hear there is a storm coming."

He had no idea.

"Wait." She looked at him then the judge. "You're ... *Now?*"

The judge arched an eyebrow at Stone. "Perhaps not. He looks as if he'd just ate a bad hamburger."

"N-no. It's just ..."

Turning to him, she put a hand on his chest. "We can talk about it."

What was there to talk about? He loved her, wanted her, wanted to be married to her.

Then why couldn't he just jump in, say "let's do it"?

200

"Thank you," Brighton said, touching the judge's arm. "We'll talk about it."

Tell her no, you idiot!

There were pleasantries. Oscar and his uncle started walking away.

"It's okay," Brighton said softly. "I know you want to marry me. But it doesn't have to be right now. C'mon. I'm ready for my Boston Crème—"

"Why not?" He couldn't breathe. Why had he said that?

She turned slowly, glanced to the ground. "Don't. Don't say that just because—"

"Why. Not?" He shifted, so they were toe to toe, his hand drifting along her waist and resting at the small of her back. He nudged her into his arms. "Like you said, we want to get married. Here's a way."

Expectation perched on her lips and eyes. "Stone ..."

"Now's as good a time as any." The terror of it slowly fell away, replaced by thrill.

"Don't say this just because—"

"I'm not. I want to do this."

"But you didn't two seconds ago."

"I just needed time to think it through, plan—"

"We'd have no wedding, no witnesses."

"Rowe's in town with my mom picking up some supplies for her place. I can call them over. The wedding can happen once this thing blows over."

"It's okay to wait," she said. "We have each other, we're not going anywhere—"

"Is that what you want? To wait?" Why did that surprise him, make him angry?

"Yes." She scowled up at him. "No." She shook her head. "Stone, I don't want you to feel pressured into doing this. I want you to marry me because you want to."

"Oh, I want to. And we both know it. I'm sick of having to

say goodbye to you each night instead of goodnight. I want you with me. I want *us* together."

"Me, too."

"Then let's do this."

She smiled. "Yeah?" Her question was wistful, hopeful.

"Yeah." Holding her hand, he pivoted.

And found the judge standing there, waiting. He laughed and motioned them toward the courthouse

CHAPTER
TWENTY-ONE

SOMEWHERE IN THE ATLANTIC

IT HAD SEEMED MUCH CLOSER. Arms and legs aching, lips and head throbbing from blisters and dehydration, Willow did her best to swim. Keep swimming … and swimming. The distance was so deceptive. Painfully deceptive. Cruelly deceptive.

What appeared to be an easy swim seemed to be taking hours. But it was land. It might take her all night to get there, but they would get there. God help her, they would. She set her gaze on the island and continued moving. The currents and wind fought her, but she would not surrender. She'd get Chiji to land. Find potable water. Maybe some berries or something to eat. She wished she'd let her dad teach her to gut fish. But she'd been too mortified at killing the fish to even think about slicing it open. Ugh. Even now, her stomach railed. But if it meant they'd stay alive …

What if we're stranded here? For … ever?

As she took turns between swimming and resting—more of the former than the latter—she let her mind wander, figure out what it would look like being stranded. Building a hut with vegetation, sitting quietly on the beach with no texts or emails to answer.

In all honesty, she would have no regrets not having technology. Not being smothered by the million thoughts and opinions plaguing social media, the meanness, the bullying. In fact, the internet was one of the main reasons human trafficking was flourishing. Websites and web hosts preferred profit over protecting the innocents. Large strides were being made by organizations like MiLE, O.U.R., Exodus Cry, DHS Blue Campaign, and others, but it was a constant looming battle. She ached for Nkechi and the others still on the trawler. After the explosion, what happened to them? She prayed the trawler had not sunk, because it would've meant certain death for Nkechi and the others.

"I … help …" Chiji dropped a hand in the water and made a pulling motion.

But it was like having one oar—his strokes were angling them in the wrong direction.

"Chiji," she said, touching his shoulder. "Please stop. You're not strong enough—"

"I am," he insisted.

"You're not strong enough to swim *with both arms,* and using only one is working against us."

His dark eyes registered his mistake and smeared grief all over it. "I … fail … you."

"Not possible." She wanted to argue more, but she needed every bit of strength to get them to dry ground. So, she focused on that. Allowed her mind to return to the fantasy she was conjuring … the little hut … Ife playing happily, her teaching him English as Chiji built them a house and found food. There were places her mind drifted that should embarrass her. Instead, they fueled her. Like her and Chiji falling in love, having a family. Being happy. They'd have to be married. But who would marry them? And how did that work if there wasn't a place to get a marriage license?

She didn't care. She'd be with Chiji. And that ... amazingly, suddenly seemed like the only place in the world she wanted to be. With him. Always. Her gaze drifted to him as she rowed with her arms, guiding them toward the island. Eyes closed, he lay there peacefully. Physical features aside—she had clearly established how gorgeous the guy was—there was also a strength about him, character that both challenged and celebrated her. Made her want to be a better person yet made it okay to be who she was already. Let her explore truths on her own, come to her own conclusions. Pushed her to think and respond. His hard-and-fast truths were sometimes difficult to take, but she appreciated that. He didn't fluff his facts with pretty speeches. Just the truth. And she liked it. And him. A lot.

Enough to envision them married.

Not long ago, she'd have walked out of this movie of her life. But she honest-to-God wouldn't be offended if God left them to figure things out on their own. Was that dumb? They'd only known each other for a few weeks. Granted, going through what they'd gone through, depending on each other for survival for ... however many days it'd been—it'd both erased and lengthened time. Made it seem as if she'd always known him. It had cemented their hearts. If she'd read all this in a book, she might've thrown it across the room. Called it unrealistic. Sappy.

But her blistered, exhausted self would take sappy.

Something scraped her toe.

Another marlin strike! She snapped up her legs with a yelp. Spun around to check for the attacker. Rather than a predator, she realized ... ground!

She blinked and focused. Tested her theory—stretched her leg, and again felt the grit of sand and rock beneath her toes. The island that had felt like lightyears away was right before her now. Though she tried to put her feet down, she realized what had touched her toe must've been some upgrowth or rock. But she aimed for the shallow inlet where various types of ferns and trees shot upward along the craggy shore.

"Chiji!" She gasped. "Chiji, we did it! Land!!" Delighted, she plotted her trajectory.

He grunted and looked, bleary-eyed, at their refuge. With what little strength he apparently had, he kicked. His arms were clumsy and flopped more than stroked.

Kicking harder, she propelled them toward the rocky beach. Finally, she put her feet under her, a laugh bubbling up through her, and drew in their buoy-raft. Her feet slipped and whacked against the rocky shoal. Determined to get past the rocks, to be able to rest—a deep, bone-rattling-snoring rest—she shoved her foot down. Pain spiked through her calf, but she kept moving. Legs like rubber, she wavered. Wobbled. "Whoa." She steadied herself. Noticed the raft was significantly lighter. It shouldn't be. It should be heaver. Over her shoulder, she saw Chiji on all fours among the rocks, head down. Moonlight caressed his shoulders and blistered, bald head.

To her relief, Ife shifted off the buoy and struggled over the rocks. Up a slight incline, he collapsed on his back among tufts of grass. Smiled.

"Thank You, God," she whispered. There was no doubt in her mind that they shouldn't have survived that many days lost at sea.

She slipped and sloshed back to Chiji, who had managed to lift his torso and a leg. Still on one knee, he wobbled. Willow hurried toward him and caught his shoulder. "It's okay. I've got you." She threaded her arm under his and around his back. Hoisted him upright.

He cried out and grabbed his side.

"Sorry. Should we—"

"Go." He gave a curt nod.

Okay then. Awkwardly, clumsily, the two of them so

ridiculously exhausted, they made their way toward Ife's patch of greenery. Trying to help Chiji to the ground, she wasn't surprised when he simply collapsed there with a grunt.

"Chineke ... is good," Chiji murmured as his eyes closed. His hand twitched toward her. "Rest ..."

It was an invitation she could not resist. Lowering herself to grass, she stared up at the sparkle of stars. Saw clouds shifting and sliding, blocking her view. As exhaustion overpowered her, she felt Ife crawl between her and Chiji. Curled toward her, he buried his face into her. Wrapping an arm around him, she turned onto her side and noted the heat radiating off him. Oh no ... She pressed her lips to his temple. Fever.

Chiji moaned and shook his head. "Water ..."

She was thirsty, too. Thirsty. So very thirsty. It struck her then—if the island wasn't populated, they were on their own. She didn't know the first thing about what was and wasn't potable water, or how to make water potable. Or which berries were poisonous. Chiji most likely knew, but they couldn't wait for him to recover enough to search out food and water.

Why couldn't it be easy? Just this once?

"God ..." Would He listen after all the time she'd given Him the cold shoulder? She had to try, didn't she? "Please, help us. We're thirsty. Tired, sick. I'm so tired. So very ... tired ... "

Get up. Find water.

It sounded like an order. Maybe even a warning. She should. It was vital. They had run out two days ago. They could not go hours longer. Ife was feverish, possibly from heat stroke. Despite the temperature of her skin, she had chills, so she likely suffered the same.

Water. She had to find water.

Willow pushed up. At least, she tried to but her arms buckled. Whimpering, she felt tears coming in a rush. If she didn't find them water, they'd die.

Again, she tried to push up. Made it to her knees, but her

legs trembled violently. She lost her strength, her balance. Canted into the dirt. She choked on a sob. The swelling of her throat muscles hurt and made crying hurt her even more. Tears slipped down, stinging her cheek where the blisters had just scraped off. Whimpers turned into full-on crying. She couldn't help it. Her skin burned. Her eyes burned. Everything burned and ached.

"Where are You?" she said, crying … She closed her eyes. Lay there, face up, tears slipping free. She just needed to get her strength. Just a moment …

Somehow, sleep finally, greedily claimed its victory.

Something drummed her face. It was prickling and fast, repetitive. What on earth could it be? Did she care? She just wanted to sleep. *Please … leave me alone …*

But it persisted. Demanded she not sleep.

Groaning around aches and a painfully dry throat, she strained to open her eyes. Looked up—and was rewarded with a splat in the eye. She snapped her eyes shut against the rain.

Rain!

Willow gasped and turned her face to the sky, opening her mouth. Let it pour into her mouth. She swallowed. Swallowed again.

She nudged Ife and Chiji awake. "Drink! It's raining—drink the rain. As much as you can."

They both did, and soon, Chiji was laughing. Not his radiant, mesmerizing laugh. This was a tired, in-pain laugh, but it was nice. Sent glorious darts through her stomach. "Chineke … Creator! Great … merciful One!" He lifted his hands—barely. "Thank You for the rain." And he drank again.

So did Willow, delirious with joy that they were able to get at least a little relief. First from the ocean and swimming, struggling every second of every day to stay alive. Now, from the excruciating thirst. He was right. Chineke was great! She cried silently, overwhelmed. Amazed.

Struggling to sit upright, she squinted to the buoys. Saw the ice chest bobbing against the rocks. Something seemed … wrong. Not right. But she didn't care. Not right now. Just had to make sure they collected some rainwater. With a groan, she crawled on all fours to the cooler, her left leg strangely heavy. Once it was full, she tugged it back toward their position and collapsed. Tugged again, water sloshing over the sides. It was too heavy. She was too tired, so she wedged it into the rocks, even managed to find a loose rock and dropped it inside, and left the lid open. Proud of herself for accomplishing that—which seemed so absurd a menial task—she glanced over the waters. Again, something nagged at the back of her mind.

But it was too hard to think. So, she maneuvered back around and returned to the guys, collapsing next to Ife, only to find his back to her. He was now snugged against Chiji—thankfully, not on the side he'd been injured—and the big warrior had his arm around the boy. If it had been any other man, Willow would be furiously possessive over Ife. But there was no finer man for Ife to seek shelter with. And maybe she even experienced a twinge of jealousy that Ife was cradled in the arms of this Nigerian hero with his strong profile.

She smiled, once more admiring Chiji. "Inside and out, you are so beautiful. How can I already be in love with you?"

To her surprise, his mouth opened and he again accepted the rainwater.

Oh gosh. He's awake! Her heart skidded into that realization, wondering if he'd heard her profession. She nearly laughed at the possibility, but that would take too much strength. Instead, she set her hand on his arm and inched closer, still watching him. Skin blistered and ashen, but the rainwater … surely it had done him some good. It had helped her.

Wait.

She could see the buoy, the ice chest. Chiji.

That meant ... *Daylight*. She tried to lift her head, but only her eyes complied. It wasn't night. Nor morning. It was already dusk. That's what had seemed off with the water—they'd

slept a whole day?

Willow grunted and closed her eyes. If she could, she'd sleep for a week! Though exhausted and aching, she had never felt happier. Safer. They must rest. Their ordeal had depleted them. In the morning, she would find food. And shelter. Yes, they needed shelter. But what was she to do about Chiji's wound?

Tomorrow. She would figure it out tomorrow. She felt sleep, a beast as powerful as the ocean, pulling her under. She was drifting ... floating ...

Back on the ocean. A storm. Lightning. Voices.

On the ship?

Were they back on the ship?

At least they were dry. And could sleep.

Yes, sleep.

No, this isn't right. They were on land ... how did they ...?

A scream punctured her dream. She snapped awake, pain writhing through her limbs. A woman stood over her, dagger in hand.

CHAPTER
TWENTY-TWO

Island in the North Atlantic Ocean

"NO!" Willow tried to sit, but agony and utter exhaustion forbade her. "No, stop!"

"Shhhh."

"What do you want?" she cried. "We have nothing."

"*Shh!*" The woman was more empathic, then spoke in a foreign tongue.

Peering down the length of her body, Willow started. She wasn't on the beach anymore. It was a shelter of some kind. The damp air hung heavy. Rain splatted the thatched roof of fronds and what looked like bamboo. "Where ...?"

"Mama Willow, it is okay."

She glanced to the side and unbelievably saw Ife standing there, looking as he had at Obioma. Healthy. Happy.

No no. That didn't make sense. *Am I dead?* Was this was a dream? Well, the woman and her dagger would make it a nightmare. Especially when the woman bent toward Willow's leg and aimed that blade to her calf.

"*No!*"

"No!" the woman snapped back, her expression sharp. She

pointed at Willow and spoke to Ife in their tongue again. Wait—were they speaking the same dialect? Curious.

"She is fixing you, Mama Willow," Ife said with a cheery nod and bright eyes. "She say you must keep still."

This made no sense. And he wanted her to let this woman drive the dagger into her leg? Willow reached toward him, half expecting her hand to pass through him. Instead, she caught his face. "Your blisters ..." Remnants of them pocked his face. "That ... that's not ... possible."

"Soso is fixing you, too. Your leg."

Confused by his words, Willow glanced down again and saw her leg was elevated. And to her shock, she was no longer wearing Chiji's clothes but a brown dress. But her leg ... her leg was swollen. Very swollen—to twice its size. She gasped, only then feeling the throb of whatever happened. "What did you do?"

The woman touched her blade to a small fire, then aimed it at Willow's leg.

"No! Sto—"

Fire erupted through her calf. Scorching agony. Willow cried out—screamed. Dropped back against the cot. Torment churned and overwhelmed her, smothering her in darkness and cold isolation.

No matter the circumstance, Chineke was great and merciful.

Though his flesh wanted to argue, Chiji could not, because one drop of poison contaminated an entire well and the ground around it. If he questioned one aspect of God, all of his Creator must be questioned. And that was a line he could not—*would not*— cross. No matter how his anger grew, watching from his own cot as the local woman named Soso lanced Willow's leg. Watching her thrash in fever-induced dreams for the last two days. Watching as she grew so still, he was forced to shift to the edge of his cot. Reach over and take her hand. Her leg had become infected from the Marlin strike, and that infection threatened to take her leg, possibly her life. How excruciating to see the woman who had not shown one moment of weakness in all their trials now lie there, screaming and fighting for her life. His gunshot wound that had threatened to kill him healed unfairly fast once the bullet had been removed. That pain had been brutal, but it paled in comparison to watching Willow suffer.

Holding her hand between his, Chiji sat at her side. Prayed. Begged God for her life. He knew better than to bargain, and just as King David had pleaded with God for the life of his illegitimate son, so Chiji pleaded with Chineke for hers. It was because of him that she was here. He had pushed her into the water. Believed MiLE and Command were near enough for a rescue. His mistake threatened her life.

And yet, Willow had saved him. Saved all three of them. He had failed. Failed the boy and the woman he had loved from a picture. She, who had no vested interest in his country and people, saved them. His Olamma. He brushed the fringe of hair from her forehead, resting his hand on her crown, his skin so stark a contrast to her pale, beautiful features.

"Come back to me," he whispered. "It is not fair—you did this thing to my heart. Show up. Steal it. I know Chineke sent you to Nigeria. To me."

"You are so beautiful inside and out. How can I already be in love with you?"

He recalled in his feverish sleep hearing those words—from her. It was so incredible, he doubted it was real. But ... he wanted it to be real. Wanted it to be true.

Her strength radiated from within, showing in strong cheekbones and fair skin. Full lips that he dreamed of kissing. And eyes like the sky over his country on a clear day.

She belongs with me.

"I beg this thing of you, Willow. Please come back." He pressed his lips to her knuckles as he battled the sting of tears.

"Is she dead?" Ife lay nearby, having slept well into the morning. It was amazing the one at greatest risk against the rage of the ocean had come away with little more than dehydration, sunburns, calluses, and rope burns from his struggle to remain atop the buoy. A warrior of the highest caliber. "You should kiss her"—he nodded at Willow—"like she kissed you. It helped you wake up. I don't want her to die."

A kiss was so simply and often traded in Western cultures, but to Chiji, it was sacred. Not something he would steal while she slept. He glanced at the boy whose sleepy eyes mirrored his tired voice. "Ifechukwu ... do you know what your name means?"

"'No one is greater than God.'"

"Yes." Chiji smiled. "And that means *no one* is greater than God, not even a sick leg."

Ife studied him. "You were one of the bad men."

It hurt to hear those words from small lips. "To help the women and children, I had to pretend, yes. And it was not something I liked. It made my heart"—he touched his chest—"want to sink to the bottom of the ocean."

"Mama Willow said you could not die." His eyes brightened. "She also said I could go to America with her."

The thought of her leaving ... Chiji traced her still features. Ached that she might return to her country after this. "She is a very good person and will make sure you are taken care of, but I would be very sad to see her leave." After what she had been put through at the hands of his countrymen, it would not surprise him if she left. Nigeria was a great country and had its evils, just like any other, but his had exerted its evil on her.

"... mm ..."

His gaze snapped to hers. Blue eyes glittered back shooting

sparks of electricity into his heart. He smiled down at her. "Hello."

She swallowed and wet her lips. "… -er … home …"

He rubbed her hand in his. "Yes. You will get better and find a way home." He pressed his lips to her knuckles, his throat thick and raw at the words that escaped. "I will make sure."

"If—" Her eyes fluttered.

"He is there. On the cot. Well. Thanks to you." He held her hand close to himself. "We are all alive because of you, Olamma. Forever am I in your debt."

A slow smile rose and faded, her eyes sliding closed again. Taking his joy with them.

Yes. She would leave. It only made sense. Go back to her family, to her mother.

The thought and grief of it pushed him from the tent. Salted island air rushed to him on a swift breeze. He leaned against the slope of earth that the lean-to had been built into. Glanced at the bamboo door. It had been their shelter, their home for the last three days as she struggled through fever and chills. Being with her, talking with Ife … he could almost imagine them a family. Could they not stay here?

Foolish. Had he not been called back to his people? How, then, could he cower here, holed up with her? Just for the love of a woman.

He would do it. If she were willing.

But she would not. And he should not.

The air rifled across his senses again. That foreboding that had awakened him in the early hours of dawn tugged at him once more. Something … something was wrong. What did they know of this place? Nothing. Simply had awakened in the lean-to with locals tending them.

Convenient.

Too convenient. Holding his bandaged side, he wandered up over a small rise. No, he did not want her to go, but he must do what he could to secure her happiness. Even if that did not include him. It would be safer for her in America right now anyway. After the incident with the Nigerian mafia, she would have a target on her head. He trudged over the rocky terrain and crested a small knoll. "You were here before me, Chineke. So I know all must turn out as You plan, but ... I cannot understand that You bring her to me, then—" The words died on his lips at what he saw.

Down the slope. Out across the glittering waters of the inlet rose a near-black stone structure with a perfect arch.

"... *find the arch of rock.*" He thought Debare had been mocking him. But he'd been trying to tell Chiji—

Wait.

As the thoughts came together and formed a terrible conclusion: *This* was where Debare had said to look. He knew this place—El Hierro Island. That meant—

Footsteps crunched heavily and quickly toward him.

Chiji glanced to the side even as the steps slowed but remained confident. Not threatening or sneaky. The reeds of the brush around him would work well for kali sticks. He bent and broke one off as the steps closed in. Then secured another. Slowly, he turned.

And the face—

His knees buckled. He crashed to the ground, eyes unable to believe who stood before him. Breath stolen. Thoughts tangled.

"Careful!" She was there, squatting before him. "Are you okay?"

Though his collapse could be explained by the harrowing journey, that was not what pushed him down. "You're ... here. How?" He grabbed her shoulders, yelping a laugh. "*How*?!"

"Shh!" Wild, frantic eyes crashed into his. "Say nothing, Chijioke. I beg you. If they discover—"

"They?"

She nodded, her face hard like stone. "The yacht." She said it as if knowing he would understand. As if he should know what that meant. And he did. "It docked on the other side an hour ago. They are coming—"

"You saw it?" That was not possible. He had seen the land around the hut—this was the only view of the sea, and it bore no yacht. "How do you know this thing?"

"Please." She tugged him back to his feet. "They *know*, Chiji. They know you and this woman are here, and they want you both dead!" She pulled him toward the knoll, in the direction of the hut. "Please—you must get her and go. Now."

He half cried, half laughed, still shocked at the face before him. "Go? Where am I to go? I can barely walk." He blinked away the shock. The confusion. "How are you here? How is this thing possible?"

"Would you shut up and listen—you *must* go!"

He started. Frowned. "If I am to go, come with me. We will leave this island together."

"Impossible. You have no idea of this thing you say!"

"I will not leave without you, Chiasoka."

"Mama Willow! Mama Willow!"

The hurried tapping and hushed panic of Ife drummed into Willow's awareness. She blinked and groaned. Shards of light stabbed her eyes.

"Mama Willow! Hurry! The bad men come."

Snapped awake by his words, she shot up—and the world canted. Regretting her hasty movement, she realized her entire body and head ached, felt ... odd. Moaning, trying to make sense of the rush of chaotic messages swarming her veins, she sat very still. *What ...?*

"Pleeeasse," Ife whimpered, shaking her arm, then tugging against it to draw her off the cot. Cot?

Wading through thick thoughts and a heavy head, "Where are ...?"

"Hurry!" Ife demanded.

His urgency shoved her past the cloud of confusion. The island. They'd made it to the island. It'd been raining. Another thought burrowed past the chaos—a throbbing, piercing ... "My leg."

Legs bouncing and face tangled in frustration, Ife whimpered. "They are here. The bad men." Tears choked off his words.

Willow drew in a sharp breath. Thought finally catching fire. "What bad men?" She really didn't have to ask. The terror in Ife's eyes told her. She swung around in front of him, her leg protesting violently. Forcing her to shift her leg out so it wasn't a weight-bearing leg. "Where, Ife? Where are they?"

"Coming from the big boat."

Drawing Ife into her arms, Willow glanced toward the door where light stabbed through the slats. Through those gaps, she saw a swath of white. Heart stuttering, she planted Ife to the side and slowly drifted toward the door, squinting. Refusing to believe what she saw.

No ... No no no. But Ife was right—the big boat was the superyacht that had appeared right as Chiji pushed her off the trawler.

With a gasp, she glanced around. "Where's Chiji?" How had the superyacht found them? And so fast.

Face buried in the crook of her shoulder, he murmured, "Out."

In the distance, voices began to pepper the air. Turned to shouts. Distressed. Shots cracked the day.

She pivoted and gathered Ife into her arms. "Hold on tight." Cupping his head and holding him close to her chest, she darted through the slat-wood door, hunkering low. Darted a look toward the huge boat and gasped. Between her and that white monstrosity, men were sweeping up the incline, raiding huts. Dragging people from shanties and small plaster structures into the open.

Willow kept moving, pulse pounding like her feet against the uneven ground. A low stone wall sectioned off a flat area into a courtyard, then surrendered to the wilds of the hilly terrain. "Chiji, where are you?" she whispered, pleading for direction. To know which way to go.

Ife pointed behind himself. "He went that way. The men go after him and the woman."

Woman?

The bad men had already found Chiji?

Willow faltered. What was she supposed to do against these men? She'd never believed in violence as an answer. Though her brothers had taught her to defend herself—skills she had used more than once in her line of work—she hated using them. There were always alternate means to reach the end.

Or so she had believed.

Until now. These men had been relentless in perpetuating evil. They did not care about words. They only spoke one language—violence.

Seizing the direction Ife pointed, Willow bolted down a hardpacked path that slowly unfurled before her and provided a view of the inlet with the stone arch, the one whose shore they'd washed up on. Voices slowed her. Then she heard his voice, the deep rumble that had spoken to her more than once.

He's okay. Thank God! She quickened her steps, hearing her own breath panting against Ife's shoulder as she hurried. Around another bend—

Willow sucked in a breath and jerked back, cowering as she folded herself beneath some scrub to hide from the two men who had Chiji on the ground. They were going to kill him. She couldn't let that happen.

But what am I supposed to do?

219

Whatever it takes. She would not let them kill Chiji. He had too much to do on this earth still. Too many lives to touch and save. That still begged the question—*what* could she do?

Think quick. She couldn't kill anyone. The thought alone made her stomach churn. But maybe ... One of the huts she'd run past ... the fire ...

Poker! She'd seen a black rod. Maybe she could knock the men out. Could she actually hurt someone? It wasn't like she'd kill them.

Not if she stayed here debating.

Crouched in a sitting position, she shifted and tucked Ife back deeper. "Stay here."

"No—"

She clapped a hand over his mouth. "Shh." She met his bulging eyes. "Chiji is in trouble. I have to help. Promise me—stay here. I'll be back."

Tears spilled over his dark eyes, but he nodded his agreement.

Willow crawled out from under the scrub and scrambled around the other side. Stumbled around a still-throbbing leg back to the hut where she'd seen the fire. Felt clammy, sweat soaking her shirt to skin. She hobbled to the fire, staying low, trying to avoid drawing the attention of any of the other men from that yacht.

She snatched the poker and hobbled back toward Chiji. "Please, please don't let me be too late." Diverting from the path, she cut through the vegetation, letting the voices guide her. Creeping closer, lower and lower until she was crawling up to a boulder. Grimacing against the pain in her leg and shaking with the sweats, she flattened her back against the rock. Then peeked around it.

Oh no.

The men now held Chiji at gunpoint as two more held him

on his knees. A well-dressed man with gold glinting from his fingers and wrist confronted Chiji with a malevolent sneer.

What was she to do against that many?

She had one stick. And not even the courage to wield it.

Tears pricked.

I'll do what I have to.

It was too crazy. They hadn't kissed. They hadn't done movies or dates. Yet, she felt as wholly committed to him as Canyon was to Dani. As Stone to Brighton.

This is crazy.

"Where is the woman? What did you do with her?"

Willow startled. The voice demanding answers wasn't Nigerian. It sounded … she wasn't even sure, but definitely not Arabic or one of the Nigerian dialects. Maybe … German? Clearly this was the rich man. Was he the yacht owner?

"Tell us or—"

"Kill me," Chiji hissed. "I will not tell you."

"Do not be a fool, Chijioke. Tell them!" urged a woman.

"What is this, Chiasoka? You defend these people when they—"

"You do not know what you do here, Chijioke. Mr. Stegenga will kill everyone if you do not cooperate."

Who was she? Why did she know his real name?

"We will torture it out of you!" A Nigerian speaker.

"Yes, take your pleasure out of him, if you will, but I'm afraid Chiasoka is wrong—cooperation has little to do with it. You know too much now, my tall Nigerian friend."

"I am not a friend to evil."

The German laughed again. "You became its embodiment. What God will forgive you for not stopping the men from raping the children? And this looker of an American you have so generously brought to me." He clicked his tongue. "What will she say when you don't come for her? You see, it is a small island—we *will* find her. And I will take great pleasure in exploring every inch of her on our two-day cruise back." He whistled and grunted, then pointed to his men. "Do what you will and leave him for the carrion."

"No!" Willow punched to her feet even as her brain caught up with her actions and told her this was stupid. She tucked the metal poker behind her back. "I'm here. Don't hurt him. Please!"

The well-dressed man turned and leered. Gray-blond hair. Blue eyes. Mid-forties. He sniffed and started toward her. "Thank you for making it easy. Now, we can kill you both and get back to business."

She did not want to hit him or hurt him. But she would. *God, if I must do this … help me.* He had enabled David to use a rock to take down a giant.

God, I'm all about the rocks …

He was nearly upon her—and beyond him, the other men were angling to shoot Chiji.

Raising the poker to strike, Willow shouted, "No!"

CHAPTER
TWENTY-THREE

HE SAW what she intended and it broke his heart. Infuriated him. That this woman who abhorred violence would engage to protect him ...

Like lightning, Chiji grabbed fistfuls of dirt and flicked them into the eyes of the gunmen. Planted his hands and swung his legs around, swiping the unsuspecting men off their feet.

A scream from Willow spiked adrenaline through his veins. Served as a homing beacon. He flipped to his feet and lunged in her direction. Caught Willow by the waist with one hand and the rod by the other. In a fluid move, he spun her behind himself and extracted the weapon from her hand. He whipped the poker at the billionaire.

It struck fast and true. Knocked the man aside. He faltered and went to a knee. But evil did not so easily surrender. The man glowered and pushed up.

Enough was enough. Chiji rushed him, determined to make sure this man would not hurt Willow or anyone else again.

Sand and rocks spat at him, the earth erupting beneath a

barrage of bullets. Drove Chiji back. He stumbled into Willow even as gunmen swarmed over the rise, firing at him. Two sprinted to the man funding this expedition and helped him back to his feet.

Chiji reached back for Willow, searching for an exfil. But combatants were closing in on three sides and the inlet had them barricaded on the fourth. There was nowhere to go.

"I'm so sorry," Willow said, her voice hoarse beneath unshed tears. "I thought I—"

"That was very stupid," the German said, pressing a handkerchief to the gash in his temple and cheekbone that gushed blood. "Chiasoka said you could be reasoned with."

"This is not *reason*—it is psychological warfare. Brutality. Violence. *Evil*." Curling an arm around Willow, Chiji tucked her close. Felt her trembling. Vowed if any of them walked away from this alive, it would be her.

"Chiasoka—that's your sister?" Willow whispered to him.

"Well, evil is very lucrative," the man sneered. "Do not worry. I will be sure this American beauty lives happily in luxury."

"Our version of happiness is very different from yours," Willow spat. "Keep your blood money."

The billionaire arched an eyebrow. "If you insist. But"—he cocked his head—"... your funeral." He lifted a hand and the men around them closed in, once more drawing up their weapons to take aim.

Willow turned her face into Chiji's shoulder. Held onto him.

Conviction digging deep into his chest, he closed his arms around her. "Do not be afraid," he whispered against her ear. "God will provide the ram." He would not give up until his last breath was gone.

"*Tschüss.*" The billionaire motioned with two fingers.

When the staccato cracks of gunfire punctured the island's tranquility, Chiji tightened his hold and vaulted backwards with her, rotating midair. Landed hard on the pebbled beach atop Willow. Hoping to shield her from the bullets.

Only … that wasn't what those weapons should sound like.

And the shots were coming from behind.

As the very familiar sound of M4A1s rattled the air and bodies thumped to the ground, Chiji sought to make sense of it. Braved a look. Stared, disbelieving at the combatants laid out. He glanced back and his eyes refused to believe what the saw.

A team of six men in wetsuits advanced with skillful confidence, weapons firm against their shoulders, and gained the shore, seemingly without disturbing the water. They moved the way his brothers-in-arms—SEALs—were taught to move, to strike. But who …?

"Want to explain why you're laid out on top of my sister?"

Body trembling from adrenaline and fear, Willow gasped at the voice.

Chiji shifted aside and let her up.

She peered up at the team of men … all dressed alike. All wet from their insertion onto the island. But only one with the pale blues of their family. *"Range?"* The absurdity that—of all brothers—Range was the one here, rescuing her … well, her brain wouldn't process it.

Chiji unfolded himself and stood, then held a hand to her, his gaze roving the Nigerians. Long strides carried him quickly to the woman, his sister. "Chiasoka."

Shaken and mouth agape, she trembled to her feet. "What …?"

"They cannot hurt you anymore."

Willow faltered, wondering that he could be so nice to a sister who had betrayed him.

Chiasoka's hands clamped onto his arms. Stared at him in shock. Then sobbed. "I'm sorry. I'm so sorry."

He held her, pursed his lips, his gaze meeting Willow's over his sister's head as he consoled her and sharing with Willow his grief, disappointment, and relief, all at once.

A face swam into view, filling her with her amazement and disbelief as her own brother removed his headgear. Willow gaped. "You ... how ...?" A shudder of relief, clogged by confusion, ran through her. "What're you doing here?"

"Saving your life." That familiar edge was there, defensive. Harsh.

Willow wilted and went to him. Hugged his wet, neoprene-clad self. "Thank you." Tears stung. Not just that he was here. But that he'd saved Chiji—them from the Nigerian firing squad. "I'm so glad ... So glad it was you."

His hug was awkward, short. "Mom would've beat me if I hadn't. Then Canyon would've finished me off."

"True," she said with a sniffling laugh. She framed his face. "I can't believe it ... How did you know to be here?"

"Didn't. Not really. It was a guess—"

"An educated guess," another black-clad operator offered.

Range shrugged. "Knew there were some trafficking hot spots along the coast, so used SATINT to explore them, then spotted the yacht, triangulated its heading ... and here we are."

She stared at him, impressed. "You always found unique ways of solving problems nobody else could."

With a grunt, he stepped back. "We should get you two off the island before you drill me with guilt bombs."

Chiji shifted back into the discussion. "The yacht—"

"Yeah." Range unzipped his suit a few inches and stretched his neck. "Taggart arranged a two-pronged effort—my team came in this side and the Spanish Navy came from the other side of the island with a full response. They're taking it now."

"Spanish?"

Range shrugged. "Canary Islands are under Spanish control." He touched his earpiece and nodded to one of his men. "Yacht's secured. Fifteen in custody so far."

"The people here and on the yacht are captives," Chiji said, "but they may be too afraid to speak to what has happened. We must help them."

"Not our problem," Range said.

"What?" Willow balked, scowling. "These people need help!"

"My team isn't even supposed to be here—and we're not. Understood?"

Willow hesitated, her experiences over the last months shaping her reaction. "Then don't be here."

Her brother cocked his head. "Excuse me?"

Willow sighed. "I only meant that you can go. You said someone was securing the yacht, so Chiji and I will make sure the survivors are safe and returned to their families."

"So you're … what?" He eyeballed Chiji for a second, then shrugged at her. "Staying?"

"Well, not here on this island, but …" Though she shouldn't have, Willow looked at Chiji, too. Saw the surprise, the hope in his dark eyes, but even more, she saw pride. He was proud of her. And that did more for her than a million words. "Ye—"

"Mama Willow! Mama Willow!"

"Ife," Willow breathed, irritated with herself for not remembering that he'd been hiding. She turned toward his voice.

One of the bodies on the ground rolled. A weapon come up. Aimed at Ife.

"No!" Adrenaline raged. She whirled, the moment powering down to an agonizingly slow speed. She swung to Ife. "Do—"

Crack!

Terror ripped through her as Ife collapsed. His little body laid out. She plunged into action. Sprinted across the beach. Up the path. Heard a shriek searing the air. Realized it was her own. She raced to him and dropped to the ground. "Ife! Ife!" Tears blurred her vision. Looked for the wound, for blood. Where had he been hit? With her medical training, she knew not to move him until she knew where he'd been hit. But ... where was the blood? "There's no blood."

Ife turned his head to her and grinned. "I won, Mama Willow!"

Willow choked on a sob as relief gushed out of her. "Ife. What ...?"

"Remember? Major Matt taught us to drop when we saw guns."

She pulled the boy into her arms. Hugged him tight. Again grieved the loss of Matt. Thanked him in heaven for teaching the children that silly game. A silly game she'd accused him of scaring the children with. A silly game that had just saved Ife's life. Now, she was the one clinging to him as she climbed back to her feet, Chiji there, his own anxiety still evident thinking the boy was lost. He gathered them both into his arms.

"I won, Chiji!" Ife pushed back and beamed at her, then frowned, twining his hand in her blond hair. "You should be happy. I won, Mama Willow."

"Yes," she breathed, relieved. "You won, and I am very happy for that." She leaned into Chiji's hold as he pressed a light kiss against her temple, startling her. Startling them both. They shared a nervous smile, then she rested her head on his shoulder.

Safe. Happy. Very happy.

"Mama Willow?" Range asked, his brow furrowed as he studied them in what basically amounted to an embrace.

"To Ife"—she smiled down at the precocious boy—"I am Mama Willow." She squinted around the setting sun to her brother. As if the sun was setting on the hard times she'd faced, her wandering in the ocean of life. "As for your question about me staying—yes. I'm staying with Chiji and Ife. I mean, here." Heat crept up her neck and into her face at the presumption of that decision. "To help ... the girls. I belong with them."

Jaw set, Range didn't look happy. "Do you? Do you really belong here?"

Hurt by his challenging tone, she frowned. "What do you care, Range? You bailed on me and the family long ago." She shouldn't be resentful but the wound stung.

"But—"

"No." What she was considering was radical for her, but conviction knitted the decision to her soul. "No buts. I'm staying."

"My mission was straight from Cord—I'm to return you to safe soil."

"Job done. I'm safe." She felt Chiji's hand on her waist, which infused her with courage. "Besides, I'm not your responsibility. I'm where I belong now."

"C'mon, Wills. We all know with you that 'where you belong' changes from year to year."

Why was her brother challenging her so much? That accusation hurt. Mostly because it contained so much truth. "You're being a jerk, Range, but ... you're also right." She swallowed, hoping Chiji wouldn't think less of her. "I didn't know what was driving that restlessness, but I do now. And ... I found the answer." She could not help but look at Chiji. "I'm staying." They had not voiced any feelings. Had not kissed. Had not been intimate. Yet, she knew ... Did he?

Chiji laced his fingers with hers, as if agreeing with her decision, as if saying, "yes, I know." He gave a slow but firm, welcoming nod. And she remembered what he'd said on the trawler. Hoped he meant more than simply at that desperate moment.

"Back home, Mom had you, Stone, Canyon, and even Leif. And"—she sniffed a laugh—"whatever you guys couldn't fix, Brooke could. I wasn't needed." There was no anger, no bitterness. Only a sense of rightness, of belonging. "But here?" She again looked at Chiji. "I'm needed here."

EPILOGUE

Imo State, Nigeria

IT WAS a dream come true that he had never dared dream. She was here, living in his family's compound. Helping with food and chores. Loving his people. Once on that island, she had spoken of her love to him when she thought him unconscious.

Now another dream dug its talons into his heart—to ask her to be his. He leaned back against the half wall surrounding the courtyard of his mom's home, watching as she played with the children she had been teaching—his nephews and nieces.

White-blonde braid down her back, lacey white shirt accenting her femininity, and jeans dusted with dirt from working in the compound garden, Willow was playing American football with them. A game she had taught, that she had said was important to her family. She was a free spirit full of laughter and vibrancy. Talented, determined, compassionate, she had so much to offer the world. Yet, she had chosen to stay. Here. *With me.*

The ball soared past the barrels they had set up as goal posts, and the children celebrated their victory. She hugged little Ife who had not left her side since the island. It did his heart good to see this. To remember how close it came to ending very differently.

After so much had happened to her, after enduring humiliation and horrible things at the hands of wicked men, Willow had told her brother—as she looked at Chiji—that she was needed. How his heart leapt! He'd spoken those words on the trawler and hoped she understood that he did not just mean right then. That he needed her in his life. Wanted her.

With Ife clinging to her waist and feet on her boots, she walked toward Chiji with the boy, the two of them laughing. Then Ife tore off for another game with the kids. "Wow." She brushed her fringe from her forehead and laughed. "So much for undying love."

Chiji extended his hand, and when she put hers in his, he drew closer. "You have mine."

She dipped her head, a pretty blush pinking her cheeks. "I … don't deserve it."

"Love is not about deserving. Love is a gift." He straightened to his full height. "I have loved you since I saw your photo."

"It doesn't work that way."

He laughed. "But it does, Olamma."

"Okay, then tell me what that nickname means."

"It means 'beautiful pearl.'"

"Because my hair is blonde?"

"Because a pearl is formed when an irritant gets under the shell of an oyster or clam. It coats it with a fluid, layer upon layer, until a beautiful pearl is formed." He framed her face with both hands. "I have seen you, Willow. Heard how much you have seen, endured, and yet … you smile. You … shine."

Tears slipped down her cheeks. "You said you needed me."

"I am glad you remembered."

"Was that—"

"Because I need you. In my life. All the time." He traced her lip with his thumb and thought to take the kiss he had wanted for a long time.

"You know," she said quietly, hugging him, "I am so glad we were in that together. I don't think I would've had the will to keep going if you hadn't been there."

"I think you mean if you didn't have to keep me alive."

"Well, I couldn't let the only man in the world who needed me die." She eased back and smiled at him, but her gaze drifted down, sadness pushing away the nice curve to her lips. "I hope Cord can find Nkechi and the twins."

His own heart twinged at that. Some of the victims had apparently been offloaded at another waystation before the superyacht had hit the Canary Islands. "I will not let him forget to keep looking."

"Neither will—"

"Incoming cars!" shouted one of his brothers-in-law.

Willow glanced to the gate, worry and fear etched in her blue eyes. "Were you expecting someone?"

"Yes." He touched her shoulder, then his hand slid down to hers. "Come. I think you will be happy."

She stopped, tugged him back until he met her gaze. "I *am* happy, Chiji. Here. With you."

He turned to her and this time did not hold back the kiss. Pressed his lips to hers.

Caressed her mouth with his. Would lie if he did not admit how much he enjoyed it. Looked forward to many more kisses as he let his lips linger on hers.

"Dude." A hand thwapped Chiji's arm. "Come up for air."

Willow startled. "Canyon!"

Her brother's scowl was garbled with that maddening smirk. "Chiji. Next time you're going to eat her face, maybe ask me first."

"This has nothing to do with you," Willow shot back with a laugh.

"Then why was I brought here?"

She opened her mouth to reply, but then frowned. Looked at him. "Good question."

With a grin, Canyon nodded to Chiji. "Guessing this guy has the answer."

Chiji held her hand. "In my country"—why was his heart pounding like a drum?—"it is a custom for a man to go to a woman's compound and ask her father for permission to marry."

Willow gasped and covered her mouth.

"But since Willow's father is dead—"

"Dude." Canyon shook his head. "There's a reason her name starts with 'will'—she has a powerful one, and if you think *anyone* could make her do something she didn't want to, you maybe should escape out the back gate while you can." He winked. "I'll distract her and you run."

"Oh, stop." Willow laughed, pushing her brother.

"See what I mean?" Canyon raised his eyebrows and motioned to her. "You ready for this kind of abuse when she doesn't get her way?"

"Canyon!"

He buried another laugh. "Sorry. In all seriousness, if you won her, then you're aces in my book. Nobody has managed that, and I had a good friend who tried for years."

Chiji's expression sobered. "Major Matt." He nodded. "His death was a big loss, not just for her, but for Obioma."

"Speaking of—hear y'all are going to open it back up."

Heart full, excited for the future, Chiji nodded. "We will have to rebuild since they burned it to the ground, but"—he looked at Willow—"she has agreed to help me."

"And you want to do that … *next level?*" Canyon arched an eyebrow. "Married. Man and wife."

"You do not have to ask my brother's permission to marry me," Willow said, but she touched Chiji's chest. "But it touches my heart that you did and included my family. They're important to me. As you are. And I know this is part of your custom."

Canyon extended his hand to him. "Welcome to the family, dude."

Chiji hesitated. "So, I have your permission? We can marry?"

Canyon glanced at his sister. "Dude's got some learning to do, doesn't he? Has to learn to speak Metcalfe." He eyed Chiji's head, which he hadn't shaved since they returned to the compound. "Guess Brooke doesn't have the darkest hair in the family anymore."

One Month Later

Obioma Compound, Imo State, Nigeria

"This is looking good." Impressed with how much they'd accomplished in so short a time, Cord Taggart smiled at Chiji and Willow as they made their way to his armored SUV with Lowell, a man the size of a tank and with a heart just as big. "I hate to lose you as an Aftercare Specialist."

Willow brushed her bangs from her face, taking in the construction happening on one end of the compound, a new gate going in on the west side, and the children playing in the center. "I'm not *completely* leaving it—I'll still be here, helping the survivors. It wasn't an easy decision, but"—her blue eyes landed on his one-time regional ops leader—"I think I made the right decision."

"If that ring on your finger is any indication ..." Cord sighed. Change was hard. This one created a gap he'd have to fill, but he knew God would provide the right people. "I know your skills and training will be beneficial here. And what happened—I know it was some kind of messed up, but at least we've got a lead on the Viper, the second in charge of Horvath's org chart. Not names yet, but we're closing in, thanks to you."

"The German?" Willow squinted at Chiji. "What did Chiasoka call him?"

"Steg-something." He jutted his jaw at him. "Did she tell you?"

Cord looked chagrined.

"What?" Willow shifted closer.

"The billionaire went MIA somewhere between the island and Spanish port. Nobody knows how or why."

"He bought someone," Chiji supplied.

"Probably, and"—he swallowed—"Chiasoka is gone, too."

Chiji roughed a hand over his face and muttered something under his breath. "Why would she do this thing?"

"It happens a lot, and it's hard to comprehend. Some would rather face the evil they know than the world they don't know." Cord shrugged those thick shoulders of his. "Or she went back for someone. That's common, but don't worry—we're working intel channels with the leads we got from the yacht. Don't worry. We're closing in on them."

"How did the hearings go?" Chiji wondered.

The hearings were the whole reason Cord had been stranded in country for the last few weeks. "Good. Good. Governor Eijofor is glad to have routed one more corrupt politician. The Ministry of Transportation official, Mr. Haruna, is behind bars, as is his son, Yemi. The governor sends her personal thanks for your help in the op against the mafia cell."

"It is bad enough that we must battle Boko Haram and the Nigerian mafia," Chiji said, earnestly, "but to battle the two in collusion ... it must stop. We are better than that."

"Well, your governor is fierce about cleaning up the system, and she says your new president is a good one for Nigeria. I hope she's right."

"I am hopeful." Chiji seemed sorrowful. "Nigeria has so much potential that has been smothered by corruption. It is why I must stay. Help my people, even if I must do it alone."

"You're not alone." Willow slid her arm around his and took his hand. "Cord, what about Range? Have you heard from him? After we left the island, I never saw him."

"Neither did I. Have a feeling he likes it that way."

"I'm still confounded—what was the U.S. Coast Guard doing here?"

"Well, USCG does help here in Africa, training their Navy for quick responses, but"—he hated that she didn't know—"your brother ... I don't think he's a Coastie anymore. Guessing he's into some deeper stuff. Black ops."

Willow frowned. "That doesn't sound like Range. You sure? He was almost a pacifist like me."

Cord snorted. "Yeah, I don't think he has that problem now."

Her eyes narrowed. *"Problem?"*

"Not what I meant. Just ... he's hard-hitting, working in the dark." He scratched his beard, remembering what he'd seen in the guy's face. "Maybe ... a little lost in that darkness."

"What do you mean?" Willow's compassion rose to the fore again. "Should I be worried about him?"

He'd always vowed to be honest, even if it hurt. "Look, I don't know what he's doing, who he's working for. But you saw the operators he showed up with. They weren't there for tea and scones."

"I know one of them," Low said. "Last I knew, he was DEVGRU. Some pretty serious slag."

"Does Canyon know?"

Cord coughed a laugh. "There's very little that brother of yours doesn't know."

Willow bobbed her head side to side. "And he wouldn't tell me."

He stuck out his hand. "Good seeing you both. Thanks for your work on this op."

Willow, sappy woman that she was, pulled him into a hug. "If you hear from Range, tell him thanks for me."

"Sure." He tried to smile. No way Range would call him again. The guy liked things on his terms, and the way MiLE had to operate, he was a wild card that ruined the game. They were better on their own turfs. "Take care."

Back in their SUV, he and Lowell headed out of the compound. Even as they wound through the nearby village, Cord thought about the Metcalfes. A family cemented on patriotism, but there were a lot of interesting dynamics happening there.

His phone rang. "Taggart."

"Hey. You owe me one, right?"

The voice—he glanced at the caller ID, but it had no identifier. Was it really— "Range?"

"Did you a solid with El Hierro. Now it's payback."

"That's not how—"

"You owe me."

Man, this guy ticked him off. "Do you—" Hold up. Hold up. Something filtered through his rising anger. An awareness, a realization: this guy hadn't talked to his family in years, and a tightknit family looked out for each other. How likely was it that he'd *ask* for help?

He wouldn't. *He'd say someone owed him.*

Swallowing his irritation, Cord stared out the window. "Okay." He had a bad feeling about where this would go. "I'm listening."

"We've got a situation out here with some drug and skin traffickers. That guy, Aqbari, I pulled to help on the op?"

"Yeah?"

"Chopped meat—and I don't mean figuratively. Now I'm suddenly not welcome in that compound."

"The one with the brothel. And that's a problem?" What did he expect Cord to do?

"Look—"

Cord did. Right out the window. As the SUV slid past a shop plastered with advertisements, he saw a face. A gorgeous, familiar face. "Wait!" He slapped Low in the driver's seat. "Stop the truck. Stop the truck."

Low nailed the brake. "What the—"

"Wait here." He pointed to the side of the street, then remembered Range. "Hey. I'll call you back." He hung up and climbed out of the truck, glancing back to where he'd seen her. Had it been his imagination?

Lowell came around from the driver's side. "What is this about?"

"Stay with the truck. I'll be right back." He jogged down the street, scanning for her. At the shop, he ducked inside, but only found locals. "You see a white woman in here?"

They just stared at him.

He bit off a curse and stepped back out. Scanned the shadows and alleys. "Where did you go ...?" Was it his imagina—

A shadow shifted across the street. Flash of pink. And that to-die-for face. His heart did the jangly thing again, pulling him across the road. Ducking between two buildings, he palmed his weapon, ready for trouble. Not from her. But this area was sketch.

He rounded the corner and found her pacing, arms folded. She stopped short, dark hair swishing over that soft pink sweater.

He grunted. Who wears a sweater in Nigeria? "What're you doing here?"

"When you said Willow was captured …" She hugged herself. "I wanted to make sure she was safe."

"Could've done that with a phone call."

"She's my little sister—I had to see with my own eyes she was okay."

"Could've sent you a photo."

Her mouth tightened.

"And since you never actually went to her, I can't see why a picture wouldn't suffice." He moved in closer. "I mean, taking time off from lawyering … that would cost a pretty penny."

She held his gaze defiantly. "What I do, the money I spend, is none of your business."

"But here's the thing, gorgeous," he said, closing the gap between them, "you keep making it my business by showing up, asking questions."

"I didn't ask *anything* of you." She had the softest smattering of freckles across the ridge of her nose, accenting those pale blue eyes, and pink, inviting lips.

How had he missed that before? "Yeah. You did." He was less than a breath away. "You stood on that street, watched us drive by. *Waited* for me. You could've run."

"Clearly should have."

A grin quirked his mouth. "But you didn't." He wanted to rest his hand on her waist. Draw her closer. Kiss some sense into her. But this was as dangerous as trying to round up Crew's military working dog, Havoc. That beast hated being cornered. Crew had more than a few stitches from the Belgian Malinois. "I'm here, Brooke."

There was this thing between them, like some crazy vortex that made his head and heart spin like a prop. Drew his mouth to hers like a winch.

Until she stepped back, her breath a little ragged like his. "Stop."

"Whatever you need—"

"I don't need anything."

"Bullspit."

Defiance flashed through that tightly controlled façade. "What? Are you going to tell me I need you?"

"I know you're going to need a job if you don't go back to New York soon."

Her eyes widened. She drew back. "How do you ..." She sucked in a breath. "You're ..."

He knew she'd go ballistic. Rage at him. And he was ready for it.

Except that wasn't what happened.

She shoved him alright. Then stepped back. Swallowed. Something happened right there that he did not like: the fight in her collapsed. "Stay out of my business, Mr. Taggart." Her tone went apathetic and distanced. Cold.

"I know whatever this is, it's connected to my line of work. And you don't know these people, Brooke. The darkness—the cruelty, the pure evil would blow your mind. Willow experienced some of it. You should've gone to her, talked to her."

"Why? To make me feel sorry for her?"

Seriously, she wasn't this shallow, was she? "No. So you could wake up and smell the danger you're sniffing. These people, this industry—they're powerful and vicious. We caught the guy we believed was at the head of this serpent, and he vanished. Right out of the jail. That doesn't just happen with a nobody. That takes money, power, connection." He softened his tone, seeing the effect his words were having. "I don't want to see you get hurt."

"Don't worry. You won't, because you won't see me again." She started down the alley.

Unwilling to be that easily deterred, he trailed her. "Just tell me what's going on. Let me help."

"I don't need help."

"If you believed that, you wouldn't keep calling me."

"It'll never happen again."

"What's happening that you left your job?"

She stopped short. Glanced back at him. "I didn't leave my job. It's a sabbatical. Everyone at the firm has to take one every ten years."

They hadn't told him that when he called. "Okay ... My mistake."

Her eyes were on him, searching. Probing. Pleading.

Pleading for what?

"Goodbye, Taggart." She darted to the left.

Cord lunged after her. Rounded the corner ... and found himself staring at an empty dirt road. Shops had customers. Locals were walking, some driving. Down the way, Low leaned against the SUV, glancing at his phone.

"Low!"

His head came up as he pushed off the truck. "Yeah?"

"Where'd she go?"

His buddy frowned. "Who?"

"Son of a ..." Cord huffed and turned a circle, again probing the shadows. She couldn't have gone far. "Brooke!" he shouted. "Brooke! You know my number. I'll be waiting."

But he had a very bad feeling there wouldn't be a call. Or an email. She'd been digging hard and relentlessly for something, answers—proof. He didn't know. But he worried she was digging her own grave.

OPERATION UNDERGROUND RAILROAD

To the children
who we pray for daily, we say:
Your long night is coming to an end.

Hold on. We are on our way.

And to those **captors and perpetrators,**
even you monsters who dare offend God's
precious children, we declare to you:
Be afraid. We are coming for you

To Those Who Have Read This Far
we plead with you: Donate to our cause

Donate. We can't do this without you.

MORE INFORMATION ON OPERATION UNDERGROUND RAILROAD

Within the Metcalfes Series, you will meet Cord Taggart and his organization, Mission: Liberate Everyone (MiLE), an organization I've loosely modeled after Tim Ballard's Operation Underground Railroad. A couple of years ago, I stumbled upon a video about a young boy name Gardy (check out Gardy's story here https://ourrescue.org/blog/search?search=gardy), stolen from his church in Haiti's Port-au-Prince and from his father, who has never given up the fight to find his son. The heart-wrenching story gripped me and wouldn't let me go. I watched hours of videos, which invariably led to Tim Ballard and his backstory, and his organization, Operation Underground Railroad. This fight against trafficking wouldn't leave me alone. So, I reached out to O.U.R. and asked if someone would talk to me, so I could be sure to write with accuracy and authenticity. I was in awe of how responsive they were, how willing they were to share their organization and their hearts. Not to brag on themselves. But rather to add to the voices screaming out against trafficking. O.U.R. has my heart. I can't venture around the globe, but I can write. And that is my contribution to O.U.R.'s endeavor and the fight against monsters selling people for sex. PLEASE. DONATE.

From the O.U.R website (www.ourrescue.org):

WE WORK WITH LAW ENFORCEMENT TO FREE SURVIVORS OF HUMAN TRAFFICKING AND EXPLOITATION. THEN WE WORK TO BREAK THE CYCLE.

Operation Underground Railroad currently supports operation and aftercare efforts in 22 countries and 34 U.S. States. Since our group is privately run, we are able to quickly respond to foreign government requests and institute investigative measures, develop intelligence and assist in enforcement operations and rescue efforts.

The O.U.R. Ops Team primarily consists of highly experienced and extensively trained current and former law enforcement personnel. Other members have a background in either the military or in intelligence work. Our goal is to develop long-term relationships with foreign governments and their law enforcement agencies responsible for combatting human trafficking and child sexual exploitation; working closely with O.U.R. Aftercare in anticipation of their rescue.

O.U.R. does not conduct or participate in investigations, operations or enforcement action in the United States. This important work is conducted by the brave men and women in law enforcement.

Domestically, O.U.R. develops relationships with law enforcement agencies and offers resources to assist them in their local efforts against human trafficking and sexual exploitation.

THE PROCESS

1. Assess the feasibility of rescue. This must take into account the willingness of local authorities to work with us since we not only want to save the children but arrest the perpetrators as well. We also want everything to be done legally and above board.

2. Research the location, the children and the background of those who are running the sex ring. We also search for vetted care facilities that will take the children once they are rescued and not only give them food and shelter but rehabilitate them as well. In some instances the children are able to return to their families.

3. Design a strategy for rescuing the children. This is the logistical part of the process. As former CIA, Navy Seals, Special Agents, etc., we have a very unique skill set to make this happen safely, efficiently and legally. We provide local law enforcement training to support and sustain anti-trafficking operations.

4. Take action. Obviously this is the most dangerous part of the operation but one well worth taking. In some instances we go undercover and arrange to "buy" a child as if we were a customer. After the purchase, we move in with the police, arrest those responsible and rescue the children. In other cases, we may act as a "client" looking for favors, etc. Again, we work with local authorities to make sure everything is done to protect the children and that the perpetrators are arrested.

5. Recover the children. These children's lives will never be the same. Their innocence has been stolen and they need help to readjust to a better world. Therapy can be provided as well as food and shelter at a pre-screened facility.

6. Arrest, try, and convict the perpetrators. We follow this process every step of the way to make sure they don't traffic children again. In many cases the perpetrators were sex slaves and victims of trafficking themselves and know no better way to survive. We hope to break this cycle.

EXODUS CRY

HTTPS://EXODUSCRY.COM/OURSOLUTION/

Exodus Cry has worked both nationally and internationally training abolitionists in outreach, hosting governmental screenings of our documentary *Nefarious*, and reaching women bound in sexual exploitation. Here's the impact we've made since starting in 2008.

Exodus Cry is committed to abolishing sex trafficking and breaking the cycle of commercial sexual exploitation while assisting and empowering its victims.

Our international work involves **uprooting the underlying causes in our culture** that allow the industry of sexual exploitation to thrive and **helping those who have been sexually exploited.**

We fight sex trafficking and all forms of commercial sexual exploitation.

Trafficking is one component of a much larger system of *violence, exploitation,* and *gender inequality* known as the **commercial sex industry.** Our strategies are designed to assist, empower, and help bring freedom to those who have been victimized, while also fighting to uproot the larger system of injustice and exploitation that made it possible.

OUR BATTLE PLAN

Exodus Cry fights sexual exploitation in the sex industry in three strategic ways:

Shifting our culture – Working to shift the culture with powerful messaging through films, videos, podcasts, conferences, and the written word.

Changing Laws – Advocating for laws that uproot commercial sexual exploitation and defend those who are sexually exploited for profit.

Reaching Out – Engaging with those who are currently bound in sexual exploitation and lovingly offering them a way out.

HOW WE'VE MADE AN IMPACT

Exodus Cry has worked both nationally and internationally training abolitionists in outreach, hosting governmental screenings of our documentary *Nefarious*, and reaching women bound in sexual exploitation. Here's the impact we've made since starting in 2008.

We've started the fight.
You can strengthen the movement and bring freedom
to those caught in the commercial sex industry.

Donate

Join the movement. Sign the pledge.

Become an Abolitionist.

THE METCALFE CHARACTERS

Stone (Metcalfes #1)
Willow (Metcalfes #2)

Cole "Tox" Russell (aka: Ndidi)
The Warrior's Seal (The Tox Files Prequel)
Conspiracy of Silence (The Tox Files #1)
Crown of Souls (The Tox Files #2)
Thirst of Steel (The Tox Files #3)
Willow (The Metcalfes #2)

He's back and out for blood.

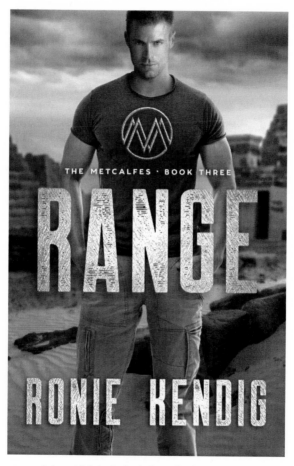

Fed up with living in the shadows of his brothers, Range
Metcalfe left his family to carve out a name for himself—one
written in the blood of many a terrorist. He always gets his guy,
and this time is no different. Except that the bad guy is a woman.
One so well protected by every power player out there that
nobody knows what she looks like. No matter the cost, Range is
going to bring her notoriety to an end.

ACKNOWLEDGMENTS

Many thanks to dear friends who helped bring this book to fruition: Rel Mollet, Kim Gradeless, and Katie Donovan. Thank you, Bethany Kaczmarek for proofing this story and your amusing comments that kept me from tears (mostly).

Thank you to Jenny from Seedlings Studio for designing such perfect covers for The Metcalfes.

Thank you, Julee Schwarzburg, for tucking this story into your tightly packed schedule and making sure it is a solid, quality story. I am so grateful to be working with you again, especially since you helped me with *Wolfsbane*—Canyon's story, the catalyst for this entire series. Love you, sweet lady! So grateful for you!

ABOUT THE AUTHOR

Ronie Kendig is an bestselling, award-winning author of over thirty books. She grew up an Army brat, and now she and her Army-veteran husband have returned to their beloved Texas after a nearly ten-year stint in the Northeast. They survive on Sonic runs, barbecue, and peach cobbler that they share—sometimes—with Benning the Stealth Golden and RMWD Cyril D002. Ronie's degree in psychology has helped her pen novels of intense, raw characters.

Website: www.roniekendig.com
Instagram: www.instagram.com/kendigronie
Facebook: www.facebook.com/rapidfirefiction
Twitter: www.twitter.com/roniekendig
Goodreads: www.goodreads.com/RonieK

BookBub: www.bookbub.com/authors/ronie-kendig
Amazon: www.amazon.com/Ronie-Kendig/e/B002SFLGQ2

ALSO BY RONIE KENDIG

The Quiet Professionals

Raptor 6

Hawk

Falcon

Titanis: A Novella

A Breed Apart

Trinity

Talon

Beowulf

The Droseran Saga

Brand of Light

Dawn of Vengeance

Shadow of Honor

Abiassa's Fire Fantasy Series

Embers

Accelerant

Fierian

Standalone Titles

Operation Zulu: Redemption

Dead Reckoning

Made in United States
North Haven, CT
22 December 2022

30021148R00159